'The television clicked itself on and said, "A news bulletin. Advance units of the Third Army report that the *Gray Dinosaur*, the ship in which Citizen Thors Provoni left the Sol System, has been located circling Proxima with no signs of life . . ." The set clicked itself off, its message delivered. A strange, almost convulsive shudder swept through Darby Shire. "They will never get him," he said through gritted teeth. "And I'll tell you why. Thors Provoni is an Old Man, the best of us, and superior to any New Men or Unusuals. *He will return to this system with help.* As he promised. Somewhere out there help exists for us, and he will find it, even if it takes eighty years. He's not looking for a world we can colonize; he's looking for *them . . .*" '

Also by Philip K. Dick in Panther Books

Philip K. Dick

Our Friends from Frolix 8

Panther

Granada Publishing Limited
First published in Great Britain in 1976 by
Panther Books Ltd
Frogmore, St Albans, Herts AL2 2NF

Copyright © 1970 by Philip K. Dick
Made and printed in Great Britain by
Hazell Watson & Viney Ltd
Aylesbury, Bucks
Set in Linotype Times

Part One

ONE

Bobby said. 'I don't want to take the test.'

But you must, his father thought. If there is going to be any hope for our family as it extends itself into the future. Into periods lying long after my death – mine and Kleo's.

'Let me explain it this way,' he said aloud, as he moved along the crowded sliding sidewalk in the direction of the Federal Bureau of Personnel Standards. 'Different people have different ability.' How well he knew that. 'My ability, for example, is very limited; I can't even qualify for a government G-one rating, which is the lowest rating of all.' It hurt to admit this, but he had to; he had to make the boy understand how vital this was. 'So I'm not qualified at all. I've got a little nongovernment job ... nothing, really. Do you want to be like me when you grow up?'

'You're okay,' Bobby said, with the majestic assurance of his twelve years.

'I'm not,' Nick said.

'To me you are.'

He felt baffled. And, as so many times of late, on the edge of despair. 'Listen,' he said, 'to the facts of how Terra is run. Two entities maneuver around each other, with first one ruling and then the other. These entities—'

'I'm not either one,' his son said. 'I'm an Old and a Regular. I don't want to take the test; I know what I am. I know what you are and I'm the same.'

Within him, Nick felt his stomach dry and shrink, and because of that he felt acute need. Looking around, he made out a drugbar on the far side of the street, beyond the traffic of squib cars and the larger, rotund public-transit vehicles. He led Bobby up a ped-ramp, and ten minutes later they had reached the far sidewalk.

5

'I'm going into the bar for a couple of minutes,' Nick said. 'I'm not well enough to take you to the Federal Building, at this particular junction of time and space.' He led his son past the eye of the door, into the dark interior of Donovan's Drugbar – a bar which he had never visited before but liked on first impact.

'You can't bring that boy in here,' the bartender informed him. He pointed to the sign on the wall. 'He's not eighteen. Do you want it to look like I sell nibbles to minors?'

'At my regular bar—' Nick began, but the bartender cut him brusquely off.

'This isn't your regular bar,' he declared, and stumped off to wait on a customer at the far end of the shadow-clouded room.

Nick said, 'You look in the shop windows next door.' He nudged his son, indicating the door through which they had just entered. 'I'll meet you in three or four minutes.'

'You always say that,' Bobby said, but he trudged off, out onto the midday sidewalk with its legions of squashed-together humanity ... for a moment he paused, glancing back, and then he continued on, out of sight.

Seating himself on a bar stool, Nick said, 'I'd like fifty milligrams of phenmetrazine hydrochloride and thirty of stelladrine, with a sodium acetyl-salicylate chaser.'

The bartender said, 'The stelladrine will make you dream of many and far-off stars.' He placed a tiny plate before Nick, got the pills and then the sodium acetyl-salicylate solution in a plastic glass; laying everything before Nick he stood back, scratching his ear reflectively.

'I hope it does.' Nick swallowed the three meagre pills – he could not afford any more this late in the month – and downed the brackish chaser.

'Taking your son for a Federal test?'

As he got out his wallet he nodded.

'You think they're rigged?' the bartender inquired.

'I don't know,' Nick said briefly.

The bartender, resting his elbows on the polished surface of the bar, leaned toward him and said, 'I think they are.' He took Nick's money; turned to the cash register to ring it up. 'I see folks going by here fourteen, fifteen times. Unwilling to accept the fact that they – or as in your case, your kid – isn't going to pass. They keep trying and it comes out the same, always. The New Men, they aren't going to let anybody else into the Civil Service. They want—' He glanced about, lowered his voice. 'They don't intend to split up the action among anybody extra beyond themselves. Hell, in government speeches they practically admit it. They—'

'They need fresh blood,' Nick said doggedly . . . said it to the bartender as he had said it to himself so many times.

The bartender said, 'They have their own kids.'

'Not enough.' Nick sipped his chaser. He could already feel the phenmetrazine hydrochloride going to work on him, building up his sense of worth, his optimism; he experienced a powerful glow deep within him. 'If it got out,' he said, 'that the Civil Service tests were rigged, this government would be voted out of office within twenty-four hours and the Unusuals would be in, replacing them. Do you think the New Men want the Unusuals to rule? My god.'

'I think they're working together,' the bartender said. And walked off to wait on another customer.

How many times, Nick thought as he left the bar, I've thought that myself. Rule first by the Unusuals, then the New Men . . . if they have actually worked this out to a fine point, he thought, where they control the personnel testing apparatus, then they could constitute, as he said, a self-perpetuating structure of power; but our whole political system is based on the fact of the two groups' mutual animosity . . . it's the basic verity of our lives – that, and the admission that due to their superiority they deserve to rule and can do so wisely.

He parted the moving mass of pedpeople, came upon his son, who stood gazing raptly into a store window. 'Let's go,' Nick said, placing his hand firmly – the drugs had made him so – on the boy's shoulder.

Not moving, Bobby said, 'There's a distance pain infliction knife they're selling. Can I have one? It'd give me more self-confidence if I was wearing that while I take the test.'

7

'It's a toy,' Nick said.

'Even so,' Bobby said. 'Please. It really would make me feel a lot better.'

Someday, Nick thought, you will not have to rule through pain infliction – rule your peers, serve your masters. You will be a master yourself, and then I can happily accept everything I see going on around me. 'No,' he said, and steered his boy back into the dense stream of sidewalk traffic. 'Don't dwell on concrete things,' he said harshly. 'Think of abstractions; think of processes of neutrologics. That's what they'll be asking.' The boy hung back. 'Move!' Nick grated, urging him forcibly on. And, physically sensing the boy's reluctance, felt the overwhelming presence of failure.

It had been this way for fifty years, now, since 2085 when the first New Man had been elected . . . eight years before the first Unusual had taken upon himself that high office. Then, it had been a novelty; everyone had wondered how the lately-evolved irregular types would function in practice. They had done well – too well for any Old Man to follow. Where they could balance a bundle of bright lights, an Old Man could handle one. Some actions, based on thought processes that no Old Man could even follow, had no analogue among the earlier variety of human species at all.

'Look at the headline.' Bobby had halted before a newspaper rack.

CAPTURE OF PROVONI REPORTED NEAR

Nick read it without interest, not believing it and at the same time not really caring. As far as he was concerned, Thors Provoni no longer existed, captured or otherwise. But Bobby seemed fascinated by the news. Fascinated – and repelled.

'They won't ever capture Provoni,' Bobby said.

'You're saying it too loud,' Nick said, his lips close to his boy's ears. He felt deeply uneasy.

'What do I care if somebody hears me?' Bobby said hotly. He gestured at the streams of men and women flowing by them. 'They all agree with me anyhow.' He glared up at his father with churning wrath.

'When Provoni left,' Nick said, 'and headed out of the Sol System, he betrayed all mankind, Superior and – otherwise.' He believed this strongly. They had argued this many times, but never had they been able to integrate their conflicting views about the man who had promised to find another planet, another useful world, on which Old Men could live ... *and govern themselves*. 'Provoni was a coward,' Nick said, 'and subpar mentally. I don't even think he was worth chasing. Anyhow, they've evidently found him.'

'They always say that,' Bobby said. 'Two months ago they told us that within twenty-four hours—'

'He was subpar,' Nick broke in sharply. 'And so he doesn't count.'

'We're subpar, too,' Bobby said.

'I am,' Nick answered. 'But you're not.'

They continued on in silence; neither of them felt like talking to the other.

Civil Service Officer Norbert Weiss withdrew a green slip from the processing computer behind his desk and read with care the information thereon.

APPLETON, ROBERT.

I remember him, Weiss thought to himself. Twelve years old, ambitious father ... what had the boy shown on the prelim test? A marked E-factor, considerably above the average. But—

Picking up his interdepartmental v-fone, he dialled his superior's extension.

Jerome Pikeman's pocked, elongated face appeared, showing the stress of overwork. 'Yes?'

'The Appleton boy will be in here shortly,' Weiss said. 'Have you made a decision? Are we going to pass him or are we not?' He held the green slip before the scanner of the fone, refreshing his superior's memory.

'The people in my department don't like his father's servile attitude,' Pikeman said. 'It's so extreme – in respect to authority – that we feel it could readily generate its negative in his son's emotional development. Flunk him.'

'Completely?' Weiss said. 'Or pro tem?'

'Flunk him forever. Totally out. We'll be doing him a favour; he probably wants to drop out.'

'The boy scored very high.'

'But not exceptional. Nothing we have to have.'

'But out of fairness to the boy—' Weiss protested.

'Out of fairness to the boy we're turning him down. It isn't an honour or a privilege to get a federal rating, it's a burden. A responsibility. Don't you find it so, Mr. Weiss?'

He had never thought about it that way. Yes, he thought; I am overtaxed by my job, and the pay is slight and, as Pikeman says, there's no honour, only a sort of duty. But they would have to kill me to make me give it up. He wondered why he felt this way.

In September of 2120 he had obtained his Civil Service status, and he had worked for the government since, under first an Unusual Council Chairman, then a New Man Chairman . . . whichever group held ultimate control, he, like other Civil Service employees, stayed on, performing their skilled functions. Skilled – and talented.

He, himself: he had since childhood defined himself legally as a New Man. His cerebral cortex showed visible Rogers nodes – and, in intelligence-testing, he displayed, on cue, the proper ability. At nine years of age he had outthought a mature Old Man; at twenty he could mentally plot a random table of one hundred numbers . . . as well as much else. For example, he could, without the use of a computer, plot the course-position of a ship subject to three gravities; by his innate mental processes he could project its locus at any given moment. He could deduce a wide variety of correlates from a given proposition, either theoretical or actual. And at thirty-two—

In a widely distributed paper he had presented objections to the classic theory of limits, showing in his own unique way, a possible return – at least theoretically – to Zeno's concept of progressively halved motion, utilizing as a fulcrum Dunne's theory of circular time.

And as a result of this he held a minor post in a minor

branch of the government's Federal Bureau of Personnel Standards. Because what he had done, although original, was not much. Not compared with the advances made by other New Men.

They had changed the map of human thought ... in fifty short years. Changed it into something which the Old Men, the persons of the past, could neither understand nor recognize. Bernhad's Theory of Acausality, for example – in 2103 Bernhad, working at the Zürich Polytechnic Institute, had demonstrated that Hume, in his enormous skepticism, had been fundamentally right: custom, and nothing else, linked events understood by the Old Men as cause-and-effect. He had brought Leibnitz's monad theory up to date – with devastating results. For the first time in human history it had become possible to predict outcomes of physical sequences on the basis of a spectrum of variable predicates, each equally true, each as much 'causal' as the next. Applied sciences had because of this taken a new form, one which the Old Men could not deal with; in their minds a principle of acausality meant chaos: they could predict nothing.

And there had been more.

In 2130 Blaise Black, a certified G-sixteen New Man, had upset Wolfgang Pauli's Synchronicity principle. He had shown that the so-called 'vertical' line of connectivity operated as a predictable factor, as easily plotted – using the new methods of random selection – as the 'horizontal' sequence. Thus, the distinction between the sequences was effectively obliterated – freeing abstract physics from the burden of a double determination – making all computations, including those derived from astrophysics, fundamentally easier. Black's System, as it was called, ended at last any reliance on Old Man theory and practice.

Contributions by Unusuals had been more specific; they had to do with operations involving actual entities. So – at least as he, a New Man, saw it – his race had contributed the underlying pinions of the reshaped map of the universe, and the Unusuals had done their work in the form of application of these general structures.

11

The Unusuals, he knew, would not have agreed with this. But that did not bother him.

I have a G-three rating, he said to himself. And I have done a little; I have added a jot to our collective knowledge. No Old Man, however gifted, could have done so. Except perhaps Thors Provoni. But Thors Provoni had been absent for years; he did not stir the sleep of either Unusuals or New Men. Provoni raged and roamed the outskirts of the galaxy, searching, in his wrath, for something vague, something even metaphysical. An answer, to so speak. A response. Thors Provoni yelled into the emptiness, dinning out his noise in hope of a response.

God help us, Weiss thought, if he ever finds it.

But he was not afraid of Provoni; neither were his peers. A few nervous Unusuals muttered among themselves as the months turned into years and still Provoni did not die and was not captured. Thors Provoni constituted an anachronism: he remained the last of the Old Men who could not accept history, who dreamed of orthodox and thoughtless action . . . he lived in a dismal past, most of it not even real, a dreamless and dead past which could not be recalled, even by a man as gifted, as educated, as active as Provoni. He is a pirate, Weiss said to himself, a quasi-romantic figure, steeped in exploits. In a sense I will miss him when he dies. After all, we emerged from the Old Men; we are related to him. Distantly.

To his superior, Pikeman, he said, 'It's a burden. You are very right.' A burden, he thought, this task, this Civil Service rating. I can't fly up into the stars; I can't pursue something which does not exist into the remote windings of the universe. How will I feel, he wondered, when we destroy Thors Provoni? My work, he thought, will be just that much more tedious. And yet I like it. I would not give it up. To be a New Man is to be something.

Maybe I'm a victim of our own propaganda, he reflected.

'When Appleton comes in with his boy,' Pikeman said, 'give little Robert the entire test . . . then tell them the rating won't be ready for another week or so. That way the blow will be less hard to endure.' He grinned starkly and added,

'And you won't have to deliver the news – it'll be in the form of a written notice.'

'I don't mind telling them,' Weiss said. But he did. Because, probably, it would not be the truth.

The truth, he thought. *We* are the truth; we create it: it is ours. Together we have drawn a new chart. As we grow, it grows with us; we change. Where will we be next year? he asked himself. No way to know ... except for the precogs among the Unusuals, and they saw many futures at one time, like – he had heard – rows of boxes.

His secretary's voice came from the intercom. 'Mr. Weiss, a Mr. Nicholas Appleton and his son are here to see you.'

'Send them in,' Weiss said, and leaned back in his large, imitation-naugahide chair, preparing to greet them. On his desk the test-form lay; he fiddled with it reflectively, seeing it, from the corner of his eye, assume various shapes. He squeezed his eyes almost shut for an instant ... and made the form, in his mind, exactly what he wanted it to be.

TWO

Kleo Appleton, in their tiny apartment, glanced swiftly at her watch and trembled. So late, she thought. And so little, little use. Maybe they'll never come back; maybe they'll say the wrong thing and be whisked off to one of those internment camps you hear of.

'He's a fool,' she said to the television set. And, from the speaker of the set, a chorus of clapping sounded as the irreal 'audience' applauded.

'Mrs. Kleo Appleton,' the 'announcer' said, 'of North Platte, Idaho, says her husband is a fool. What do you think about that, Ed Garley?' A fat round face appeared on the screen as television personality Ed Garley pondered a witty reply. 'Would you say it's perfectly absurd for a grown man to imagine for an instant that—'

She shut off the set with a wave of her hand.

From the stove, in the far wall of the living room, the smell of ersatz apple pie drifted. She had spent half her week's wage coupons on it, along with three yellow ration stamps. And they're not here for it, she said to herself. But I guess that isn't so important. In comparison to everything else. This was, perhaps, the most important day in her son's life.

She needed someone to talk to. While she waited. The TV set, this time, would not do.

Leaving the apartment, she crossed the hall, knocked at Mrs. Arlen's door.

It opened. Frowsy-haired, middle-aged Mrs. Rose Arlen peered out, turtle-like. 'Oh, Mrs. Appleton.'

Kleo Appleton said, 'Do you still have Mr. Cleaner? I need him. I want to get everything right so it'll look nice when Nick and Bobby get back. You see, Bobby is taking the test, today. Isn't that wonderful?'

'They're rigged,' Mrs. Arlen said.

14

'The people who say that,' Kleo said, 'are people who've failed the test, or someone related to them has. There are countless people who pass every day, most of them children like Bobby.'

'I'll bet.'

Frostily, Kleo said, 'Do you have Mr. Cleaner? I'm entitled to three hours of use a week and I haven't had him this week at all.'

With reluctance, Mrs. Arlen puttered off, was gone for a few moments, and then returned pushing pompous, lofty Mr. Cleaner, the internal maintenance man of the building. 'Good day, Mrs. Appleton,' Mr. Cleaner whined tinnily, seeing her. 'Well plug me in but it's nice to see you again. Good morning, Mrs. Appleton. Well plug me in but it's—'

She pulled him across the hall and into her own apartment.

To Mrs. Arlen, Kleo said, 'Why are you so hostile to me? What did I ever do to you?'

'I'm not hostile,' Rose Arlen said. 'I'm just trying to wake you up to the truth. If the test was on the level, our daughter Carol would have passed. She can hear thoughts, at least a little; she's a genuine Unusual, as much as anyone in Civil Service classifications. A lot of rated Unusuals, they lose their ability because—'

'I'm sorry; I have to clean.' Kleo firmly shut the door, turned to look for an outlet in which to plug in Mr. Cleaner—

She halted. And stood unmoving.

A man, small and grubby-looking, with beaked nose and thin, agile features, wearing a seedy cloth coat and unpressed trousers, confronted her. He had entered the apartment while she had been talking to Mrs. Arlen.

'Who are you?' Kleo asked, and felt her heart labor with fear. She sensed about the man a furtive atmosphere; he seemed ready to dodge out of sight . . . his eyes, narrow and dark, peeped nervously here and there, as if, she thought, he's making sure he knows all the ways out of the apartment.

The man said huskily, 'I'm Darby Shire.' He stared at her fixedly, and on his face the hunted expression grew. 'I'm an old friend,' he said, 'of your husband's. When will he be home, and can I stay here until he comes?'

'They'll be home any minute now,' she said. She still did not move; she kept as far away from Darby Shire – if that was really his name – as possible. 'I have to clean the apartment before they get back,' she said. But she did not plug Mr. Cleaner in. She kept her gaze, her scrutiny of Darby Shire, unaltered. What's he so afraid of? she wondered. Are they after him, the Public Security Service? And if so, what has he done?

'I'd like a cup of coffee,' Shire said. He ducked his head, as if avoiding the pleading quality in his own voice. As if he did not approve of himself asking for anything from her, but needing it, having to have it, any way.

'May I see your identab?' Kleo said.

'Be my guest.' Shire rummaged in the bulging pockets of his coat, brought out a handful of plastic cards; he tossed them onto the chair beside Kleo Appleton. 'Take as many as you want.'

'*Three* identabs?' she said, incredulously. 'But you can't own more than one. It's against the law.'

Shire said, 'Where is Nick?'

'With Bobby. At the Federal Bureau of Personnel Standards.'

'Oh, you have a son.' He smiled crookedly. 'You can see how long it's been since I last had anything to do with Nick. Is the boy New? Unusual?'

'New,' Kleo said. She made her way across the living room to the v-fone. Lifting the receiver she began to dial.

'Who are you calling?' Shire asked.

'The Bureau. To see if Nick and Bobby have left already.'

Striding towards the v-fone, Shire said, 'They won't remember; they won't know who you're talking about. Don't you understand how they are?' He reached, cut off the v-fone's circuit. 'Read my book.' Groping among his various pockets, he came up with a paperback book, bent, with wrinkled pages and stains, its cover torn; he held it out to her.

'God, I don't want it,' Kleo said with revulsion.

'Take it. Read and understand what we must do to rid ourselves of the New and Unusual tyranny that blights our lives, that makes a mockery of everything man tries to do.' He fumbled with the greasy, torn book, searching for a particular page. 'Can I have a cup of coffee now?' he asked plaintively. 'I can't seem to find the reference I want; it's going to take some time.'

She pondered a moment, then strode off into the kitchen cubicle, to heat water for the instant, ersatz coffee.

'You can stay five minutes,' Kleo said to Shire. 'And if Nick isn't back by then you'll have to leave.'

'Are you afraid of getting caught here with me?' Shire asked.

'I – just find myself getting tense,' she said. Because I know what you are, she thought. And I've seen bent, mutilated books like that before, dreary books carried here and there in dirty pockets, pawed over in stealth and in secret. 'You're a member of RID,' she said aloud.

Shire grinned crookedly. 'RID is too passive. They want to work through the ballot box.' He had found the reference he wanted, but now he looked too weary to show it to her; he merely stood there, holding onto his book. 'I spent two years in a government prison,' he said presently. 'Give me some coffee and I'll leave; I won't wait for Nick. He probably can't do anything for me anyhow.'

'What did you think he could do? Nick doesn't work for the government; he doesn't have any—'

'That's not what I need. I'm out legally; I served my term. Could I stay here? I don't have any money or any place to go. I thought of everyone I could remember who might help me and then I thought of Nick by a process of elimination.' He accepted the cup of coffee, handing her his book in return. 'Thanks,' he said as he greedily sipped. 'Do you know,' he said, wiping his mouth, 'that the entire structure of power on this planet is going to crumble away from rot? Internal rot . . . we'll be able, some day, to push it over with a stick. A few key men – Old Men – here and there both inside and outside the Civil Service apparatus and—' He made a violent, sweeping gesture. 'It's all in my book. Keep it and

17

read it; read how the New Men and the Unusuals manipulate us via their control of all the media and of—'

'You're insane,' Kleo said.

'Not any longer.' Shire shook his head, his rat-like features twisting with intensity, a swift and emotional repudiation of her words. 'When they arrested me three years ago I was clinically and legally insane – paranoia, they said – but before they would release me I had to take more psych tests, and now I'm able to prove my sanity.' He fumbled about in his many pockets once more. 'I even have the official documentation with me, I carry it around.'

Kleo said, 'They should check on you again.' God, she thought. Is Nick never going to get home?

'The government,' Shire said, 'is planning a programme of sterilization of all Old Men males. Did you know that?'

'I don't believe it.' She had heard many such wild rumours, but none of them ever turned out to be true . . . or anyhow most of them. 'You say that,' she said, 'to justify force and violence, your own illegal activities.'

'We have a Xerox copy of the bill; it's already been signed by seventeen Councilmen out of—'

The television set clicked itself on and said, 'A news bulletin. Advance units of the Third Army report that the *Gray Dinosaur*, the ship in which Citizen Thors Provoni left the Sol System, has been located circling Proxima with no signs of life. At present, tugs of the Third Army are engaged in grappling that apparently abandoned spaceship, and it is believed that Provoni's body will be discovered within the next hour. Stay near your set for further bulletins.' The television clicked itself off, its message delivered.

A strange, almost convulsive shudder swept through Darby Shire; he grimaced, clutched with his right arm . . . he bit savagely into empty air, then, his eyes gleaming, he turned back to face Kleo. 'They will never get him,' he said through gritted teeth. 'And I'll tell you why. Thors Provoni is an Old Man, the best of us, and superior to any New Men or Unusuals. *He will return to this system with help.* As he promised. Somewhere out there help exists for us, and he will find it, even if it takes eighty years. He's not looking for

18

a world we can colonize; he's looking for *them*.' He eyed Kleo searchingly. 'You didn't know that, did you? Nobody does – our rulers have control of all information, even about Provoni. But that's what it's all about; Provoni will make us no longer alone and no longer in the control of mutational opportunists exploiting their so-called "abilities" as a pretext for grabbing power here on Terra and holding it forever.' He wheezed noisily, his face writhing with intensity; his eyes had glazed over with his own fanaticism.

'I see,' she said. Repelled, she turned away.

'Do you believe?' Shire demanded.

Kleo said, 'I believe you're a devout supporter of Provoni; yes, I believe that.' And I believe, she thought, that you are once again clinically and legally insane, as you were a couple of years ago.

'Hi.' Nick, with Bobby lagging after him, entered the apartment. He perceived Darby Shire. 'Who's this?' he asked.

'Did Bobby pass?' Kleo asked.

'I think so,' Nick said. 'They'll notify us by mail within the next week. If we had failed they would have told us right away.'

Bobby said remotely, 'I failed.'

'Do you remember me?' Darby Shire asked Nick. 'After so much time has passed?' The two men surveyed each other. 'I recognize you,' Darby said in a hopeful tone of voice, as if inviting Nick to recognize him, too. 'Fifteen years ago. In Los Angeles. The county hall of records; we were both clerical assistants to Horse Faced Brunnell.'

'Darby Shire,' Nick said. He held out his hand; they shook.

This man, Nicholas Appleton thought, is deteriorated. What a dreadful change – but fifteen years is a long time.

'You look exactly the same,' Darby Shire said. He held his tattered book towards Nick. 'I'm recruiting. For example, I tried just now to recruit your wife.'

Seeing the book, Bobby said, 'He's Under Man.' The boy's voice held excitement. 'Can I see it?' he asked, reaching for the book.

19

'Get out of here,' Nick said to Darby Shire.

'You don't think you could—' Shire began, but he cut him off savagely.

'I know what you are.' Nick grabbed Darby Shire by the shoulder of his ragged coat; he propelled him forcibly towards the door. 'I know you're hiding from the Public Security people. Get out.'

Kleo said, 'He needs a place to stay. He wanted to stay here with us for a while.'

'No,' Nick said. 'Never.'

'Are you afraid?' Darby Shire asked.

'Yes.' He nodded. Anyone caught circulating Under Man propaganda – and anyone associated with him in any way – was automatically deprived of his right to take future Civil Service tests. If the PSS caught Darby Shire here, Bobby's life would be destroyed. And, in addition, they all might be fined. And sent to one of the relocation camps for an indefinite period. Subject to no real judicial review.

Darby Shire said quietly, 'Don't be afraid. Have hope.' He drew himself up – how short he is, Nick thought. And ugly. 'Remember Thors Provoni's promise,' Darby Shire said. 'And remember this, too: your boy isn't going to get a Civil Service rating anyhow. So you have nothing to lose.'

'We have our freedom to lose,' Nick said. But he hesitated. He did not quite push Darby Shire out of the apartment and into the public hallway. Suppose Provoni does come back, he said to himself, as he had pondered many times before. I don't believe it; Provoni is being captured right now. 'No,' he said, 'I don't want to have anything to do with you. Ruin your own life; keep it to yourself. And – go away.' He propelled the smaller man out into the hall, now; several doors had popped open and the various inhabitants, some of whom he knew, some of whom he did not, gawked with interest at what was happening.

Darby Shire eyed him, then, calmly, reached into an inner pocket of his shabby coat. He seemed taller, now, and more in command of himself . . . and the situation. 'I'm glad, Citizen Appleton,' he said as he brought forth a slim, flat, black case and snapped it open, 'that you have taken the

20

attitude you have. I am making spot checks in this building, random selections, so to speak.' He showed Nick his official identab: it glowed dully, enhanced by artificial fire. 'PSS occifer Darby Shire.'

Inside him, Nick felt coldness at work, numbing him. Making him silent. He could think of nothing to say.

'Oh, god,' Kleo said in dismay; she came up beside him, and so, after a pause, did Bobby. 'But we said the right thing, didn't we?' she asked Darby Shire.

'Exactly right,' Shire said. 'Your responses were uniformly adequate. Good day.' He returned his flat-pak of identification back to his inner coat pocket, smiled momentarily, and, still smiling, flowed through the ring of gawking people. In a moment he had gone. Only the ring of nervous bystanders remained. And – Nick and his wife and son.

Nick shut the hall door, turned to face Kleo. 'You can never rest up,' he said thickly. How close it had been. In another moment ... I might have told him to stay, he realized. For old time's sake. After all, I did know him. Once.

I suppose, he thought, that's why they picked him to make a spot loyalty check on me and my family. Good lord, he thought. It left him terrified and shaking; with unsteady steps he made his way towards the bathroom, to the medicine cabinet in which he kept his supply of pills.

'A little fluphenazine hydrochloride,' he murmured, reaching for the reassuring bottle.

'That's three of those you've taken today,' Kleo said, wife-wise. 'Too many. Stop.'

Nick said, 'I'll be okay.' Filling the bathroom water glass, he rapidly, mutely took the round tablet.

And, inside him, felt dull anger. He experienced a transitory flash of rage, at the system, at the New Men and the Unusuals, at the Civil Service – and then the fluphenazine hydrochloride hit him. The anger ebbed away.

But not completely.

'Do you think our apartment is bugged?' he asked Kleo.

' "Bugged"?' She shrugged. 'Evidently not. Or we'd have

been called in a long time ago because of the awful things Bobby says.'

Nick said, 'I don't think I can take much more.'

'Of what?' Kleo said.

He did not say. But he knew, down inside himself, who and what he meant. And his son knew, too. They now stood together – but how long, he wondered, will I feel this way? I will wait and see if Bobby passed his Civil Service test, he said to himself. And then I'll decide what to do. God forbid, he thought. What am I thinking? What's happening to me?

'The book's still here,' Bobby said; bending, he picked up the torn, creased paperback which Darby Shire had left behind. 'Can I read it?' he asked his father. Thumbing through it he said, 'It looks like it's real. The police must have gotten it off an Under Man they caught.'

'Read it,' Nick said savagely.

THREE

Two days later, a letter from the government made its appearance in the Appletons' mail box. Nick opened it at once, his heart vibrating with expectation. It was the test results, all right; he scanned through the several pages – a Xerox copy of Bobby's paper was included – and came at last to the determination.

'He failed,' Nick said.

'I knew I would,' Bobby said. 'That's why I never wanted to take it in the first place.'

Kleo began to snivel.

Nick said nothing, thought nothing; he was empty and numbed. A hand, colder than that of death itself, gripped his heart, killing off all emotion.

FOUR

Picking up his line-one fone, Willis Gram, Council Chairman of the Extraordinary Committee For Public Safety, bantering said, 'How's the capture of Provoni coming, Director? Any new news?' He chuckled. God knew where Thors Provoni was. Probably dead long ago, on some airless planetoid far away.

Police Director Lloyd Barnes said stonily, 'Are you speaking of media releases, sir?'

He laughed. 'Tell me what the TV and the papers are blabbing about now.' He could, of course, turn his own TV set on, without having even to get out of bed. But he enjoyed raking his stuffed-shirt Police Director over the coals re the Thors Provoni situation. The color of Barnes' face usually proved interesting in a morbid sort of way. And, being an Unusual of the highest order, Gram could enjoy firsthand the chaos in the man's mind when it came to anything dealing with the topic of the runaway traitor.

After all, it had been Director Barnes who had released Thors Provoni from a Federal prison ten years ago. As rehabilitated.

'Provoni is going to narrowly slip through our fingers again,' Barnes said gloomily.

'Why don't you say he's dead?' It would have enormous psychological consequences on the population – and along the lines he would have liked to see.

'If he shows up here again, the basis of our situation would be jeopardized. By merely showing up—'

'Where's my breakfast?' Gram asked. 'Tell them to bring it in.'

'Yes sir,' Barnes said, nettled. 'And what do you want? Eggs and toast? Fried ham?'

'Is there really ham available?' Gram asked. 'Make it ham, with three chicken eggs. But make sure nothing's ersatz.'

Not enjoying his servant-role, Barnes muttered, 'Yes sir,' and got off the line.

Willis Gram lay back against the pillows; one of his personal men immediately manifested himself and expertly propped the pillows up exactly as they should have been. Now where's the damn paper? Gram asked himself, and held out his hand to receive it; another of his personal staff-members noted his gesture and adroitly produced the current three editions of the *Times*.

For a time, he leafed through the first sections of the great old newspaper – now government-controlled. 'Eric Cordon,' he said at last, making a motion with his right hand to show that he wished to dictate. At once a scribe appeared, portable transcriber in hand. 'To all council members,' Gram said. 'We cannot claim Provoni's death – for reasons which Director Barnes has pointed out – but we can deliver Eric Cordon. I mean we can execute him. And what a great relief that will be.' Almost, he thought, like getting Thors Provoni himself. Throughout the Under Men network, Eric Cordon was the most admired organizer and speaker. And there were, of course, his many books.

Cordon was a true Old Man intellectual, a theoretical physicist who could inspire a great group-response among other disenchanted Old Men who longed for the ancient days. Who would, if he could, put the clock back fifty years. Cordon, however, despite his unique forensic ability, was a thinker, not a doer – as was Provoni: Thors Provoni the man of action who had roared off to 'get help', as Cordon, his onetime friend, had reported in endless speeches, books and grubby tracts. Cordon was popular, but – unlike Provoni – Cordon was not a public menace. With his execution, he would leave a void which he had really never properly filled. He was, despite his public appeal, strictly small-fry.

But much of the Old Men population did not understand that. Hero worship surrounded Eric Cordon. Provoni was an abstract hope; Cordon existed. And he worked and wrote and spoke here on Earth.

Picking up the line-two fone he said, 'Get me Cordon on the big screen, Miss Knight.' He hung up, settled back in his bed and once again snooped into the articles in the newspaper.

'Further dictation, Council Chairman?' the scribe inquired, after an interval of time.

'Oh yes.' Gram pushed the newspaper aside. 'Where was I?'

' "I mean we can execute him. And what a—" '

'To continue,' Gram said, clearing his throat. 'I want all department heads – are you getting this? – to grasp and understand the reasons behind my desire to finish off whatshisname.'

'Eric Cordon,' the scribe said.

'Yes.' Gram nodded. 'Why we must destroy Eric Cordon is as follows. Cordon is the link between the Old Men of Earth and Thors Provoni. As long as Cordon is alive, people feel the presence of Provoni. Without Cordon they have no contact, real or otherwise, with that ratty space bastard out there somewhere. In a sense, Cordon is the voice for Provoni while Provoni is gone. I admit that this might backfire; the Old Men might riot for a time ... but on the other hand this might bring the Under Men out of hiding where we could get at them. In a sense, I'm about to deliberately spark a premature show of force by the Under Men; there will be wild waves as soon as Cordon's death is announced, but ultimately—'

He broke off. On the big screen, which comprised the far wall of his great bedroom, a face had begun to ignite. A thin, esthetic face with hollows about the jaw: a weak jaw, Gram reflected as he saw the jaw move with speech. Rimless glasses, meager hair in the form of carefully combed strands across an otherwise bald head.

'Sound,' Gram instructed, as Cordon's lips continued to move inaudibly.

'. . . pleasure,' Cordon boomed, as the sound came on too loudly. 'I know how busy you are, sir. But if you wish to speak to me—' Cordon gestured elegantly. 'I am ready.'

To one of his bedside aides, Gram said, 'Where the hell is he now?'

'In Brightforth Prison.'

'You getting enough to eat?' Gram asked the image on the big screen.

'Very much so, yes.' Cordon smiled, showing teeth so even as to seem – and probably were – false.

'And you're free to write?'

Cordon said, 'I have the materials.'

'Tell me, Cordon,' Gram said energetically, 'why do you write and say those damn things? You know they're not true.'

'Truth is in the eye of the beholder.' Cordon chuckled in his thin, humorless way.

'You know that trial a few months ago,' Gram asked, 'where you were sentenced to sixteen years in prison for treason? Well, goddam it, the judges have gone back and eradicated the specifications of your punishment. They've now decided on the death penalty.'

No expression appeared on Cordon's bleak face.

'Can he hear me?' Gram asked an aide.

'Oh yes, sir. He hears you, all right.'

Gram said, 'We're going to execute you, Cordon. You know, I can read your mind; I know how afraid you are.' It was true; inside Cordon quaked. Even though their contact remained purely electronic, with Cordon himself actually two thousand miles away. Psionic capacities like this always baffled the Old Men – and, frequently, the New Men as well.

Cordon said nothing. But it was obvious that he grasped the fact that Gram had begun to feel him out telepathically.

'Down underneath,' Gram said, 'you're thinking, "Maybe I should bolt. Provoni is dead—" '

'I don't think Provoni is dead,' Cordon broke in, showing outrage: his first genuine facial expression.

'Subconsciously,' Gram said. 'You're not even aware of it.'

'Even if Thors were dead—'

'Oh, come off it,' Gram said. 'You know and I know that if Provoni were dead you'd drop your agitation and propaganda enterprises and creep off out of public sight for the rest of your damn ineffectual life.'

A buzzer in the communications apparatus to Gram's

26

right all at once squeaked into life. 'Pardon me,' Gram said, and pressed a switch.

'Your wife's attorney is here, Council Chairman. You left word that he was to be let in no matter what you were doing. Shall I send him on in, or—'

'Send him in,' Gram said. To Cordon he said, 'We'll notify you – Director Barnes, most probably – an hour before your scheduled death. Goodbye, I'm busy now.' He made a motion and the wall-size screen dribbled into opaqueness.

The central bedroom door opened and a slim, tall, well-dressed gentleman with a short beard strode briskly into the room, briefcase in hand. Horace Denfeld, who always dressed this way.

'Do you know what I read in Eric Cordon's mind just now?' Gram said. 'Subconsciously, he wishes he'd never joined the Under Men, and here he is, the leader of it – to the extent that they have a leader. I'm going to obliterate their existence, starting with Cordon. Do you approve of my ordering Cordon's execution?'

Seating himself, Denfeld unzipped his briefcase. 'According to Irma's instructions, and my professional advice, we have changed several clauses – minor ones – in the separate maintenance agreement. Here.' He handed a folio, a document, to Gram. 'Take your time, Council Chairman.'

'What will happen when Cordon is gone?' Gram asked as he unfolded the legal size sheets of paper and began reading here and there; in particular he scanned the passages marked in red.

Denfeld said offhandedly, 'I couldn't even manage to guess, sir.'

' "Minor clauses",' Gram mocked with bitterness as he read. 'Jeez Christ, she's upped the child support from two hundred pops a month to four.' He shuffled among the pages, feeling the edges of his ears glow with wrath – and with stunned dismay. 'And the alimony up from three thousand to five. And—' He reached the last sheet; it was strewn with red lines and sums penciled in. 'Half my travel expenses – she gets that. And *all* of what I make for paid speeches.'

His neck had become grimy and soggy with warm, stinging sweat.

'But she's allowing you to keep all your earnings from written material which you—'

'There isn't any written material. Who do you think I am, Eric Cordon?' He tossed the papers brusquely onto the bed; for a time he sat steaming ... partly from what he had just now read and partly because of the attorney, Horace Denfeld, who was a New Man; low as he was in the general New Man standings, Denfeld considered all Unusuals – including the Council Chairman – merely a pseudo evolvement. Gram could pick it up from Denfeld's mind: that low, constant level of superiority and contempt.

Gram said, 'I'll have to think it over.' I'll show it to my own attorneys, he said to himself. The best government attorneys there are: those in the tax branch.

'I want you to consider one thing, sir,' Denfeld said. 'In a way, it may seem to you that it's unfair of Mrs. Gram to ask so—' He searched for the word. 'So large a share in your property.'

'The house,' Gram agreed. 'And the four apartment buildings in Scranton, Pa. All that, and now this.'

'But,' Denfeld pointed out smoothly, his tongue flitting about his lips like a paper streamer dancing in the wind, 'it is essential that your separating from your wife must at all costs be kept secret – *for yourself*. For the fact that a Council Chairman of the Extraordinary Committee For Public Safety cannot let a breath of ... well, shall we say *la calugna*—'

'What's that?'

'Scandal. There can't be a scandal for any high-ranking Unusual or New Man anyhow, as you well know. But this, plus your position—'

'I'll resign,' Gram grated, 'before I sign that. Five thousand pops alimony a month. She's insane.' He raised his head and scrutinized Denfeld. 'What happens to a woman when she's getting a separate maintenance or a divorce? She – they – want everything, nailed down or otherwise. The house, the apartments, the car, all the pops in the world—' God, he

28

thought, and rubbed his forehead wearily. To one of his servants he said, 'Get me my coffee.'

'Yes sir.' The aide fiddled with the coffee maker, handed him his black, strong espresso cup.

To the aide, and to everyone in the room, Gram said, appealing to them, 'What can I do? She's got me.' He placed the folio of documents in the drawer of his bedside desk. 'There's nothing more to discuss,' he said to Denfeld. 'My attorneys will let you know my decision.' He glowered at Denfeld, whom he did not like at all. 'Now I have other business.' He nodded to an aide, who put his firm hand on the attorney's shoulder and guided him toward one of the doors leading out of the bedroom.

After the door had shut behind Denfeld, Gram lay back, meditating and drinking his coffee. If only she'd break a law, he said to himself. Even a traffic law – anything to get her behind in her relationship to the police. If we caught her jaywalking we could make it stick; she could resist arrest, use foul and obscene language in public, be a public menace by virtue of the fact that she had deliberately flouted the law ... and, he thought, if only Barnes' people could catch her on a felony rap; for example buying and/or drinking alcohol. Then (his own attorneys had explained this) we could hit her with an unfit mother suit, take the children, put the blame on her in a true divorce action – which, under those circumstances, we could make public.

But, as it stood, Irma had too many things on him. A contested divorce would make him look bad indeed, what with what Irma could scrape together out of the gutter.

Picking up his line-one fone he said, 'Barnes, I want you to get hold of that cop dame, that Alice Noyes, and send her in here. Maybe you should come along, too.'

Police occifer Noyes headed the team which had been trying, for almost three months, to get something on Irma. Twenty-four hours a day, his wife was monitored by police video and audio gadgetry ... without her knowledge, of course. In fact, one video camera scanned the happenings in Irma's bathroom, which unfortunately had not turned up anything to speak of. Everything Irma said, did, everyone she saw, every place she went – all on reels of tape at PSS Central in Denver. And it added up to nothing.

She's got her own police, he realized gloomily. ExPSS flatheads who roamed about with her when she went shopping or to a party or to Dr. Radcliff, her dentist. I've got to get rid of her, he said to himself. I should never have married an Old Man wife. But it had happened long ago, when he did not hold the high position which had become his later on. Every Unusual and every New Man sneered at him in private, and he did not like it; he read thoughts, lots of them, emanating from many, many people, and buried there somewhere lay the contempt.

It was exceptionally great among the New Men.

While he lay waiting for Director Barnes and occifer Noyes, he examined the *Times* once again, opening it at random to one of its three hundred pages.

And found himself confronted by an article on the Great Ear project ... an article which called the byline of Amos Ild, a very well-placed New Man: someone Gram could not touch.

Well, the Great Ear experiment is just rolling merrily along, he thought sardonically as he read.

Thought to be beyond the scope of probability, work on the first purely electronic telepathic listening device advances at a reassuring rate, officials of McMally Corporation, the designer and builder of Great Ear, as it has come to be called, said today in a press conference attended by many skeptical observers. 'When Great Ear goes into operation,' Munro Capp opined, 'it will be capable of telepathically monitoring the thought-waves of tens of thousands of persons, and with the ability – not found among Unusuals – to unscramble these enormous flood-tides of ...

He tossed the newspaper away; it fell with a noisy thump to the deep pile of the carpeted floor. Those New Men bastards, he said savagely to himself, his teeth grinding impotently. They'll pour billions of pops into it, and after Great

Ear they'll build a device which can replace precog Unusuals, then all the rest, one by one. There'll be poltergeist machines rolling along the streets and buzzing through the air. *We won't be needed.*

And ... instead of the strong and stable two-party government which they now had, there would be a one-party system, a monolithic monster with New Men holding all key posts, at all levels. Goodbye to Civil Service – except to tests for New Man cortical activity, that double-domed neutrologics with such postulates as, A thing is equal to its opposite and the greater the discrepancy, the greater the congruity. Christ!

Maybe, he thought, the whole structure of New Man thought is a gigantic put-on. *We* can't understand it; the Old Men can't understand it; we take their word for it that it's a whole new step upward in the evolution of human brain-functioning. Admittedly, there are those Rogers nodes, or whatever. There is a physical, different structure of their cerebral cortex. But ...

One of his intercoms clicked on. 'Director Barnes and a woman police occifer are—'

'Send them in,' Gram said. He leaned back, made himself comfortable, folded his arms and waited.

Waited to tell them his new idea.

FIVE

At eight-thirty in the morning, Nicholas Appleton showed up at his job and prepared to begin the day.

The sun shone down on his shop, his little building. Therein he rolled up his sleeves, put on his magnifying glasses, and plugged in the heating iron.

His boss, Earl Zeta, stumped up to him, hands in the pockets of his khaki trousers, an Italian cigar dangling from his overgrown lips. 'What say, Nick?'

31

'We won't know for a couple of days,' Nick said. 'They're going to mail us the results.'

'Oh yeah, your kid.' Zeta put a dark, large paw on Nick's shoulder. 'You're cutting the grooves too light,' he said. 'I want them down into the casing. Into the damn carcass.'

Nick, protestingly, said, 'But if I go any deeper—' The tire will blow if they back over a warm match, he said to himself. It's equal to shooting them down with a laser rifle. 'Okay,' he said, the fighting strength oozing out of him; after all Earl Zeta was the boss. 'I'll go deeper,' he said, 'until the iron comes out the other side.'

'You do that and you're fired,' Zeta said.

'Your philosophy is that once they buy the squirt—'

'When their three wheels hit the public pavement,' Zeta said, 'our responsibility ends. After that, whatever happens to them is their own business.'

Nick had not wanted to be a tire regroover . . . a man who took a bald tire and, with the red hot iron, carved new grooves deeper and deeper into the tire, making it look adequate. Making it look as if it had all the tread it needed. He had inherited the craft from his father, who had learned it from his own father. Down the years, father, to son; hating it as he did, Nick knew one thing: he was a superb tire regroover and always would be. Zeta was wrong; he already burned deeply enough. I'm the artist, he thought; I should decide how deep the grooves should go.

Leisurely, Zeta snapped on his neck radio. Cheap and noisy music – of a sort – blurred out of the seven or eight speaker-systems spread over the heavy man's bulging body.

The music ceased. A pause, and then an announcer's voice, speaking in professionally disinterested tones. 'PSS spokesmen, representing Director Lloyd Barnes, announced a short while ago that police prisoner Eric Cordon, long imprisoned for acts hostile to the people, has been transferred from Brightforth Prison to the termination facilities in Long Beach, California. When asked if this meant that Cordon is to be executed, PSS spokesmen avowed that no decision as to that has been reached. Well-informed sources outside the PSS are openly saying that this heralds Cordon's execution, pointing out that of the last nine hundred PSS prisoners transferred at various times to the Long Beach detention facilities, almost eight hundred were eventually executed. This has been a bulletin from—'

Convulsively, Earl Zeta clutched at the switch of his body radio; he missed it, clenched his fist spasmodically, shutting his eyes and rocking back and forth. 'Those bastards,' he said between his teeth. 'They're murdering him.' His eyes opened; he grimaced, his face showing violent and deep pain ... then, by degrees, he obtained control over himself; his anguish seemed to ease. But it did not go away; his tubby body remained tensed as he stared at Nick.

Nick said, 'You're an Under Man.'

'For ten years you've known me,' Zeta grated. He got out a red handkerchief and carefully mopped his forehead. His hands were shaking. 'Listen, Appleton,' he said, managing to make his voice more natural, now. More steady. Yet the shaking continued down deep in the man, out of sight. Nick sensed it, knew it was there. Hidden and buried, out of fear. 'They're going to get me, too. If they're executing Cordon they'll just go on and wipe all of us out, all the way down to minnows like me. And we'll go into those camps, those damn, lousy, rotten detention camps on Luna. Did you know about them? That's where we're going. We – my people. Not you.'

'I know about the camps,' Nick said.

'Are you going to turn me in?'

Nick said, 'No.'

'They'll get me anyway,' Zeta said bitterly. 'They've been compiling lists for years. Lists a mile long, even on microtapes. They've got computers; they've got spies. Anyone could be a spy. Anyone you know or have ever talked to. Listen, Appleton – Cordon's death means we're not just fighting for political equality, it means we're fighting for our actual physical lives. Do you understand that, Appleton? You may not like me very much – God knows we don't get along with each other – *but do you want to see me murdered*?'

'What can I do?' Nick said. 'I can't stop the PSS.'

Zeta drew himself up, his dumpy body rigid with the agony of despair. 'You could die along with us,' he said.

'Okay,' Nick said.

' "Okay"?' Zeta peered at him, trying to understand him. 'What do you mean?'

'I'll do what I can,' Nick said. He felt numbed by what he was saying. Everything was gone, now: the chance for Bobby had been effectively voided, and a race of tire regroovers would go on forever.

I should have waited, he thought. This just simply happened to me; I didn't expect it – I don't really understand it. It must be because Bobby failed. And yet I'm here saying this, telling Zeta this. It's been done.

'Let's get over to my office,' Zeta said hoarsely, 'and open a pint of beer.'

'You have liquor?' He could not imagine it, the penalty was so terribly great.

'We will drink to Eric Cordon,' Zeta said, and led the way.

SIX

'I have never drunk alcohol before,' Nick said as they sat facing one another across the table. He had begun to feel terribly odd. 'You read in the papes all the time that it causes people to go berserk, to suffer complete changes of personality, suffer brain damage. In fact—'

'Scare stories,' Zeta said. 'Although, it's true you should go easy at first. Take it slow; let it just slide down.'

'What's the penalty for drinking alcohol?' Nick asked. He found himself having trouble forming words.

'A year. Mandatory, without possibility of parole.'

'Is it worth it?' The room, around him, seemed unreal; it had lost its substantiality, its concreteness. 'And isn't it habit-forming? The papes say once you start, you can never—'

'Just drink your beer,' Zeta said; he sipped his, downing it without apparent difficulty.

34

'You know,' Nick said, 'what Kleo would say about my having alcohol?'

'Wives are like that.'

'I don't think so. She's like that, but some aren't.'

'No, they're all that way.'

'Why?'

'Because,' Zeta said, 'their husband is the source of all their financial money.' He belched, grimaced, leaned back in his swivel chair, the beer bottle gripped in one large hand. 'To them – well, look at it this way. Suppose you had a machine, a very complex delicate machine, which when it was working properly it pumped out, fed out, a line of pops. Now, supposing that machine—'

'Is that really how wives feel about their husbands?'

'Sure.' Zeta burped again, handed Nick the bottle of beer.

'It's dehumanization,' Nick said.

'Sure it is. Bet your purple and green ass it is.'

'I think Kleo worries about me because her father died when she was very young. She's afraid all men are—' He searched for the word but could not find it; by now his thought-processes were erratic, filmed over and peculiar. He had never experienced anything like this before, and it frightened him.

'Just be calm,' Zeta said.

Nick said, 'I think Kleo is vapid.'

' "Vapid"? What's "vapid"?'

'Empty.' He gestured. 'Maybe I mean passive.'

'Women are supposed to be passive.'

'But it interferes—' He stumbled over the word and felt his face redden with embarrassment. 'It interferes with their maturing.'

Zeta leaned toward him. 'You're saying all this because you're scared of her disapproval. You say she's "passive" and yet that's exactly what you want, now, in regard to this. You want her to go along; I mean, approve of what you're doing. But why tell her at all? Why does she need to know?'

'I always tell her everything.'

'Why?' Zeta said loudly.

'That's the way it's supposed to be,' Nick said.

'When we finish this beer,' Zeta said, 'you and I are going somewhere. I won't say where – it's just a place. Where, if we get lucky, we can pick up some material.'

'You mean Under Men material?' Nick asked, and felt coldness tug at his heart; he felt himself being steered into risky waters. 'I already have a booklet a friend posing as a—' He broke off, unable to construct his sentence. 'I'm not going to take any risks.'

'You already have.'

'But it's enough,' Nick said. 'Already. Sitting here drinking this beer and talking the way we've been talking.'

Zeta said, 'There is only one "talking" that matters. The talking of Eric Cordon. The real stuff; not the forgeries that are being circulated around on the street, but what he does say, what it's all about. I don't want to tell you anything: I want *him* to tell you. In one of his booklets. I know where we can pick one up.' He rose to his feet. 'I'm not talking about the "words of Eric Cordon". I'm talking about the *true* words of Eric Cordon, his admonitions, parables, the plans, known only to those who are truly members of the world of free men. Under Men in the truest sense; the real sense.'

'I don't want to do anything Kleo won't approve of,' Nick said. 'A husband and wife have to be honest with each other; if I go ahead with this—'

'If she doesn't approve, get yourself another wife who can.'

'You mean that?' Nick asked; his brain had become so fogged over now that he could not tell if Zeta was serious. And, if he did mean what he said, whether he was right or not. 'You mean this could split us,' he said.

'It's split a lot of marriages before. Anyhow, are you so happy with her? You said before, "She's vapid." Your exact words. And *you* said it, not me.'

'It's the alcohol,' Nick said.

'Of course it's the alcohol. "*In vino veritas*,",' Zeta said, and grinned, showing his brownish teeth. 'That's Latin; it means—'

'I know what it means,' Nick said; he felt anger, now, but he did not know what toward. Was it toward Zeta? No, he thought, it's Kleo. I know how she would react to this. We

36

shouldn't ask for trouble. We'll wind up in a detention dome on Luna, in one of those dreadful work camps. 'What comes first?' he asked Zeta. 'You're married, too; you have a wife, and you have two children. Is your respon—' Again his tongue failed to function properly. 'Where's your first loyalty? To them? Or to political action?'

'Toward men in general,' Zeta said. He raised his head, held the beer bottle to his lips, and finished the last of the beer. He then slammed it violently down on the table. 'Let's get moving,' he said to Nick. 'It's like the Bible says: "You shall know the truth, and the truth shall make you free." '

' "Free"?' Nick asked, also rising – and experiencing difficulty in doing so. 'That's the last thing Cordon's booklets are going to make us. A track will get our names, find out we're buying Cordonite writing, and then—'

'Always looking over your shoulder for tracks,' Zeta said scathingly. 'How can you be alive that way? I've seen hundreds of people buy and sell pamphlets, sometimes a thousand pops' worth at one time and' – he paused – 'sometimes the tracks do worm their way in. Or a prowl car catches sight when you're passing over some pops to a dealer. And then, like you say, it's in prison on Luna. But you have to take the risk. Life itself is a risk. You say to yourself, "Is it worth it?" and you answer, "Yes, it is. Goddam it, yes it is." ' He put on his coat, opened the door of the office and stepped out into the sunlight. Nick, after an extensive pause – seeing that Zeta was not looking back – followed after him, slowly. He caught up with him at Zeta's parked squib. 'I think you ought to begin looking for another wife,' Zeta said; he opened the door of the squib and squeezed his bulk in behind the tiller. Nick, getting in also, slammed the door on his side. Zeta grinned as the squib shot up into the morning sky.

'That's really none of your business,' Nick said.

Zeta did not answer; he concentrated on his driving. Turning his head he said to Nick, 'I can drive badly now, we're clean. But on the way back we'll have the stuff, so we won't get a PSS occifer flagging us down for speeding or erratic turning. Right?'

'Yes,' Nick said, and felt the numbing fear inside him rise. It had become inevitable, the path they were following; he could not now get out of it. Why not? he asked himself. I know I have to go through with it, but why? To show that I'm not afraid that a track will burst us? To show that I'm not dominated by my wife? For all the wrong reasons, he thought . . . and mainly because I've been drinking alcohol, the most dangerous substance – short of Prussic acid – you can imbibe. Well, he thought, so be it.

'Nice day,' Zeta said. 'Blue sky, no clouds to duck behind.' He soared upward enjoying himself; Nick shrank numbly back against the seat and merely sat, helpless, as the squib oozed forward.

At a payfone, Zeta made a call; it consisted of only a few half-articulated words. 'He's holding?' Zeta asked. 'He's there? Okay. Yeah, right. Thanks. Bye.' He hung up. 'That's the part I don't like,' he said. 'When you make the fonecall. All you can do is figure that so many million fonecalls are made in one given day that they can't monitor them all.'

'But Parkinson's Law,' Nick said, trying to cover his fear with jollification. ' "If a thing can happen—" '

Zeta, getting back into the squib, said, 'It hasn't happened yet.'

'But eventually.'

'Eventually,' Zeta pointed out, 'death will get us all.' He cranked up the engine of the squib and they zoomed upward again. Presently, they were flying over a sprawling residential section of the city; Zeta peered down, scowling. 'All the goddam houses look exactly alike,' he muttered. 'It's so frigging hard to see from the air. But that's good; he's stuck right in the middle of ten million loyal believers in Willis Gram and Unusuals and New Men and all the rest of that crap.' The squib dived suddenly. 'Here we go,' Zeta said. 'You know, that beer affected me – it actually did.' He grinned at Nick. 'And you look like a stuffed owl; you look like you could turn your head completely around.' He laughed.

They came to rest on a roof landing field.

Grunting, Zeta got out; Nick did so, too, and they made their way to the escalator. In a low voice, Zeta said to him, 'If the occifers stop us and ask what we're doing here, we say we're bringing some guy back his squib keys which we forgot to give him when we fixed his squib.'

'That makes no sense,' Nick said.

'Why doesn't it make any sense?'

'Because if we had his squib keys he wouldn't have been able to fly back here.'

'Okay, we say it's a second set of keys he asked us to order for him, for his wife.'

At the fiftieth floor, Zeta stepped from the escalator; they made their way down a carpeted hall, seeing no one. Zeta paused all at once, briefly looked around, then knocked on a door.

The door opened. A girl stood confronting them, a small, black-haired girl, pretty in an odd, tough way; she had a pug nose, sensual lips, elegantly formed cheekbones. About her hung the glow of feminine magic; Nick caught it right away. Her smile, he thought, it lights up: it illuminates her whole face, bringing it to life.

Zeta did not seem pleased to see her. 'Where's Denny?' he asked in a low but distinct voice.

'Come in.' She held the door aside. 'He's on his way.'

Looking uneasy, Zeta entered, motioning Nick to follow him. He did not introduce either of them to the other; instead he strode through the living room, into the bedroomette, then into the kitchen area of the living room, prowling like an animal. 'Are you clean here?' he demanded suddenly.

'Yes,' the girl said. She looked up into Nick's face, a jump of about a foot. 'I've never seen you before.'

'You're not clean,' Zeta said; he stood reaching down into the waste tube; he came up abruptly with a package which had been taped to the inside of the tube. 'You kids are nuts.'

'I didn't know it was there,' the girl said in a sharp, hard voice. 'Anyhow, it was fixed so that if a track busted down the door, we could flick it down the tube just by touching it, and there'd be no evidence.'

'They plug the tube,' Zeta said. 'Catch it down around the second floor, before it hits the furnaces.'

'My name's Charley,' the girl said to Nick.

'A girl named Charley?' he asked.

'Charlotte.' She held out her hand; they shook. 'You know, I think I know who you are. You're Zeta's tire regroover.'

'Yes,' he said.

'And you want a genuine booklet? Are you paying for it or is Zeta? Because Denny isn't going to lay out any more credit; he'll want pops.'

'I'm paying for it,' Zeta said. 'This time, anyhow.'

'That's how they always do it,' Charley said. 'The first booklet is free; the next is five pops; the next is ten; the—'

The apartment door opened. Everyone ceased moving, ceased breathing.

A pretty boy stood there, bulky, well-dressed, with tangled blond hair, large eyes, an expression of intensity constricting his face so that in spite of his prettiness he had an ugly, cruel intensity to him. He surveyed Zeta briefly, then Nick, for several silent moments. He then shut the door after him, Ferok-bar locked it, walked across the room to the window, peered out, stood chewing on the edge of his thumbnail, radiating, all about him, ominous vibrations, as if something awful, something which would destroy everything, was about to happen . . . as if, Nick thought, he's going to do it. He's going to beat up all of us himself. The boy emanated an aura of strength, but it was a sick strength; it was overripe, as were his enlarged eyes and tangled hair. A Dionysus from the gutters of the city, Nick thought. So this was the dealer. This is the person from whom we get authentic tracts.

'I saw your squib on the roof,' the boy said to Zeta, as if announcing the discovery of some evil act. 'Who's this?' he asked, inclining his head toward Nick.

'Someone – who I know – who wants to buy,' Zeta said.

'Oh, really?' The boy, Denny, walked toward Nick, studied him at closer range. Studying his clothes, his face; judging me, Nick realized. As if some eerie kind of combat is involved, the nature of which was, to him, totally unclear.

All at once, Denny's protruding, large eyes moved rapidly, he stared at the couchette, at the wrapped booklet lying on it.

'I dug it out of the waste tube,' Zeta said.

'You little bitch,' Denny said to the girl. 'I told you to keep this place clean. You understand?' He glowered down at her; she gazed up, lips half-parted anxiously, her eyes unblinking with alarm. Turning rapidly, Denny picked up the booklet, tore the wrappings from it, studied it. 'You got this from Fred,' he said. 'What'd you pay for it? Ten pops? Twelve?'

'Twelve,' Charley said. 'You're paranoid. Stop looking like you think one of us is a track. You always think someone is a track if you don't personally—'

'What's your name?' Denny asked to Nick.

'Don't tell him,' Charley said.

Turning to her, Denny raising his arm, drew back; she faced him calmly, her face inert and hard. 'Go ahead,' she said. 'Hit me and I'll kick you where it'll hurt for the rest of your life.'

Zeta said, 'He's an employee of mine.'

'Oh, yes,' Denny said sardonically. 'And you've known him all your life. Why don't you simply say he's your brother?'

'It's the truth,' Zeta said.

'What do you do?' Denny asked Nick.

'I regroove tires,' Nick said.

Denny smiled; his entire manner changed, as if the trouble had cleared. 'Oh, yeah?' he asked, and laughed. 'What a job. What a vocation. Handed down to you by your father?'

'Yes,' Nick said, and felt hate; it was all he could do to keep it from showing, and he wanted to keep it from showing; he felt afraid of Denny – perhaps because the others in the room were, and he was picking it up from them.

Denny held out his hand to Nick. 'Okay, tire regroover, you want to buy a nickel or a dime booklet? I've got both.' He reached inside his leather jacket and brought out a bundle of tracts. 'This is good stuff,' he said. 'All authentic; I know the guy who prints them. I've seen Cordon's original manuscript there in the plant.'

41

'Since I'm paying for it,' Zeta said, 'it'll be a nickel booklet.'

'I suggest *THE MORALS OF PROPER MAN*,' Charley said.

'You do?' Denny said sardonically, eyeing her. She met his gaze, as before, without flinching; Nick thought. She is as hard as he is. She is able to withstand him. But why? he wondered. Is it worth it, to be near such a violent person. Yes, he thought; I can feel the violence, and the volatility. He is apt, at any time, to do anything, any minute. He has an amphetamine personality. Probably he takes massive doses of one of the amphetamines, either orally or by injection. Or maybe, to do the job he does, he has to be this way.

'I'll take that one,' Nick said. 'The one she suggests.'

'She's roped you in,' Denny said. 'Like she ropes in everybody, every man, anyhow.' To Nick he said, 'She's a stupid. She's a stupid, short bitch.'

'You fairy,' Charley said.

'The lesbian talks,' Denny said.

Zeta got out a five-pop bill and handed it to Denny; clearly he wanted to conclude the transaction and leave.

'Do I bother you?' Denny asked Nick, abruptly.

He said, carefully, 'No.'

'Some people I bother,' Denny said.

'Of course you do,' Charley said. She reached out, took the handful of booklets from him, found the proper one and handed it to Nick, smiling her illuminating smile at the same time. Sixteen, he thought; no older than that. Children playing at the game of life and death, hating and fighting, but – probably sticking together when there is trouble. The animosity between Denny and the girl masked, he decided, a deeper attraction. Somehow, they functioned in tandem. A symbiotic relationship, he conjectured; not pleasant to look on but nonetheless real. A Dionysus from the gutter, he thought, and a small, pretty, tough girl able to – or trying to – cope with him. Hating him, probably, and yet unable to leave. Probably because he is, to her, so attractive physically, and, in her eyes, a real man. Because he is tougher than she

42

is, and that she respects. Because she herself is so tough she knows what it means.

But what a person to be melded to. Like a sticky fruit in too warm a climate, he had melted; his face was soft and molten and only the blazing glare of his eyes held his features in conformity.

I would have thought, he thought, that those distributing and selling Cordon's writing would be idealistic, noble. But apparently not. His work is illegal; it attracts those who naturally handle illegal things, and they are a type themselves. The objects they peddle don't in themselves matter; it is strictly the fact that they are illegal, and people will pay a good, a very good, price.

'Are you sure this place is clean now?' Denny asked the girl. 'You know, I live here; I'm here ten hours a day. If they find anything here—' He prowled about, suspicious in an animal-like way: a brooding suspiciousness, replete with hatred.

Suddenly, he picked up a floor lamp. He examined it, then got from his pocket a coin; he unscrewed three screws and the baseplate came loose in his hands. And, from the hollow shaft of the lamp, appeared three rolled-up booklets.

Denny turned toward the girl, who stood unmoving, her face calm – virtually so, anyway; Nick saw her lips press tightly together as if she were preparing herself for something.

Lifting his right arm, Denny hit her, hit at her eye but missed. She had ducked, but not far enough; the blow caught her on the side of the head above the ear. And, with startling speed, she grabbed his extended arm, lifted his wrist and bit him, bit deep into his flesh. Denny screamed, flailing at her, trying to free his wrist from her teeth.

'Help me!' Denny yelled at Nick and Zeta. Nick, not knowing what to do, started toward the girl, hearing himself mumble at her, telling her to let go, telling her she might bite through a nerve and leave his hand paralyzed. Zeta, however, seized her by the jaw, inserted his big, dark-stained fingers into the hinges and pried her jaws open; Denny at once withdrew his arm, examined the bite; he seemed dazed, and then, immediately after, the violence returned to his face. And now it was a murderous violence; his eyes bulged as if about to pop literally from his head. He bent, picked up the lamp, lifted it high.

Zeta pinned him, gasping; he held the boy in a huge grip, and at the same time gasping to Nick, 'Get her out of here. Take her somewhere he can't find her. Can't you see? *He's an alcohol addict.* They'll do anything. Go!'

In a trance, Nick took hold of the girl's hand and led her rapidly from the apartment.

'You can take my squib,' Zeta, panting, yelled after him.

'Okay,' Nick said; he tugged the girl along – she came willingly, small and light – and he reached the elevator, stabbed at the button.

'We better run off up to the roof,' Charley said. She seemed calm; she, in fact, smiled up at him with her radiant smile which made her face so exquisitely lovely.

'Are you afraid of him?' Nick asked as they got onto the escalator and began to sprint up it, two steps at a time. He still held her gripped by the wrist, and she still managed to keep up with him. Lithe, spirit-like, she combined an animal-like ability to move swiftly with an almost supernatural gliding quality. Like a deer, he thought, as they continued on up.

Far below them on the escalator, Denny appeared. 'Come back!' he yelled his voice shaking with agitation. 'I'm going to have to go to a hospital to get this bite looked at. Drive me to the hospital.'

'He always says that,' Charley said placidly, unstirred by the boy's pitiful whine. 'Just ignore him and hope he can't run faster than us.'

'Does he do that to you very often?' Nick panted as they reached the roof field and sprinted in the direction of Zeta's parked squib.

'He knows what I'll do,' Charley said. 'You saw what I did – I bit him and he can't stand to be bitten. Have you ever been bitten by a full-grown person? Have you ever thought what it would feel like? And I can do another thing – I stand against the wall and sort of hold myself there with my arms out, so I'm tight against something, and then I kick, with both

44

feet. I'll have to show you sometime. Just remember: never try to touch me when I don't want to be touched. No man is going to do that and get away with it.'

Nick got her into the squib, ran around to the driver's side, slid in behind the tiller. He started up the motor, and there, at the escalator exit, stood Denny, wheezing. Seeing him, Charley laughed in delight, a girlish laugh; she put both hands to her mouth and rocked from side to side, her eyes shining. 'Oh God,' she said, 'He's so angry. And there's nothing he can do. Take off.'

Pressing down on the power knob, Nick took off; the squib, old and battered as it was, had a well souped-up motor which Zeta had built himself; he had modified every moving part. So, in his own squib, Denny would never catch him. Unless of course, Denny had souped up his own squib.

'What do you know about his squib?' he asked Charley, who sat smoothing down her hair and arranging herself tidily. 'Has he—'

'Denny can't do anything involving manual labor. He hates to get his hands greasy. But he's got a Shellingberg 8, with the B-3 engine. So he can go very fast. Sometimes, if there's no other traffic, like late at night, he opens it up all the way to fifty.'

'No problem,' Nick said .'This old clinker will reach seventy or even seventy-five. If Zeta's word can be trusted.' The squib was moving rapidly, now, weaving in and out of the mid-morning traffic. 'I'll lose him,' Nick said. Behind him he saw a Shellingberg, painted bright purple. 'Is that him?' he asked her.

Twisting around to see, Charley said, 'Yes, that's it. Denny owns the only purple Shellingberg 8 in the United States.'

'I'll get into heavy cross-city traffic,' Nick said, and began to descend to the level frequented by short-hop squibs. Almost at once, two innocuous squibs filled in behind him as he tailgated the squib ahead. 'And I'll turn here,' he said, as the balloon marked HASTINGS AVE appeared bobbingly on his right. He turned, became – as he had hoped – utterly involved in the slow rows of squibs looking for parking places ... most of them driven by women out on shopping trips.

No sign of the purple Shellingberg 8. He peered in all directions, trying to catch sight of it.

'You've lost him,' Charley said matter-of-factly. 'He depends on speed – you know, free speed high up out of traffic – but down here—' She laughed, her eyes shining with what seemed to him delight. 'He's too impatient; he never drives down here.'

Nick asked, 'So what do you think he'll do?'

'Give up. He'll get over being mad in a couple of days, anyhow. But for about forty-eight hours he'll be homicidal. That really was stupid of me to hide those booklets in the lamp; he's right. But I still don't like being hit.' Meditatively, she rubbed the side of her head where he had hit her. 'He hits hard,' she said. 'But he can't stand to be hurt back; I can't really hit him and make it work – I'm too small – but you saw me bite.'

'Yes,' he said. 'The all time great bite of the century.' He did not wish to dispute *that*.

'It's very nice of you,' Charley said, 'a total stranger, helping me like this, when you don't even know me. You don't even know my name.'

'I'll settle for Charley,' he said. It seemed to fit her.

'I didn't get your name,' the girl said.

'Nick Appleton.'

She laughed her bubbling glee from between the fingers of her hands. 'That's the name a character in a book would have. "Nick Appleton." A private track, maybe. Or on one of those TV shows.'

'It's the kind of a name that denotes competency,' Nick said.

'You *are* competent,' she admitted. 'I mean you got us – me – out of there. Thank you.'

'Where are you going to spend the next forty-eight hours?' Nick asked. 'Until he cools off?'

'I have another apartment; we use that, too. We transfer stuff from one to the other, in case a PSS s-and-s warrant gets served on us. Search and seizure, you know. But they don't suspect us. Denny's family has a lot of money and influence, and one time a track started probing around, and a top PSS official, a friend of Denny's dad, called to tip us off. That's the only time we've had any thouble.'

Nick said, 'I don't think you should go to the other apartment.'

'Why not? All my things are there; I have to go there.'

'Go where he won't find you. He might kill you.' He had read articles about the personality changes often suffered by alcohol addicts. How much feral cruelty often came out, a virtually psychopathic personality structure, blended with the fast moving quality of mania and the suspicious rage of paranoia. Well, now he had seen one, seen an alcohol addict. And he did not like it. No wonder the authorities had made it illegal – *really* illegal: an alcohol addict usually found himself, if caught, in a psychodidactic work camp for the rest of his life. Unless he could pay for a major lawyer who in turn could pay for expensive testing of the individual, with the idea of proving that the period of addiction was over. But of course it was never over. An alc-hound remained what he was forever, even after Platt's surgery on the diencephalon, the area of the brain which controlled oral cravings.

'If he kills me,' Charley said, 'I'll kill him. And, basically he's more afraid than I am. He has a lot of fears; most of what he does he does out of fear – out of panic, I should say. He's in a constant hysterical panic.'

'What if he hasn't been drinking?'

'He's still scared, and that's why he drinks . . . but he isn't violent unless he drinks; he just wants to run away and hide. But he can't do that – because he believes people are watching him and know he's a dealer – so then he drinks; that's when it occurs.'

'But by drinking,' Nick said, 'he draws attention to himself; that's the very thing he's trying to avoid. Isn't it?'

'Maybe not. Maybe he wants to get caught. He's never done a lick of work in his life before dealing in tracts and booklets and minitapes; his family always supported him. And now he takes advantage of the cred – what's the word?'

'Credulity,' Nick said.

'Does that mean like when you want to believe?'

'Yes.' It was reasonably close.

47

'So he takes advantage of their credulity, because people, a lot of people, superstitiously believe in Provoni, you know? About his coming back? All that shrnap you find in Cordon's writings?'

Nick, incredulous, asked, 'You mean to say that you people who deal in Cordon's writings, you people who sell it—'

'We don't have to believe it. Does the man who sells someone a pint of liquor have to be an alcohol addict himself?'

The logic, correct as it was, appalled him. 'It's for money,' he said. 'You probably don't even read what's in those tracts; you just know them by name. Like a clerk working in a warehouse.'

'I've read a few.' She turned to face him, still massaging her forehead. 'God, I've got a headache. Do you have any darvon or codeine at your place?'

SEVEN

'No,' he said, filled with abrupt, alert unease. She wants to stay with me, he thought, for the next couple of days. 'Listen,' he said, 'I'll take you to a motel, one picked at random; he'll never find you. I'll pay for it for two nights.'

'Hell,' Charley said, 'there's that master location-meter and control center that processes the name of everyone checked into every motel and hotel in North America; for two pops he can use it just by picking up a fone.'

Nick said, 'We'll use a fake name.'

'No.' She shook her head.

'Why not?' His unease became greater; he felt, all at once, as if she were sticking to him like flypaper: he couldn't pry her loose.

'I don't want to be alone,' Charley said, 'because if he *does* find me in some motel room, alone, he'll beat the hell out of me; nothing like you saw, but really. I have to be with some-

48

one; I have to have people who—'

'I couldn't stop him,' Nick said, truthfully. Even Zeta, for all his strength, hadn't been able to hold onto Denny for more than a few minutes.

'He won't fight with you. It's just that he doesn't want anybody, any third party, to see what he does to me. But—' She paused. 'I shouldn't try to get you involved. It's not fair to you. Suppose a fight broke out at your place, and we were all bursted by the PSS, and they found that tract on you that you got from us . . . you know the penalty.'

'I'll throw it away,' he said. 'Now.' He rolled down the window of the squib, reached into his cumberbund for the small book.

'So Eric Cordon comes second,' Charley said, in a neutral voice, a voice without censure. 'First comes protecting me from Denny. Isn't that funny? It's really funny!'

'An individual is more important than theoretical—'

'You're not hooked yet, sweet. You haven't read Cordon; when you do, you'll feel different. Anyhow, I have two tracts in my purse, so it wouldn't make any difference.'

'Throw them away.'

'No,' Charley said.

Well, he thought, the stuff has hit the fan. She won't give up the pamphlets and she won't let me leave her off at a motel. What do I do now? Just drive around and around in this damn in-city traffic until I run out of fuel? And there's always the chance that Shellingberg 8 will show up and we'll be finished right then and there; he'll probably ram us and kill us all. Unless the alcohol has worn off by now.

'I have a wife,' he said, simply. 'And a child. I can't do anything that—'

'You did it. By letting Zeta know that you wanted a tract; you were in it the minute you and Zeta knocked on the door of our apartment.'

'Before that, even,' Nick said, nodding; it was true.

So fast, he thought. A commitment made in the blink of an eye. But it had been there a long time, building up. The news of Cordon's pending murder – and that was what it was – had brought him to a decision, and at that moment,

Kleo and Bobby were in danger.

On the other hand, the PSS had just now spot-checked him, using Darby Shire as bait. And he – and Kleo – had passed it. So from the standpoint of statistical probabilities, there wasn't a good chance he'd be investigated soon, again.

But he could not fool himself. They probably watch Zeta, he thought. And they know about the two apartments. They know all there is to know; it's just a question of when they want to make their move.

In that case, it really was too late. He might as well go all the way; have Charley stay with him and Kleo for a couple of days. The couch in the living room made into a cot; they had had friends stay overnight.

But this situation differed, sharply, from those instances.

'You can stay with my wife and me,' he said, 'if you get rid of the tracts you're carrying. You don't have to destroy them – can't you just drop them off at some place you're familiar with?'

Charley, without answering, picked up one of the pamphlets, turned the pages, then read aloud. ' "The measure of a man is not his intelligence. It is not how high he rises in the freak establishment. The measure of a man is this: how swiftly can he react to another person's need? And how much of himself can he give? In giving that is true giving, nothing comes back, or at least—" '

'Sure; giving gives you something back,' Nick said. 'You give somebody something; later on he returns the favor by giving you something in return. That's obvious.'

'That's not giving; that's barter. Listen to this. "God tells us—" '

'God is dead,' Nick said. 'They found his carcass in 2019. Floating out in space near Alpha.'

'They found the remains of an organism advanced several thousand times over what we are,' Charley said. 'And it evidently could create habitable worlds and populate them with living organisms, derived from itself. But that doesn't prove it was God.'

'I think it was God.'

Charley said, 'Can I stay at your place tonight and maybe, if it's necessary – and *only* if it's necessary – maybe to-morrow night. Okay?' She glanced up at him, her bright smile bathed in the light of innocence. As if, like a little cat, she were asking for a saucer of milk, nothing more. 'Don't be afraid of Denny, he won't hurt you. If he beats up any-body, it'll be me. But he's not going to be able to find your apartment; how could he? He doesn't know your name; he doesn't know—'

'He knows I work for Zeta.'

'Zeta isn't afraid of him. Zeta could beat him to a pulp—'

'You contradict yourself,' Nick said, or at least so it seemed; perhaps the alcohol was still affecting him. He wondered when it wore off, an hour? Two? Anyhow, it appeared that he was flying his squib adequately; at least no PSS occifer had flagged him down or grappled onto him with tractor beams.

'You're afraid of what your wife will say,' Charley said. 'If you bring me home. She'll think lots of things.'

'Well, there's that,' he said. 'And also the law called "statutory rape". You're not twenty-one, are you?'

'I'm sixteen.'

'There, you see—'

'Okay,' she said merrily. 'Land and drop me off.'

'Do you have any money?' he asked.

'No.'

'But you'll manage?'

'Yes. I can always manage.' She spoke without rancor; she did not seem to blame him for his hesitation. Maybe this sort of thing has happened before between them, he re-flected. And others, like myself, have been lured in. With the best intentions in mind.

'I'll tell you what may happen to you if you take me to your place,' Charley said. 'You can be bursted for being in the same room with Cordonite material. You can be bursted for statutory rape. Your wife, who will also be arrested for being in the same room with Cordonite material, will leave you, and will never understand or forgive you. And yet you can't just let me off, even though you don't know me, be-cause I'm a girl and I have nowhere to go to—'

'Friends,' he said. 'You must have friends you could go to.' Or are they too much afraid of Denny? he wondered. 'You're right,' he said, then. 'I can't just let you off.'

Kidnapping, he thought; I could also be charged with that, if Denny felt like calling the PSS. But – Denny could not, would not, do that, because then, in return, he would be nailed as a peddler of Cordonite material. He can't take that chance.

'You're a strange little girl,' he said to Charley. 'In some ways you're naïveté itself and in other ways you're tough as a warehouse rat.' Did selling illegal material make her like this? he wondered. Or did it happen the other way around ... she had grown up hard, toughened, and hence had gravitated to such work. He glanced at her, now, sizing up her clothes. She is too well-dressed, he thought; those are expensive garments. Maybe she is greedy – this is a way of earning enough pops to satisfy that greed. For her, clothes. For Denny, the Shellingberg 8. Without this they would merely be teenagers, going to school in jeans and shapeless sweaters.

Evil, he thought, in the service of good. Or were Cordon's writings good? He had never seen an authentic Cordon tract before; now, presumably, he had one and he was free to read it himself and decide. And let her stay if it's good? he wondered. And if it isn't, toss her out to the wolves, to Denny and the prowl cars with their telepathic Unusuals listening constantly.

'I am life,' the girl said.

'What?' he said, startled.

'To you, I am life. What are you, thirty-eight? Forty? What have you learned? Have you done anything? Look at me, look. I'm life and when you're with me, some of it rubs off on you. You don't feel so old, now, do you? With me here in the squib beside you.'

Nick said, 'I'm thirty-four and I don't feel old. As a matter of fact, sitting here with you makes me feel older, not younger. Nothing is rubbing off.'

'It will,' she said.

'You know this from experience,' he said. 'With older men. Before me.'

Opening her purse she got out her mirror and cheekstick; she began to stroke elaborate lines from her eyes, across her cheekbones, to the rim of her jaw.

'You use too much makeup,' he said.

'All right, call me a two-pop whore.'

'What?' he asked, staring at her, his attention momentarily túrned away from the mid-morning traffic.

'Nothing,' she said. She closed up her cheekstick, placed it and the mirror back in her purse. 'Do you want some alcohol?' she asked. 'Denny and I have a lot of contacts for alc. I might even be able to get you some – what's it called – oh yes, scotch.'

'Made in some fly-by-night distillery out of God knows what,' Nick said.

She began to laugh helplessly; she sat, head down, her right hand over her eyes. 'I can picture a distillery flapping through the midnight sky, on its way to a new location. Where the PSS won't find it.' She continued laughing, holding onto her head as if the idea of it refused to leave her.

'You can go blind from alcohol,' Nick said.

'Smoke. *Wood* alcohol.'

'How can you be sure it isn't that?'

'How can you be sure of anything? Denny may catch us any time and kill us, or the PSS may do it ... it's just not likely, and you have to go by what's likely, not what's possible. *Anything* is possible.' She smiled up at him. 'But that's good, don't you see? It means you can always hope; he says that, Cordon – I remember that. Cordon says it again and again. He really doesn't have much of a message, but I remember that. You and I might fall in love; you might leave your wife and I'd leave Denny, and then he'd go outright insane – he'd go on a drinking binge – and he'd kill all of us and then himself.' She laughed, her light eyes dancing. 'But isn't it great? Don't you see how great it is?'

He didn't.

'You'll see,' Charley said. 'Meanwhile, don't talk to me

53

for the next ten or so minutes, I have to figure out what to tell your wife.'

'I'll tell her,' Nick said.

'You'd foul it all up. *I'll* do it.' She squeezed her eyes shut, concentrating. He drove on, then, turning in the direction of his apartment.

EIGHT

Fred Huff, personal assistant to PSS Director Barnes, placed a list on his superior's desk and said, 'Pardon me, but you asked for a daily report on apartment 3XX24J and here it is. We used standard tapes of voices to identify those who came by. Only one person – one new person, I mean – came by. A Nicholas Appleton.

'Doesn't sound like much,' Barnes said.

'We ran it through the computer, the one we lease from the University of Wyoming. It made an interesting extrapolation as soon as it had all previous material on this Nicholas Appleton, his age, occupation, background, is he married, does he have any children, has he ever—'

'He's never broken the law before in any manner whatsoever.'

'You mean he's never been caught. We asked the computer that, too. What are the chances, given this particular man, that he would knowingly violate the law, at the felony level. It said probably no, he would not.'

'He did when he went to 3XX24J,' Barnes said caustically.

'So noted; hence the application from the computer for a prognosis. Extrapolating from his case, and others similar to it during the last few hours, the computer declares that the news of Cordon's impending execution has already swelled the ranks of the Cordonite underground by forty percent.'

'Balls,' Director Barnes said.

'That's how it works out statistically.'

54

'You mean they've joined in protest? Openly?'

'Not openly, no. In protest, yes.'

'Ask the computer what the reaction will be to the announcement of Cordon's death.'

'It can't compute. Not enough data. Well, it computed, but in so many possible ways as to tell us nothing. Ten percent: a mass uprising. Fifteen percent: a refusal to believe that—'

'The greatest probability is what?'

'A belief that Cordon is dead, but that Provoni is not; that he's alive and will return. Even without Cordon. You must remember that thousands – authentic or forged – writings by Cordon are being circulated everywhere on Earth every minute of the day. His death isn't going to end that. Remember the famous revolutionary of the twentieth century, Ché Guevara. Even though dead, the diary which he left behind—'

'Like Christ,' Barnes said. He felt depressed; he had begun to brood. 'Kill Christ and you get the New Testament. Kill Ché Guevara and you get a diary that's a book of instructions on how to gain power all over the world. Kill Cordon—'

A buzzer on Barnes' desk buzzed.

'Yes, Council Chairman,' Barnes said into the intercom. 'I have occifer Noyes with me.' He nodded to her and she rose from the leather-covered chair facing his desk. 'We'll come in.' He motioned to her, feeling at the same time a stiff dislike of her.

He did not like policewomen in general, and especially those who liked to wear the uniform. A woman, he had mused long ago, should not be in uniform. The female informers did not bother him, because in no way were they required to surrender their femininity. Police occifer Noyes was sexless – in actual, physiological fact. She had undergone Snyder's operation, so that both legally and physically speaking, she was not a woman; she had no sex organs as such, no breasts; her hips were as narrow as a man's, and her face was fathomless and cruel.

'Just think,' Barnes said to her as they walked down the

55

corridor – past the double rows of weapons-police guards – and came to Willis Gram's massive, ornate oak door, 'how good you'd feel if you had after all managed to get something on Irma Gram. Too bad.' He nudged her as the door opened and they entered Gram's bedroom office. In his huge bed, Gram lay, buried in piles of sections of the *Times*, an expression of cunning on his face.

'Council Chairman,' Barnes said, 'this is Alice Noyes, the special occifer who has been in charge of obtaining material relating to the moral habits of your wife.'

'I've met you before,' Gram said to her.

'Correct, Council Chairman,' Alice Noyes said, nodding.

Gram said calmly, 'I want my wife murdered, by Eric Cordon, on live world-wide TV.'

Barnes stared at him. Peacefully, Gram stared back, the look of animal cunning still on his face.

After a pause Alice Noyes said, 'It would, of course, be easy to snuff her. A fatal squib accident during a shopping tour to Europe or Asia, she makes them all the time. But by Eric Cordon—'

'That's the inventive part,' Gram said.

After a pause, Alice Noyes said, 'Respectfully, Council Chairman, are we supposed to work out the project or do you have ideas as to how we should or could proceed? The more you tell us, the better our position, operationally, would be, all the way down to the working level.'

Gram eyed her. 'By all that, do you mean do I know how to do it?'

'I'm puzzled, too,' Director Barnes said, at this point. 'I am trying, first of all, to imagine the effect this would have on the average citizen, if Cordon did a thing of this sort.'

'They'd know that all the love and gift-giving and mutual help and empathy and cooperation among Old Men, New Men and Unusuals – they'd know it was so much bombastic bilge. And I'd be rid of Irma. Don't forget that part, Director; don't forget that part.'

'I'm not forgetting that part,' Barnes said, 'but I still don't see how it can be done.'

56

'At Cordon's execution,' Gram said, 'all top officials of the government will be present, including wives – my wife. Cordon will be brought out by a dozen or so armed police guards. The TV cameras will be getting it all; don't forget that. Then all of a sudden, by just one of those flukes that happens, Cordon grabs a hand weapon from an occifer, aims it at me, but misses me and snuffs Irma, who will of course be sitting beside me.'

'Jesus God,' Director Barnes said heavily; he felt enormous weight gather over him, bowing him down. 'Are we supposed to alter Cordon's brain so he's compelled to do it? Or do we just ask him to, if he'd mind—'

'Cordon will already be snuffed,' Gram said. 'The day before at the latest.'

'Then how—'

Gram said, 'His brain will be replaced by a synthetic neuro-control turret which will direct him to do what we want him – or it, rather – to do. That's easy enough. We'll get Amos Ild to install it.'

'The New Man who's building the Great Ear?' Barnes asked. 'You intend to ask *him* to help you do this?'

'It's like this,' Gram said. 'If he doesn't, I'll cut off all funds for the development of the Great Ear. And we'll get some other New Man capable of scooping out Cordon's brain—' He halted – Alice Noyes had shuddered. 'Sorry. Remove his brain, then, if you prefer it put that way. In any case, it's the same thing. What do you say, Barnes? Isn't this brilliant?' He paused. There was silence. 'Answer me.'

'It would help,' Barnes said carefully, 'to discredit the Under Man movement. But the risk is too great. The risk outweighs the possible gain; you have to look at it that way . . . with all due respects.'

'What risk?'

'First of all, you'll have to bring a top-level New Man into this, which makes you dependent on them, which you absolutely don't want to be. And those laboratory synthetic brains they're making in their research centers – they're not dependable. It might go berk and shoot everyone, including you. I wouldn't want to be out there when that thing emerges

57

with a gun and starts through its programming; I want to be a million miles away, for the sake of my own hide.'

'You don't like the idea, then,' Gram said.

'My statement could be so construed,' Barnes said, pulsing inside with indignation. Which Gram, of course, picked up.

'What do you think, Noyes?' Gram asked the police-woman.

'I think,' Noyes said, 'that it's the most fantastically brilliant plan I've ever encountered.'

'See?' Gram said to Barnes.

Curious, Barnes said to her, 'When did you arrive at that conclusion? A moment ago when the Council Chairman talked about—'

'It was merely his choice of words, that to-do with scooping,' Noyes said. 'But now I see it in perspective.'

'It's the finest idea that has ever come to me in all the years I've spent in the Civil Service and this top office,' Gram said proudly.

'Maybe so,' Barnes said wearily. 'Maybe it is.' Which, he thought, is a commentary on you.

Picking up Barnes' thoughts, Gram scowled.

'Just a fleeting, dubious thought,' Barnes said. 'A doubt which I'm sure will presently be gone.' He had momentarily forgotten about Gram's telepathic ability. But even if he had remembered, he nonetheless would have thought the thought.

'True,' Gram said, nodding as he picked up this, too. 'Do you want to resign, Barnes?' he asked. 'And disassociate yourself from this?'

'No sir,' Barnes said respectfully.

'All right.' Gram nodded. 'Get hold of Amos Ild as soon as possible, make sure he understands that it's a state secret, and ask him to get started on an artificial analogue to Cordon's brain. Get the encephalograms cranking out, or however it is they go about it.'

'Encephalograms,' Barnes said, nodding in agreement. 'A massive, intensive study of Cordon's mind – brain, whichever.'

Gram said, 'You've got to remember the image Irma has

vis-à-vis the public. We know what she's really like, but they think of her as a kindly, generous, philanthropic do-gooder who sponsors charities and generally beautifying public works, such as floating gardens in the sky. But we know—'

'So,' Barnes interrupted, 'the public will think that Cordon has murdered a harmless, loving person. A terrible crime, even in the eyes of Under Men. Everyone will be glad when Cordon is "killed" immediately after his vicious, senseless act. That is, if Ild's brain is good enough to fool the Unusuals, the telepaths.' In his mind he could imagine the synthetic brain sending Cordon ricocheting about the hanging arena, mowing people down by the hundreds.

'No,' Gram said, picking up his thoughts once again. 'We'll gun him down immediately. There's no chance of a foul-up there. Sixteen armed men, all crack shots, will fire on him instantaneously.'

'Instantaneously,' Barnes said dryly, 'after he's managed to shoot one particular person out of a crowd of thousands. He would have to be a damn good shot.'

'But they'll think he was after me,' Gram reminded him. 'And I'll be sitting in the front row . . . Irma with me.'

'In any case, he isn't going to be gunned down "instantaneously",' Barnes pointed out. 'A second or two will have to elapse, while he makes his shot. And if he's a little off – you're sitting right beside her.'

'Hm,' Gram said, chewing his lip.

'A slip of inches,' Barnes said, 'and it would be you, not Irma. I think your attempt to combine your problems with the Under Men and Cordon and your problems with Irma into one big colorful operatic smash-finale is a little too—' He pondered. 'There's a Greek word for it.'

'*Terpsichore*,' Gram said.

'No,' Barnes said. '*Hubris*. Trying too much; going too far.'

'I still agree with Council Chairman Gram,' Alice Noyes said in her brisk, cold-crimson voice. 'Admittedly, it's daring. But it will solve so much. A man who rules, as does the Council Chairman, must be able to make such a decision, to try daring maneuvers to keep the structure functioning. In this one act—'

'I'm resigning as Police Director,' Barnes said.

'Why?' Gram asked, surprised; obviously no thoughts passing through Barnes' mind had forewarned him of this – the decision came out of nowhere.

'Because it will probably mean your death,' Barnes said. 'Because Amos Ild will program it to get you, not Irma.'

'I have an idea,' Alice Noyes said. 'As Cordon is led to the center of the arena, Irma Gram will descend from her place, carrying one white rose. She will hold it out to Cordon, and at that moment he will grab a weapon from a too-lax guard and shoot her.' She smiled thinly, her usually dim eyes glittering. 'That ought to undermine them forever. An act of senseless viciousness like that; only a madman would kill a woman bringing him a white rose.'

'Why white?' Barnes asked.

'Why what white?' Noyes asked.

'The rose, the goddam rose.'

'Because it's a symbol of innocence,' Noyes said.

Willis Gram, still chewing on his lip, still scowling, said, 'No, that won't do. He's got to seem to be trying to get me, because he would have a motive for getting me. But what motive would he have for killing Irma?'

'To kill she, who you most love.'

Barnes laughed.

'What's funny?' Gram demanded.

'Maybe it'll work,' Barnes said. 'That's what's so funny about it. And "To kill she, who you most love." Can I quote you on that, Noyes? A model sentence all school children should learn; it parses so well.'

'Academics,' Noyes said scathingly.

Hoarsely, his face red, Gram said to Barnes, 'I don't care about her grammar. I don't care about my grammar. I don't care about anybody's grammar. All I care about is that this is a good plan and she agrees, and you've resigned as of now. So you have no further vote on the matter . . . anyhow, if I decide to accept your resignation. I'll have to think about it. I'll tell you sometime; you can wait.' His voice submerged itself into an autistic mumble at that point as he mulled over the matter under scrutiny. All at once, he glanced up at Barnes and said, 'You're in a strange mood. You usually go along with everything I suggest. What's gotten into you?'

'3XX24J,' Barnes said.

'What's that?'

'A sample Under Men apartment we're watching. We've been doing a statistical analysis with the Wyoming computer as to the characteristics of those who come and go.'

'And you just got news you don't like.'

'I got a very small piece of news,' Barnes said. 'One average citizen, who apparently heard that Cordon is going to be executed, all at once stepped across the line. Someone we had just tested, as a matter of fact. The computer didn't like that at all. Such a swing, such amplitude in loyalty, and in such a short time ... announcing Cordon's execution may have been a mistake – a mistake which we can still redeem. The "judges" could change their minds again.' He added sardonically, but straight-faced, 'I have an idea of a minor alteration in your plan, Council Chairman. Have Cordon's weapon a fake, too, along with him. He points the gun and "fires", and then at the same moment a sharpshooter hidden nearby Irma takes the actual shot at her. That way the chances of hitting you can be reduced practically to zero.'

'A good thought,' Gram said, nodding.

'You would take such a suggestion seriously?' Barnes asked.

'It's a good suggestion. It overrides the element which you brought up, as to what—'

Barnes said, '*You must untangle your public life from your private life.* You've got them all mixed in together.'

'And I'll tell you something else,' Gram said, still red-faced and hoarse. 'That lawyer Denfeld – I want some Cordon tracts and pamphlets planted around his apartment and then I want to see a burst where he's caught red-handed. And we'll stick him away in Brightforth Prison, along with Cordon. They can talk to one another.'

'Denfeld can talk,' Alice Noyes said. 'And Cordon can

write it all down. And the rest of the prisoners can read it.'

'I think,' Gram said, 'it's a masterstroke of my innate genius to solve my public and private problems with one act, it fits the requirements of Occam's Razor, if you see what I mean. Do you see what I mean?'

Neither Barnes nor Noyes answered. Barnes was wondering how to withdraw his resignation – made hastily and without thought for future possibilities. And, as he thought this, he realized that, as always, Willis Gram was listening in.

'Don't worry,' Gram said. 'You don't need to resign. But you know, I really like that touch about a sharpshooter placed near Irma and me, ready to pick her off when Cordon fires his fake gun. Yes, that appeals to me; thanks for the contribution.'

'You're welcome,' Barnes said, and held down his aversion and his rapidly boiling thoughts.

'I don't care,' Gram said, 'what you think. I only care what you do. Feel as hostile as you want, it doesn't matter, just so long as you give this project your complete and immediate attention. I want it done soon . . . Cordon might die on us or something. We need a name for the project. A code term. What'll we call it?'

'Barabbas,' Barnes said.

'I don't catch the meaning, but it's fine with me,' Gram said. 'All right; from now on it's Operation Barabbas. We'll absolutely refer to it as that in both written and oral interchanges.'

' "Barabbas," ' Alice Noyes echoed. 'That was a situation in which the wrong one of two people was murdered.'

'Oh,' Gram said. 'Well, it still sounds good enough to me.' He plucked fretfully at his lower lip. 'What was the name of the person who was innocent who they snuffed?'

'Jesus of Nazareth,' Barnes said.

'Are you drawing an analogy?' Gram demanded. 'That Cordon is like Christ?'

'It's been done,' Barnes said. 'Anyhow, let me make another point. All Cordon's writings have opposed force and compulsion and violence. It's inconceivable that he'd try to kill someone.'

'That's the point,' Gram said patiently. 'The whole point. It will discredit everything he's written. It'll show him up as a hypocrite; it'll undermine all his tracts and booklets. Do you see?'

'It'll backfire,' Barnes said.

'You really don't like my solutions to things,' Gram said, gazing at him searchingly.

'I think,' Barnes said, 'that in this case – you're being highly injudicious.'

'What's that mean?' Gram asked.

'Ill-advised.'

'Nobody advised me, it's my own idea.'

Director Barnes gave up at that point; he let his brooding thoughts take over and his tongue became silent.

Nobody seemed to notice.

'So it's on with Project Barabbas,' Gram said heartily, and smiled a wide, happy smile.

NINE

At the sound of their special knock, Kleo Appleton opened the door of the apartment. Home in the middle of the day? she wondered. Something must have happened.

And then she saw, with him, a small girl, probably in her late teens, well-dressed, with much makeup, and a white-toothed smile, as if of recognition.

'You must be Kleo,' the smiling girl said. 'I'm very glad to meet you, after what Nick has said about you.' She and Nick entered the apartment; the girl gazed around at the furniture, the wall colors: she appraised the decor expertly, seeing everything. It had the effect of making Kleo nervous and self-conscious, whereas, she realized, it ought to be the other way around. Who is this girl? she wondered.

'Yes,' she said. 'I'm Mrs. Appleton.'

Nick shut the door behind the two of them. 'She's hiding from her boyfriend,' he said to his wife. 'He tried to beat her up and she got away. He can't trace her here because he doesn't know who I am or where I live, so she's safe here.'

'Coffee?' Kleo asked.

' "Coffee"?' Nick repeated.

'I'll put on some coffee,' Kleo said. She surveyed the girl and saw how pretty she was, despite her heavy makeup. And how little she was. The girl probably had trouble finding clothes small enough to fit her . . . a trouble I wish I had, Kleo reflected.

'My name is Charlotte,' the girl said. She had seated herself on the living room couch and was unbuckling her greaves. The wide, positive smile never left her face; she gazed up at Kleo with what seemed almost to be love. Love! For someone she had never seen before in her life.

'I said she could stay here overnight,' Nick said.

'Yes,' Kleo said. 'The couch makes into a bed.' She made her way to the kitchen area and poured three cups of coffee.

'What do you take in your coffee?' she asked the girl.

'Look,' Charlotte said, springing lithely up and coming toward her. 'Don't go to any trouble for me, honest. I don't need anything, except a place to stay a couple of days that's a place Denny doesn't know about. And we lost him, we shook him off in all that traffic. So there's really no chance of a—' She gesticulated. 'A scene. I promise.'

'You still didn't tell me what you want in your coffee.'

'Black.'

Kleo handed her a cup.

'This is wonderful coffee,' Charlotte said.

Carrying two cups, Kleo went back to the living room, gave Nick his cup, seated herself on a black plastic chair. Nick and the girl, like two people in adjoining seats at a movie, sat down side by side on the couch.

'Have you called the police?' Kleo asked.

'Call the police?' Charlotte asked, with a puzzled expression. 'No, of course not. He does this all the time; I just get out and wait – I know how long it lasts. And then I go back. The police? And have them arrest him? He'd die in jail. He has to be free; he has to go on sailing over great spaces, very fast, in that squib of his, the Purple Sea Cow we call it.' She then sipped her coffee, earnestly.

Kleo pondered. She had mixed feelings, chaotic feelings. *She's a stranger*, she thought. We don't know her; we don't know even if she's telling the truth about her boyfriend. Suppose it's something else? Suppose the police are after her? But Nick seems to like her; he seems to trust her. But if she is telling the truth, of course we ought to let her stay here. And then Kleo thought, She certainly is pretty. Maybe that's why Nick wants her to stay here; maybe he's got a – she searched for the word. A special interest in her. If she wasn't so pretty, would he still want to let her in here to stay with us? But that did not sound like Nick. Unless he was unaware of his true feelings; he knew he wanted to help the girl but he didn't actually know why.

I guess we should take the chance, Kleo decided.

'We'd be very happy to have you stay with us,' she said aloud, 'for as long as you need to.'

At this, Charlotte's face grew radiant with pleasure.

'I'll take your coat,' Kleo said, as the girl wriggled out of it – Nick gallantly offering her help.

'No, you don't have to do that,' Charlotte said.

Kleo said, 'If you're going to be staying here' – she took the coat from Charlotte – 'you'll have to hang up your coat.' She carried it to the single closet of the apartment, opened the door, reached for a hanger . . . and saw, in one of the coat pockets, a hastily rolled up pamphlet. 'Cordonite writing,' she said aloud, as she took it from the pocket. 'You're an Under Man.'

Charlotte ceased smiling; she looked anxious now, and it was obvious that her thoughts were moving rapidly as she hurriedly searched for an answer.

'Then that whole story about her boyfriend,' Kleo said, 'it's a lie. The tracks are after her; that's why you want to hide her here.' She carried the coat, and the pamphlet, back to Charlotte. 'You can't stay here,' she said.

Nick said, 'I would have told you, but—' He gestured. 'I knew you'd react this way. And I was right.'

'It's true about Denny,' Charlotte said in a mild, steady voice. 'It *is* him I'm hiding from. The tracks aren't after me. And you just had a random check, Nick told me. This apartment won't be coming up again for – hell, for months. Maybe years.'

Kleo stood holding out Charlotte's coat to her.

'If she goes,' Nick said, 'I go with her.'

'I wish you would,' Kleo said.

'You mean that?' Nick asked.

'Yes, I mean it.'

Charlotte rose to her feet. 'I'm not going to split the two of you up. It isn't fair – I'll go.' She turned to Nick. 'Thank you anyway,' she said. She accepted her coat, put it on, moved toward the door. 'I understand how you feel, Kleo,' she said as she opened the door. She smiled her bright – but now frozen – smile. 'Goodbye.'

Nick moved rapidly – he strode after her, stopped her at the door by seizing her by the shoulder.

'No,' Charlotte said, and with what seemed unusual force

by a woman, she twisted loose. 'So long, Nick. Anyhow we shook the Purple Sea Cow. That was fun. You're a good driver; a lot of guys have tried to shake Denny off when he's in his ship, but you're the only one who's actually managed to do it.' She patted him on the arm and walked briskly out into the hall.

Maybe it is true about her boyfriend, Kleo thought. Maybe he did try to beat her up; maybe we ought to let her stay. Anyway. In spite of the fact . . . but, she thought, they didn't tell me: not her, not Nick. Which amounts to a lie, by omission. She thought, I've never known Nick to do that before. Here he's put us in all this danger and he hasn't said – I just happened to see the pamphlet in her coat.

And, she thought, he might actually leave with her, as he says. Then he really must be involved with her, she thought. They can't have just met: it wouldn't be reasonable for anyone to go so far in giving help to a stranger . . . except that in this case the stranger is beautiful, small and helpless. And men are that way. There is a weakness in their structure which comes out in situations like this. They no longer think or act reasonably; they do what they think of as 'chivalry'. At whatever cost to themselves, and, in this case, to their wife and child.

'You can stay,' she said to Charlotte, following after her into the hall, as the girl stood struggling to get her coat back on; Nick stood blankly, as if he could no longer follow – and hence participate in – the situation.

'No,' Charlotte said. 'Goodbye.' She ran, then, in full flight down the corridor, like a wild bird.

'God damn you,' Nick said to Kleo.

'God damn you, too,' Kleo said, 'trying to bring her in here to get us bursted. God damn you for not telling me.'

'I would have told you when the opportunity arose,' he said.

'Aren't you going after her?' Kleo asked. 'You said you would.'

He stared at her, his face mobile with wrath, his eyes small and crammed with darkness. 'You've sentenced her to forty years in a work camp on Luna; she'll roam the streets with no money and no place to go, and eventually a prowl car will stop and they'll question her.'

'She's a smart girl; she'll get rid of the pamphlets,' Kleo said.

'They'll still get her. For something.'

'Then go on and make sure she's all right. Forget us; forget Bobby and me and go see if she's okay. Go ahead. *Go!*'

His jaw retracted, as if, she thought, he is going to hit me. Look what he has learned already from his new girl friend, she thought. Brutality.

However, he did not hit her. Instead, turning, he ran up the corridor after Charlotte.

'You bastard!' Kleo yelled after him, giving not a damn who in the building heard her. Then, returning to the apartment, she slammed and locked the door; she put the night bolt in place, so that even with his key he could not open the door again.

They walked hand-in-hand along the busy street with its many shops, through heavy sidewalk traffic, neither of them speaking.

'I wrecked your marriage,' Charley said after a time.

'No you didn't,' Nick said. And it was true: his showing up with the girl had brought to the surface only that which was already there. We lived a life of scrabbling fear, he thought, a life of worry and pitiful terrors. Fear Bobby wouldn't pass his test; fear of the police. And now – the Purple Sea Cow, he thought. All we have to do is worry about it strafing us. Thinking that, he laughed.

'What's funny?' Charley said.

'I was imagining Denny dive-bombing us. Like with one of those old Stukas they used back in World War Two. And everybody scattering to get out of the way, thinking war had broken out with North-West Germany.'

Hand-in-hand they walked, each wrapped for a time in his own thoughts. Then, all at once, Charley said, 'You don't have to hang around me, Nick. Let's cut the cord; you go back to Kleo – she'll be glad to see you. I know women; I know how fast they get over being mad, especially at something like that, where what menaces her – in other words, me – is gone. Right?'

It was probably true, but he did not answer; he had not as yet found his way out of the tangle of his own thoughts. What, in toto, had happened to him today? He had discovered that his boss Earl Zeta was an Under Man; he had joined with Zeta in drinking alcohol; they had gone to Charley's – or Denny's – apartment; there had been a fight, and he had gotten out of there with Charley, rescuing her, a complete stranger, with the help of his bulky, strong boss.

And then the business with Kleo.

'Are you sure the PSS doesn't know about your apartment?' he asked Charley. In other words, he thought, have they picked me as a suspect, yet?

'We're very careful,' Charley said.

'Are you? You left that pamphlet in your coat for Kleo to find. That wasn't very frosty.'

'I was all unhooked. From slipping the Purple Sea Cow. I never do things like that, usually.'

'Do you have any more on you? In your purse?'

'No.'

He took her purse from her and looked through it. It was true. He then searched the pockets of her coat, as they walked along. True of her coat, too. But Cordon's writing also circulated in the form of microdots; she could have several of them on her, and, if they picked her up, the track boys of the PSS would find them.

I guess I don't trust her, he decided. After she let that happen with Kleo. Obviously, if she could do it once—

He thought, then. Probably the tracks are watching the apartment, monitoring it in some way. Who comes in; who goes out. *I* came in; *I* went out. So, if that's the case, I'm listed.

So it's already too late to go back to Bobby and Kleo.

'You look so grim,' Charley said, in a merry, what-the-hell voice.

'Christ,' he said, 'I've crossed the line.'

'Yes, you're an Under Man.'

'Wouldn't that make anybody look grim?'

Charley said, 'It should fill you with joy.'

'I don't want to go to a detention work camp on—'

'But it's not going to end that way, Nick. Provoni is coming back and everything will be okay.' Holding his hand, she swung her head, cocked it, peered at him birdwise. 'Cheer up, and stand up straight! Look happy! Be happy!'

My family, he thought, is broken and by her. We have nowhere we can go – they'd find us in a motel easily – and—

Zeta, he thought. He can help me. And the responsibility, to a great extent, is his: Zeta set off everything that's happened today.

'Oh,' Charley said, blinking as he tugged her to a ped overpass. 'Where are we going?'

'To the United Front Slightly Used Squibs lot,' Nick said.

'Oh, you mean to Earl Zeta. Maybe he's back at the apartment, fighting with Denny. No, I guess Denny must have gotten away by now; anyhow, that's what we thought when you were driving, because of that one sight of him on the roof. Oh, good; now I can enjoy some more of your driving ability. Do you know, as good as Denny is, and he's really good, you're better? Have I told you that before? Yes, I guess I did.' She seemed rattled. And, all at once, ill at ease.

'What's the matter?' he asked as they entered the up-ramp which would take them to the fiftieth level lot where he had parked his squib.

'Well,' she said, 'I'm afraid Denny will be looking there. Hanging around, skulking, watching. Just *watching*.' She snarled out the word, savagely, startling him – he hadn't seen this side of her before. 'No,' she said, 'I can't go there. You go alone. Let me off somewhere, or I'll just take the down-ramp and—' She made a whisking motion with the flat of her hand. 'Out of your life forever.' Once more she laughed, in the manner that she had always before. 'But we can still be friends. We can communicate by postcard.' She laughed. 'We'll always know one another, even if we never meet again. Our souls have meshed, and when souls have meshed, one can't be destroyed without the other dying.' She was laughing uncontrollably, now, virtually hysterically; she pawed at her eyes, giggling through her flattened hands. 'That's what Cordon teaches and it's so funny; it's just so goddam funny.'

He took hold of her hands and lifted them away from her face. Her eyes shone with brilliance, star-like eyes fixed on his own, searching deeply into his, as if obtaining her response not from what he said but from what his own eyes showed.

'You think I'm nuts,' she said.

'Beyond doubt.'

'Here you and I are in this awful situation, and Cordon is going to be executed and all I can do is laugh.' She had ceased, now, but with visible effort; her mouth trembled as it held the laughter back. 'I know a place where we can get some alcohol,' she said. 'Let's go there; then we can really get blurfled.'

'No,' he said. 'I'm blurfled enough now.'

'That's why you did what you did, choosing to go with me and leaving Kleo. Because of the alc Zeta gave you.'

'Is that it?' he asked. Perhaps it was. It was well-known that alcohol produced personality changes, and he certainly had not been acting in his usual fashion. But it was an unusual situation; what would have been his 'usual' reactions to what had happened to him today?

I have to take charge of this situation, he thought. I have to get this girl under control – or leave her.

'I don't like to be bossed,' Charley said. 'I can see you're about to boss me around, tell me what I can and can't do. Like Denny does. Like my father did. Someday, I'll have to tell you some of the things my father did to me . . . then maybe you'll understand better. Some of the things, the awful, things, he made me do. Sexual things.'

'Oh,' Nick said. Which might explain her lesbian tendencies, if Denny was actually right in so describing her.

Charley said, 'I think what I'll do with you is take you to a Cordonite printing center.'

'You know where one is?' he asked incredulously. 'Then the tracks would give their eyeteeth to—'

'I know. They'd love to catch me. I know about it through Denny. He's a bigger dealer than you realize.'

'Would he expect you to go there?'

'He doesn't know I know. I followed him one time – I thought he was sleeping with some other girl, but it wasn't that: it was a printing center. I sneaked off and pretended I'd never left the apartment; it was late at night and I pretended to be asleep.' She took his hand, squeezed it. 'This is a particularly interesting plant because they turn out Cordonite material for children. Like, "That's right! It's a horse! And when men were free they rode horses!" Like that.'

'Lower your voice,' Nick said. There were others riding the upramp and her vibrant, adolescent voice carried, augmented by her enthusiasm.

'Okay,' she said, obediently.

'Isn't a Cordonite printing plant at the top of the order of the organization?' he asked.

'There is no organization, there's only mutual bonds of brotherhood. No, one of the printing plants isn't at the top; what's at the top is the receiving station.'

'Receiving station? What does it receive?'

'Messages from Cordon.'

'From Brightforth Prison?'

Charley said, 'He has a transmitter stitched inside his body that they haven't found yet, even with the x-rays they took. They found two, but not this one, and through this one we get daily meditations, his evolving thoughts and ideas, which the printing plants start cranking out as rapidly as possible. And from there, the material is passed to the distribution centers, where pushers pick it up and carry it off and try to get people to buy it.' She added, 'As you can guess, there's a high mortality rate among the pushers.'

'How many printing plants do you have?' he asked.

'I don't know. Not many.'

'Do the authorities—'

'The pissers – pardon me, the PSS – locate one once in a while. But then we set up another, so the number remains generally the same.' She paused, pondering. 'I think we'd better go in a taxi rather than in your squib. If it's all right with you.'

'Any special reason why?'

'I'm not sure. They may have monitored your license number; we usually try to reach the printing plants in rented cars. Taxis are the best.'

'Is it far from here?' he asked.

'You mean like miles off in the country? No, it's in the middle of town, in the busiest part. Come on.' She hopped onto the downramp and he followed. A moment later they reached street level; the girl at once began peering into the traffic in search of a cab.

TEN

A cab floated leisurely from the traffic and came to rest at the curb beside them. Its door slid open and they entered.

'Feller's Luggage Emporium,' Charley said to the driver. 'On 16th Avenue.'

'Um,' the driver said, and lifted his ship up and once more into the flow of traffic, except, this time, going the other way.

'But Feller's Luggage—' Nick began, but invisibly Charley dug her elbow into his ribs; he took the hint and lapsed into silence.

Ten minutes later, the cab left them off. Nick paid, and the cab floated on like a child's painted toy.

'Feller's Luggage,' Charley said, surveying the aristocratic building. 'One of the oldest and most respected retail establishments in the city. You thought it would be a warehouse behind a gas station on the edge of town. Swarming with rats.' She took his hand, led him through the automatically-opening doors and onto the carpeted floor of the world famous shop.

A smartly dressed salesman approached them. 'Good afternoon,' he said, affably.

Charley said, 'I have a set of luggage put away. Synthetic

73

ostrich hide, four pieces. My name is Barrows. Julie Barrows.'

'Would you please step this way?' the salesman said to her, turning and walking with dignity toward the rear of the store.

'Thank you,' Charley said. Again she dug Nick in the ribs, this time gratuitously. And smiled up at him.

A heavy metal door slid aside, revealing a small room in which a variety of pieces of luggage rested on plain wooden shelves. The door through which they had come now slid quietly shut. The salesman waited a moment, consulting his watch, then carefully wound the watch . . . and, swiftly, the far wall of the room divided, showing a greater room beyond. A heavy pounding reached Nick's ears, major printing machinery was at work, and he could see it now. As little as he knew about printing, he knew this: it was totally modern, the best there was, and quite expensive. The Under Men presses did not consist of mimeograph machines, not in the least.

Four soldiers in gray uniforms and wearing gas masks surrounded them, all holding lethal Hopp's tubes. 'Who are you?' one of them, a sergeant, asked – asked hell. Demanded.

'I'm Denny's girl,' Charley said.

'Who's Denny?'

'You know.' Gesturing, Charley said, 'Denny Strong. He operates in this area at the distribution level.'

A scanner swept back and forth, surveying them.

The soldiers conferred, speaking into lip-level microphones and listening through earfone buttons in their right ears. 'Okay,' the sergeant in charge said at last. He turned his attention back to Nick and Charley. 'What do you want here?' he demanded.

'A place to stay for a while,' Charley said.

Nodding toward Nick, the occifer said, 'Who's he?'

'A convert. He came over to us today.'

Nick said, 'Because of the announcement of Cordon's execution.'

The soldier grunted, pondered. 'We're housing just about everyone already. I don't know . . .' He chewed his lower lip, frowning. 'Do you also want to stay here?' he asked Nick.

'For a day or so. No longer.'

Earnestly, Charley said, 'You know Denny has those psychopathic rages, but generally as far as lasting—'

'I don't know Denny,' the soldier said. 'Can you two occupy the same room?'

'I – guess so,' Charley said.

'Yes,' Nick said.

'We can give you sanctuary for seventy-two hours,' the sergeant said. 'Then you'll have to move on.'

'How big is this place?' Nick asked him.

'Four square city blocks.'

He believed it. 'This is not a nickel and dime operation,' he said to the soldiers.

'If it were,' one of them said, 'we wouldn't have much of a chance. We print tracts by the million, here. Most are ultimately confiscated by the authorities, but not all. We use the junk mail principle; even if one-fiftieth are read – and all the others thrown away – it's worth the cost; it's the way to do it.'

Charley said, 'What's come from Cordon now that he knows he's going to be executed? Or does he know? Have they told him?'

'The receiving station would know,' the soldier said. 'But we won't hear from them for a few more hours; there's generally a lapse while the material is edited.'

'Then you don't print Cordon's words exactly as they come from him,' Nick said.

The soldiers laughed. And did not answer.

'He rambles,' Charley explained.

Nick said, 'Is there going to be any attempt to agitate for a stay of execution?'

'I doubt if that's been decided,' one of the soldiers said.

'It wouldn't have any effect,' another said. 'We'd fail; they would execute him and we'd all be in detention camps.'

'So you're going to let him die?' Nick asked.

'We have no control over it,' several soldiers said at once.

Nick said, 'Once he's dead, you'll have nothing to print; you'll have to shut down.'

The soldiers laughed.

'*You've heard from Provoni,*' Charley said.

A silence, and then one of the soldiers, the sergeant, said, 'A garbled message. But authentic.'

The soldier beside him said quietly, 'Thors Provoni is on his way back.'

Part Two

ELEVEN

'That puts a new light on things,' Willis Gram said gloomily. 'Read the intercepted message again.'

Director Barnes read from the copy before him. ' "Have found . . . who will . . . their help will . . . and I am . . ." That's all that came through well enough to be transcribed. Static got the rest.'

'But all the answers are there,' Gram said. 'He's alive; he's coming back; he has found someone – not something, but someone, because he used the word "their". He says, "Their help will . . ." and what's missing probably is the rest of a sentence reading, "Their help will be enough." Or words to that effect.'

'I think you're being too pessimistic,' Barnes said.

'I have to be. Anyhow, hell, I've got the evidence to be pessimistic about. They've been waiting for word from Provoni all this time and now it's come. Their printing plants will have the news all over the planet in the next six hours, and there's no way we can stop them.'

'We can bomb their main printing plant on 16th Avenue,' Director Barnes said; he was all for that. He had waited months for permission to destroy the huge Under Men plant.

'They'll patch this into the TV circuit,' Gram said. 'Two minutes – then we'll find their transmitter and that'll be the end of that, but they'll have gotten their damn message across.'

'Then give up,' Barnes said.

'I'm not going to give up. I'm never going to. I'll have Provoni killed within an hour of the time he lands on Earth, and whoever it is he's brought to help them – we'll snuff them, too. Damn nonhuman organisms, they probably have six legs and a tail that stings. Like a scorpion.'

'And they'll sting us to death,' Barnes said.

'Something like that.' In his bathrobe and slippers, Gram paced moodily about his bedroom office, his arms locked behind him, stomach protruding. 'Doesn't it seem to you to be a betrayal of the human race, Old Men, Under Men, New Men, Unusuals – everyone? To bring in a nonhumanoid life form which'll probably want to colonize here once it's destroyed us?'

'Except,' Barnes pointed out, 'it's not going to destroy us; we're going to destroy it.'

'You just never know for sure about these things,' Gram said. 'They might gain a foothold. That's what we have to prevent.'

Barnes said, 'From a calculation of the distance from which the message came, it's computed that he – and they – won't be here for two more months.'

'They may have a faster-than-light drive,' Gram said shrewdly. 'Provoni may not be aboard the *Gray Dinosaur*; he may be on one of their ships. And hell, the *Gray Dinosaur* is fast enough; remember, it was the prototype of a whole new line of interstellar transportation type ships; he got the first one and away he went.'

'I'll admit this,' Barnes said. 'Provoni may have modified the ship's drive; he may have beefed it up. He always was a tinkerer. I wouldn't rule it out entirely.'

'Cordon will be executed immediately,' Gram said. 'Get it done now. Notify the media, so they can be present. Round up sympathizers.'

'Ours? Or theirs?'

Gram spat out, 'Ours.'

'In addition,' Barnes asked, scratching out notes on a pad of paper, 'may I have permission to bomb the 16th Avenue printing plant?'

'It's bomb proof,' Gram said.

'Not exactly. It's divided, like a beehive, into—'

'I know all about it – I've read your damn plodding, tiresome memos about it for months. You have a thing about that 16th Avenue printing plant, don't you?'

'Shouldn't I? Shouldn't it have been destroyed long ago?'

78

'Something keeps me from doing it.'

'Why?' Barnes said.

Presently Gram said, 'I worked there, once. Before I rose in the Civil Service. I was a spy. I know almost everyone there; they were onetime friends. They never found out about me ... I didn't look like I do now. I had an artificial head.'

'Christ,' Barnes said.

'What's the matter with that?'

'It's just so – absurd. We don't do that any more; we haven't done that since I took office.'

'Well, this was before you took office.'

'So they still don't know.'

'I'll give you the authority to break down the wall of the place and arrest all of them,' Gram said. 'But I won't give you permission to bomb them. But you'll see I'm right; it won't make any difference; they'll have the news of Provoni *on the air*. In two minutes, they'll blanket the Earth – two minutes!'

'The second their transmitter goes on the air—'

'Two minutes. Anyhow.'

Presently Barnes nodded.

'So you know I'm right. Anyhow, go ahead with the execution of Cordon; I want it done by six o'clock tonight, our time.'

'And the business about the sharpshooter and Irma—'

'Forget that. Just get Cordon. We'll snuff her later. Maybe one of the nonhumanoid life forms could smother her with its sack-like, protoplasmic body.'

Barnes laughed.

'I'm serious,' Gram said.

'You have a lurid idea of what the nonhumanoids are going to turn out to look like.'

'Blimps,' Gram said. 'They'll look like blimps. Only with tails. It's the tails you have to watch for, that's where the poison is.'

Barnes rose. 'May I leave now and start the procedure re Cordon's execution? And the attack on the 16th Avenue Under Men printing plant?'

'Yes,' Gram said.

Lingering at the door, Barnes asked, 'Would you like to attend the execution?'

'No.'

'I could have a special box made up for you from which you could see but into which no one—'

'I'll watch it on closed-circuit TV.'

Barnes blinked. 'Then you don't want it telecast over the regular planet-web system? For everybody to see?'

'Oh, yeah,' Gram said, glumly nodding. 'Of course; that's half of it, isn't it? All right, I'll simply watch it like everyone else does. That's good enough for me.'

'As to the 16th Avenue printing plant . . . I'll have a list made up of everyone we catch there, and you can go over the list—'

'And see how many old friends are on it,' Gram finished.

'You might want to visit them in prison.'

'Prison! Does everything have to end there or end as an execution? Is that right?'

'If you mean, Is that what happens? then the answer is yes. But if you mean—'

'You know what I mean.'

Barnes, reflecting, said, 'This is a civil war we're fighting. During his time, Abraham Lincoln imprisoned hundreds upon hundreds of men, without due process, and still he's remembered as the greatest of the U.S. presidents.'

'But he was always pardoning people.'

'You can do that.'

'Okay,' Gram said cannily. 'I'll free everyone from the 16th Avenue printing plant that I knew. And they'll never find out why.'

'You're a good man, Council Chairman,' Barnes said. 'To extend your loyalties even to those who are now actively working against you.'

'I'm a slimy bastard,' Gram grated. 'You know it; I know it. It's just that – well, hell. We had a lot of good times together; we used to get a million laughs out of what we printed. Laughs, because we put funny stuff into it. Now it's all solemn and stodgy. But when I was there, we – aw, the

80

hell with it.' He lapsed into silence. What am I doing here? he asked himself. How did I get into a position like this, with all this authority? I never was meant for it.

On the other hand, he thought, *maybe I was.*

Thors Provoni awoke. And saw nothing, only depth of blackness surrounding him. I'm inside it, he realized.

'That is true,' the Frolixan said. 'It upset me when you went to sleep – as you call it.'

'Morgo Rahn Wilc,' Provoni said, into the darkness. 'You're a worrier. We sleep every twenty-four hours; we sleep from eight to—'

'I know that,' Morgo said. 'But consider how it appears: you gradually lose your personality, your heart beat drops, your pulse slows . . . it looks very much like death.'

'But you know it isn't,' Provoni pointed out.

'It's the mental functioning that changes so much, that makes us uneasy. You're not aware of it, but unusual and violent mental activity takes place while you sleep. First, you enter a world that to some extent is familiar to you . . . in your mind you are where genuine personal friends, enemies, and socially-contacted figures speak and act.'

'In other words,' Provoni said, 'dreams.'

'This sort of dreaming forms a kind of recapitulation of the day, of what you've done, whom you've thought about, talked with. That does not alarm us. It is the next phase. You fall into a deeper interior level; you encounter personages you never knew, situations you've never been in. A disintegration of your self, of you as such, begins; you merge with primordial entities of a god-like type, possessing enormous power; while you are there you are in danger of—'

'The collective unconsciousness,' Provoni said. 'That the greatest of the human thinkers Carl Jung discovered. Abreaction past the moment of birth, back into other lives, other places . . . and populated by archetypes, as Jung—'

'Did Jung stress the point that one of these archetypes could, at any time, absorb you? And a reformation of your self would never reoccur? You would be only a talking, walking extension of the archetype?'

'Of course he stressed it. But it's not at night in sleep that the archetype takes over, it's during the day. When they appear during the day – that's when you're destroyed.'

'In other words when you sleep while awake.'

Grudgingly, he said, 'True.'

'So, when you are asleep we must protect you. Why do you object to my enfolding of you during this period? I am concerned for your life; you are so made that you would throw it away in a single gamble. Your trip to our world – a terrible gamble, one you should not have made, statistically speaking.'

'But I made it,' Provoni said.

The darkness had begun to withdraw as the Frolixan left him. He made out the metal wall of the ship, the large hamper used as a hammock, the half-closed hatch to the control room. His ship, the *Gray Dinosaur*: his world for so long. His cocoon, within which he slept a good part of the time.

They would wonder at the fanatic now, he thought, if they could see him stretched out in his hammock, a week of beard on his face, his hair down to his shoulders, his body grimy, his clothing rancid and grimier still. Here he is, the savior of man. Or rather of some part of mankind. The part which had not been suppressed until – he wondered what it was like, now. Had the Under Men gotten any support? Or were most Old Men resigned to their meager status? And Cordon, he thought. What if the great speaker and writer is dead? Then probably it all died with him.

But now they know – my friends anyhow, know – that I found the help we need and that I am returning. Assuming they got my message. And assuming they could decode it.

I, the traitor, he thought. The caller upon the unhuman for support. Opening up Earth to an invasion by creatures which otherwise would never have noticed it. Will I go down in history as the most evil of men – or savior? Or perhaps something less extreme, down there in the middle. The subject of a quarter page entry in the *Britannica*.

'How can you call yourself a traitor, Mr. Provoni?' Morgo asked.

'How indeed.'

'You have been *called* a traitor. You have been called a *savior*. I have examined every particle of your conscious self, and there is no lusting after the vainglory of greatness; you have made a difficult voyage, with virtually no hope of success, and you have done it for one motive only: to help your friends. Isn't it said in one of your books of wisdom, "If a man give up his life for his friend—" '

'You can't complete that quotation,' Provoni said, amused.

'No, because you don't know it, and all we have ever had to go on is your mind – on its contents, down to the collective level, which worries us so at night.'

'*Pavor nocturnus*,' Provoni said. 'Fear at night; you have a phobia.' He got shakily from his hammock, stood dizzily swaying, then shuffled to the food-supply compartment. He pressed a button, but nothing emerged. He pressed a second button. Still nothing emerged. He felt, then, panic; he pressed buttons at random ... and at last a cube of R-ration slid into the receptacle.

'There is enough to get you back to Earth, Mr. Provoni,' the Frolixman assured him.

'But,' he said savagely, grinding his teeth, 'just barely enough. I know the calculations; I may have to go through the last few days with no food at all. And you're worried about my sleep; Christ, if you're going to worry, worry about my gut.'

'But we know you'll be all right.'

'Okay,' Provoni said. He opened the cube of food, ate it, drank a cup of redistilled water, shuddered, wondered about brushing his teeth. I stink, he thought. All of me. They'll be appalled. I'll look like someone trapped in a submarine for four weeks.

'They'll understand why,' Morgo said.

'I want,' Provoni said, 'to take a shower.'

'There is not enough water.'

'Can't you – get me some? Somehow?' On a number of times in the past, the Frolixan had provided him with chemical constituents, building blocks he needed for more complicated entities. Surely, if it could do this it could synthesize

83

water ... there, around the *Gray Dinosaur*, where it had placed itself.

'My own somatic system is short on water, too,' Morgo said. 'I was thinking of asking you for some.'

He laughed.

'What is funny?' the Frolixan asked.

'Here we are, out here between Proxima and Sol, on our way to save Earth from the tyranny of its oligarchy of elite rulers, and we're busy trying to cadge a few quarts of water from each other. How are we going to save Earth if we can't even synthesize water?'

'Let me tell you a legend about God,' Morgo said. 'In the beginning he created an egg, a huge egg, with a creature inside it. God tried to break the eggshell open to let the creature – the original living creature – out. He couldn't. But the creature which He had made had a sharp beak, constructed for just such a task, and it chipped its way out of the egg. And hence – all living creatures have free will, now.'

'Why?'

'Because we broke the egg, not He.'

'Why does that give us free will?'

'Because, dammit, we can do what He can't.'

'Oh.' Provoni nodded, grinned, then, in amusement at the Frolixan's idiomatic English, learned, of course, from himself. It knew Terran language, only to the extent that he knew them: a reasonably adequate span of English – but not what Cordon possessed – plus a little Latin, German, Italian. It could say 'goodbye' in Italian, and seemed to enjoy doing so; it always signed off with a solemn *ciao*. He himself preferred 'Biz you later,' but evidently the Frolixans considered that substandard ... and by his own standards. It was an idiom from the Service which he couldn't get rid of. It was, like much else in his mind, a clutter of fleas: hopping fragments of thoughts and ideas, memories and fears, that had taken up residence evidently for good. It was up to the Frolixans to sort it all out, and they had so done, it would seem.

'You know,' Provoni said, 'when we get to Earth, I'm

going to find, somewhere, a bottle of brandy. And sit down on the steps—'

'What steps?'

'I just see a big gray public building, with no windows, like the Internal Revenue Service, something really dreadful, and I see myself sitting on the steps, wearing an old dark-blue coat, drinking brandy. Right out in the open. And people will come by and they will mutter, "Look, that man's drinking in public." And I'll say, "I'm Thors Provoni." And then they'll say, "He deserves it. We won't turn him in." And they won't.'

'There will be no arrest made of you, Mr. Provoni,' Morgo said. 'Then or any other time. We'll be with you from the moment you land. Not merely me, as we have here now, but my brothers. The brotherhood. And they—'

'They'll take over Earth. And then spit me out to die.'

'No, no. We have shaken hands on it. Don't you remember?'

'Maybe you lied.'

'We can't lie, Mr. Provoni. I explained that to you, and so did my supervisor, Gran Ce Wanh. If you don't believe me, and you don't *believe* him, an entity over six million years old—' The Frolixan sounded exasperated.

'When I see it,' Provoni said, 'I'll believe it.' He grimly drank a second cup of reconstituted water, even though the red light above the water-source was on ... and had been on for a week.

TWELVE

The special courier saluted Willis Gram and said, 'This came in marked Code One. For you to read immediately, if you will, with all respect, Council Chairman.'

Grunting, Willis Gram opened the envelope. Typewritten on a single sheet of ordinary sixteen-weight paper ran one sentence.

Our agent at the 16th Ave printing plant reports a second call from Provoni, and that he has been successful.

My mother's broken back, Gram said to himself. Successful. He glanced up at the courier and said, 'Bring me some straight methamphetamine hydrochloride. I'll take it orally in a capsule; make sure it's a capsule.'

A little surprised, the courier saluted again and said, 'Yes, Council Chairman.' He left the bedroom-office, and Gram found himself alone. I'll kill myself, he said to himself. Depression filled him, bursting him until he sagged like a popped balloon. Even before Cordon is dead, he thought. Well, let's get Cordon.

He pressed a button on his intercom. 'Send in a commissioned occifer; anyone – it doesn't matter.'

'Yes sir.'

'Have him bring his side arm with him.'

Five minutes later, a nattily dressed major entered the room, snapped a polished and professional salute. 'Yes, Council Chairman.'

'I want you to go to Eric Cordon's jail cell at the Long Beach facilities,' Gram said, 'and I want you personally, with your own gun, the gun I see at your belt, there, to shoot Cordon until he is dead.' He held out a slip of paper. 'This gives you my authorization.'

'Are you sure—' the occifer began.

'I am sure,' Gram said.

'I mean sir, are you sure—'

'If you won't, I'll go myself,' Gram said. 'Go.' He made a curt, abrupt gesture toward the main doors of his office.

The major departed.

No TV coverage, Gram said to himself. No audience. Just two men in a cell. Well, Provoni has forced me to do it; I can't have both of them around at the same time. It's really – in a sense – Provoni who is killing Cordon.

I wonder what kind of life forms they are? he asked himself. That Provoni found?

The bastard, he said to himself.

He flicked switches, cursed, managed to find the one which lit the camera monitoring Cordon's cell. The thin, ascetic face, the gray glasses, grayer – and thinning – hair ... the college professor who writes, Gram said to himself. Well, I am going to personally watch as that major – whoever he is – shoots him.

On the screen, Cordon sat as if asleep ... but obviously he was dictating, probably to the 16th Avenue plant. Emanate your pontifications, Gram thought grimly, and waited.

A quarter of an hour passed. Nothing happened; Cordon continued to emanate. And then, all at once, surprising both Cordon and Willis Gram, the cell door slid back. The natty, spick-and-span major entered, briskly.

'Are you Cordon, Eric?' the major asked.

'Yes,' Cordon said, standing.

The major – a young man, really, with pinched, sharply-cut features – reached for his weapon. He lifted the gun up and said, 'Under the authorization of the Council Chairman I have been instructed to come here to this place and snuff you. Do you wish to read the authorization?' He dug into his pocket.

'No,' Cordon said.

The major fired his gun. Cordon fell backward, forced by the beam of destructive power back in a sliding motion that brought him against the far wall of the cell. Then, by degrees, he slid down, until he sat like some abandoned doll – its legs apart, its head down, arms lifeless.

Speaking into the proper microphone before him, Gram said, 'Thank you, major. You can leave now. You have nothing else to do. By the way – what is your name?'

'Wade Ellis,' the major said.

'A citation will be made up for you,' Gram said, and broke the circuit. Wade Ellis, he thought. It's done. He felt ... what? Relief? Obviously. God, he thought; how simple it was. You order a soldier, who you've never seen before, whose name you didn't even know, to go snuff one of the most influential men on Earth. And he does!

It created, in his brain, an appalling imaginary conversation. The interchange would go like this:

Person A: Hi, my name's Willis Gram.

Person B: My name's Jack Kvetck.

Person A: I see you're a major in the army.

Person B: You bet your bird.

Person A: Say, Major Kvetck, would you snuff someone for me? I forget his name ... wait I'll look through this stack of papers.

And so forth.

The door of the room flew open; Police Director Lloyd Barnes rushed in, red-faced with anger and disbelief. 'You just now—'

'I know,' Gram said. 'Do you have to tell me? Do you think I don't know?'

'Then it really was your order, as the barracks commander at the prison said.'

'Yep,' he said, stoically.

'How does it feel?'

'Look,' Gram said. 'A second message came through from Provoni. It specifically states that he is bringing an unTerran life form with him. This isn't speculation, this is fact.'

'You just don't feel you can handle Cordon and Provoni at the same time,' Barnes said with fury.

'You bet your ass! That's right!' Gram said fiercely; he waggled a finger at Barnes. 'In fact, that's it in a nutshell. So don't give me a hard time about it; it was necessary. Could *you* – all of you double-domed super-evolved New Men – have coped with the two of them here on Earth, working together? The answer is no.'

'The answer,' said Barnes, 'would have been a dignified execution, with all the protocols observed.'

'And while we're giving him his last meal and all that, some irradiant fish-like gigantic entity lands in Cleveland and snatches up every Unusual and New and goes *snufffff*. Right?'

After a pause Barnes said, 'Do you plan to declare a planet-wide emergency?'

'Mayday?'

'Yes. In the most extreme sense.'

Gram pondered. 'No. We'll alert the military, the police, then key News and Unusuals – they have a right to know what the actual situation is. But nothing to the frigging rabble, all those Old Men and Under Men.' But, he thought, the 16th Avenue printing plant will tell them anyway. No matter how quickly we attack it. All they have to do is flash the messages from Provoni to slave transmitters and lesser printing plants . . . which, hell, they've undoubtedly already done.

'The commando team, Green A, backed by B and C, are on their way to the 16th Avenue printing plant,' Barnes said. 'I thought you'd like to know.' He inspected his wristwatch. 'In roughly half an hour they'll assault the first line of defense of the plant. We've arranged closed-circuit TV coverage, so you can watch.'

'Thanks.'

'You mean that ironically?'

'No, no,' Gram said. 'I mean what I say; I said thanks and I mean thanks.' His voice rose. 'Does everything have a hidden meaning? Are we a bunch of bomb-plotters sneaking about in the dark, using code words? Is that it? Or are we a government?'

Barnes said, 'We're a legal, functioning government. Faced by sedition within and invasion from without. We're taking protective measures in both directions. For example, we can station ships of the line deep in space, where they can reach Provoni's ship with their missiles as it re-enters the Sol System. We can—'

'That's the military's decision, not yours. I'll have the Ultimate Peace Council of Chiefs assemble in the Red Room' – he checked his own watch, an Omega – 'at three this afternoon.' He pressed a button on his desk.

'Yes sir.'

'I want the Chiefs to assemble in the Red Room at three this afternoon,' Gram said. 'Class A priority.' He turned his attention back to Barnes.

'We'll round up as many Under Men as we can,' Barnes said.

'Fine,' Gram said.

'Do I have permission to bomb their other printing plants? At least the ones that we know of?'

'Fine,' Gram said.

'You still sound sardonic,' Barnes said uncertainly.

'I'm just terribly, terribly pissed off,' Gram said. 'How can a human being instigate a situation in which nonhuman life forms – aw, the hell with it.' He lapsed into silence. Barnes waited for a time, then reached to turn on one of the TV screens facing Gram.

The screen showed weapons-police firing miniaturized missiles at a rexeroid door. Smoke, and armed police, were everywhere.

'They're not in yet,' Gram said. 'Rexeroid – that's a tough substance.'

'They just now started.'

The rexeroid door disintegrated into molten streams that burst into the air in the form of flaming pellets, like Martian sky birds. Clack-clack-clack came the sound of firing, by the police and by what now appeared to be uniformed soldiers within. The police, taken by surprise, scurried for cover, then tossed paralysis gas grenades and the like. The smoke tended to obscure everything, but gradually it became apparent that the police were moving ahead.

'Get the bastards,' Gram said, as a two-man bazooka team le: go directly at the line of soldiers within. The bazooka shell zoomed past the soldiers and exploded within the great clot of printing machinery within. 'There go the presses,' Glam said, feeling glee. 'Well, that's that.'

90

The police had now infiltrated into the central chamber of the printing plant itself. The TV camera followed them, focusing on a battle in cameo between two green-clad police and three gray-clad soldiers.

The noise level dropped. Fewer weapons were being fired, and fewer people could be seen moving. The police were beginning to round up press personnel, meanwhile still trading pistol shots with the few Under Man soldiers alive and armed.

THIRTEEN

In the small, private room which the press personnel had given them, Nick Appleton and Charley sat rigidly, neither speaking; mute, they listened to the sounds of fighting, and to himself Nick thought, No seventy-two hour sanctuary after all. Not for us, not one bit. It's all over now.

Charley rubbed her sensual lips, then, abruptly, bit the back of her hand. 'Jesus,' she said. 'Jesus!' she shouted, on her feet in an animal-like stance. 'We don't have a chance!'

Nick said nothing.

'Speak!' Charley snarled, her face ugly with impotent rage. 'Say something! Blame me because I brought you here, say *anything* – don't just sit there staring at the frigging floor.'

'I don't blame you,' he said, lying. But there was no point in blaming her; she had no way of knowing that the police would all at once attack the printing plant. After all, it had never happened before. She had merely extrapolated from known facts. The printing plant was a refuge; many people had come here and gone.

The authorities knew all the time, Nick thought. They're doing this now because of the news about Provoni's return. Cordon. God, he thought, God in heaven, they probably killed him right away. The signal of Provoni's return has set off a carefully planned, complex blitz, planet-wide, by the

91

establishment. They're probably rounding up every New Man they've got a file on. And it all has to be done – the printing plants bombed, the Under Men rounded up, Eric Cordon killed – before Provoni gets here. It forced their hand; it brought out their actual physical heavy cannon.

'Listen,' he said, getting up to stand beside Charley; he put his arm around her and hugged her spare, hard body against him. 'We'll be in a relocation camp for a time but eventually, when this is resolved one way or another—'

The door of the room flew open. A cop, his uniform covered with gray particles like dust – which were incinerated human bone – stood there, aiming a B-14 Hopp's rifle at them. Nick at once raised his hands, then grabbed Charley's hands and lifted them up and out, opening her fingers to show that she had no weapon.

The cop fired his B-14 at Charley; she slumped, inert, against Nick. 'Unconscious,' the cop said. 'Tranquiler depth.' And fired his B-14 at Nick.

FOURTEEN

Peering at the TV screen, Police Director Barnes said, 'So 3XX24J.'

'What's that?' Gram said irritably.

'In that room: that man with the girl. The two the greener just laid out. That was the sample person which the computer thought meant that—'

'I'm trying to see some of my old buddies,' Gram said, shaking him off. 'Shut up and watch; just watch. Or is that asking too much?'

Barnes said curtly, 'The Wyoming computer selected him as the prototype Old Man who, because of the announcement of Cordon's impending execution would – and did – go over to the Under Men. Now we've caught him, although oddly, I don't think that's his wife. Now, what would the Wyoming computer say . . .' He began to pace. 'What would its response be to the fact that we've caught him? That we have taken possession of the representative Old Man who—'

'Why do you say it's not his wife?' Gram asked. 'Do you think he's shacking up with that broad, that not only has he become an Under Man but he's also left his wife and already found someone else? Ask the computer that; see what it makes of that.' The girl, he thought, is pretty, in a tomboyish sort of way. Hm, he thought. 'Can you see to it that the girl isn't hurt?' he asked Barnes. 'Are you able to communicate with the commando teams there in the plant?'

Reaching for his belt, Police Director Barnes brought a microphone to his lips, said, 'Captain Malliard, please.'

'Yes, Malliard here, Director.' A puff-puffing voice, showing great agitation and stress.

'The Council Chairman asks me to ask you to see to it that the man and girl—'

'Just the girl,' Gram interrupted.

'—that a girl in a side room who has just been put out by a greener with a B-14 Hopp's tranquilizing rifle, be protected. Let's see, I'll try to establish the coordinates.' Barnes peered owl-wise, sideways, at the screen. 'Coordinates 34, 21, then either 9 or 10.'

'That would be to my right and a little forward of my own position,' Malliard said. 'Yes, I'll take charge at once. We have done a good job, Director – in twenty minutes we've taken virtual control of the plant, with a minimum loss of life on both sides.'

'Just keep your eye on the girl,' Barnes said, and returned the microphone to his belt.

'You're wired up with tools like a telefone linesman,' Gram said to him.

Barnes said frostily, 'You're doing it again.'

'Doing what again?'

'Mixing up your private life with your public life. That girl.'

'She has a strange face. Pushed in, like an Irish mug.'

'Council Chairman, we face an invasion by alien life forms; we face a mass insurrection which may—'

'You see a girl like that once in twenty years,' Gram said.

'May I ask one favor?' Barnes asked.

'Sure.' Willis Gram felt good, now; the efficiency of the police in taking over the 16th Avenue printing plant pleased him, and his libido had been clicked to the on position at seeing the odd girl. 'What favor?'

'I want to have you – with myself present – talk to the man, the man from 3XX24J . . . I want to know if his dominant feeling is positive, in that they've heard from Provoni, and Provoni is bringing help with him, or if his morale has been broken by being picked up in the police commando raid. In other words—'

'An average sampling,' Gram said.

'Yes.'

'Okay. I'll take a look at him, but it better be soon; it better be before Provoni gets here. *Everything* has to be done before Provoni and his monsters arrive. Monsters.' He shook his head. 'What a renegade. What a dispiteous, low-class, self-serving, power-hungry, ambitious, unprincipled renegade. He ought to go down in the history books with that statement about him.' He liked that description of Provoni. 'Jot that down,' he said to Barnes. 'I'll have that put in the next edition of the *Britannica*, just like I said it. Word for word.'

Sighing, Police Director Barnes got out his tablet of paper and painstakingly wrote the sentence down.

'Add to that,' Gram said, 'mentally-disturbed, fanatically radical, a creature – note that: a creature, not a man – who believes any means whatsoever is justified by the end. And what is the end in this case? A destruction of a system by which authority is put and *kept* in the hands of those physically constructed so as to have the ability to rule. It is rule by the most competent, not the most popular. Which is better, the most competent or the most popular? Millard Fillmore was popular. So was Rutherford B. Hayes. So was Churchill. So was Lyons. But they were incompetent, which is the whole point. Do you see my point?'

'In what way was Churchill incompetent?'

'He advocated mass night-bombings of residential areas,

94

of civilian populations, instead of hitting key targets. It prolonged World War Two an extra year.'

Director Barnes said, 'Yes, I see the point.' He thought, I don't need a lesson in civics . . . a thought which Gram immediately picked up. That, and much else besides.

'I'll see this man from 3XX24J at six o'clock our time tonight,' Gram said. 'Bring him in. Bring them both in together – the girl, too.' He caught more unpleasant dissenting thoughts from Barnes but ignored them. Like most telepaths, he had learned to ignore the great body of inchoate thoughts in people: hostility, boredom, outright disgust, envy. Thoughts, many of which the person himself was unaware of. A telepath had to learn to have a thick skin. In essence, he had to learn to relate to a person's conscious, positive thoughts, not the vaguely-defined mixture of his unconscious processes. At that region, almost everything could be found . . . and in almost anyone. Every clerk-typist who passed through his office had fleeting thoughts of destroying his superior and taking his place . . . and some aimed much higher than that; there existed fantastic delusional systems of thought in some of the most meek-mannered men and women – and these were, for the most part, New Men.

Some, who harbored truly deranged thoughts, he had quietly hospitalized. For the good of everyone concerned . . . especially himself. For, several times, he had picked up thoughts of assassination, and from the most surprising sources, both big and little. Once, a New Man technician, installing a series of video links in his private office, had lengthily pondered shooting him – and had carried the gun by which to do it. Again and again it came up: an endless theme which had come into existence when the two new classes of men had manifested themselves fifty-eight years ago. He was used to it . . . or was he? Perhaps not. But he had lived with it all his life, and he did not foresee losing his ability to adapt now at this late point in the game – this point at which Provoni and his nonhuman friends were about to intersect his own life-line.

'What's the name of the man from apartment 3XX24J?' he asked Barnes.

'I'd have to research that,' Barnes said.

'And you're sure the girl isn't his wife?'

'I briefly saw stills of his wife. Fat, nasty – a shrew, from what we got off the video tape from the deck installed in their apartment. The standard 243 deck that's in all those quasi-modern apartments.'

'What does he do for a living?'

Barnes peered up at the ceiling, licked his lower lip and said, 'A tire regroover. At a used squib lot.'

'What the hell's that?'

'Well, they take in a squib, let us say, and examination shows the tread almost worn off the tires. So he takes a hot iron and digs new, fake tread into what remains of the tire.'

'Isn't that illegal?'

'No.'

'Well, it is now,' Gram said. 'I just passed a law; make a note of that. Tire regrooving is a crime. It's dangerous.'

'Yes, Council Chairman.' He scratched a note on his pad, thinking, We are about to be overwhelmed by alien beings and this is what Gram is thinking about: tire regrooving.

'You can't overlook the minor items in the welter of the major ones,' Gram said, in answer to Barnes' thought.

'But at a time like this—'

'Make it a posted misdemeanor without delay,' Gram said. 'See that every used squib lot gets printed – mark that: printed – word of it by Friday.'

'Why don't we induce the aliens to land,' Barnes asked sardonically, 'and then have this man dig into their tires so that when they try to roll along the ground-surface the tires pop and they're killed in the resulting accident?'

'That reminds me of a story about the English,' Gram said. 'During World War Two, the Italian government was terribly worried – and rightly so – about the English landing in Italy. So it was suggested that at each of the hotels where the English were staying they should be terribly overcharged. The English, see, would be too polite to complain; instead they'd leave – leave Italy entirely. Have you heard that story.'

'No,' Barnes said.

'We're really in a hell of a mess,' Gram said. 'Even though

96

we killed Cordon and knocked out that 16th Avenue printing plant.'

'Correct, Council Chairman.'

'We're not going to be able even to get all the Under Men, and these aliens may be like the Martians in H. G. Wells' *THE WAR OF THE WORLDS*; they'll eat Switzerland in one big bite.'

'Let's reserve further speculation until we actually encounter them,' Barnes said. From him, Gram picked up weary thoughts, thoughts of a long rest . . . and, at the same time, a realization that there was not going to be a rest, long or otherwise, for any of them.

'I'm sorry,' Gram said, in answer to Barnes' thoughts.

'It's not your fault.'

Moodily, Gram said, 'I ought to resign.'

'In favor of whom?'

'Let you double-domes find someone. Of *your* type.'

'This could be considered at a council.'

'Nope,' Gram said. 'I'm not going to resign. There will be no council meeting to discuss it.'

He caught from Barnes a fleeting thought, quickly suppressed. *Maybe there will be. If you can't handle these aliens, plus the internal uprising.*

Gram thought, They'll have to kill me to get me out of office. Find some way to snuff me. And it's hard to snuff telepaths.

But they're probably looking for a way, he decided.

It was not a pleasant thought.

FIFTEEN

Consciousness returned, and Nick Appleton found himself sprawled on a green floor. Green: the color of the pissers, the state police. He was in a PSS detention camp, probably a temporary one.

Raising his head, he squinted around him. Thirty, forty

men, many with bandages, many cut and bleeding. I guess I'm one of the lucky ones, he decided. And Charley – she would be with the women, raising her voice to bitch shrilly at her captors. She will put up a good fight, he realized; she will kick them in the testicles when they come to carry her off to the permanent relocation camps. I, of course, will never see her again, he thought. She glowed like stars; I loved her. Even for that little while. It's as if I had a glimpse, saw past the curtain of mundane life, saw how and what I needed to be happy.

'You don't happen to have any pain pills on you?' a youth next to him asked. 'I've got a broken leg and it's causing me one hell of a lot of fucking pain.'

'Sorry, no,' Nick said. He returned to his thoughts.

'Don't sound pessimistic,' the youth said. 'Don't let the pissers get to you, inside.' He tapped his head.

'The knowledge that I may spend the rest of my life in a relocation camp on Luna or in southwestern Utah keeps me from smiling,' Nick said caustically.

'But,' the youth said, with a blissful, radiant smile, 'you heard the news Provoni's back, and with help.' His eyes shone, despite the pain of his leg. 'There will be no more relocation camps. "The veil of the tent is rent, and the heavens shall roll up like a scroll."'

'We've waited over two thousand years since that was written,' Nick said. 'And it hasn't happened yet.' He thought, Not one full day as an Under Man and behold! What has become of me.

A tall, lean man, squatting nearby, a deep and untreated gash about his right eye, said, 'Do either of you know if they got the message from Provoni to any of the other printing plants?'

'Oh, sure.' The golden-haired youth's eyes flamed up with trust and belief. 'They knew at once; all our communications operator had to do was click a switch on.' He beamed at Nick and the tall, lean man. 'Isn't it wonderful?' he asked. 'This; even this.' He indicated the others in the badly-lit, badly-ventilated cell. 'It's magnificent. It's beautiful!'

'It turns you on?' Nick asked.

'I'm not familiar with the literature from previous centuries,' the youth said, dismissing with scorn Nick's anachronism. 'I can live with it! All this – it's mine. Until Thors Provoni lands. He will land soon and the heavens will—'

An ununiformed police official came up to them, consulted a clipboard. 'You're the visitor to 3XX24J?' he asked Nick.

'I'm Nick Appleton,' Nick said.

'To us you're a man who visited an apartment number at a certain time on a certain day. Hence you are 3XX24J, are you not?' Nick nodded. 'Get up and come with me,' the police minion said, and started briskly away. Nick, with difficulty, managed to rise to a disfigured standing position; gradually he followed after the cop, wondering – with fear – what was happening.

As the cop unlocked the door of the cell – using a complex electronic wheel system, a spinning at great velocity of numbers – one of the men seated on the floor, his back against the wall, said to Nick, 'Good luck, brother.'

The man beside that man lifted a transistor tab from his ear and said, 'The news just came over the media. They've killed Cordon. They did it, they actually did it. "He died of a chronic liver ailment," they say, but it's not that – Cordon didn't have no liver complaint. They shot him.'

'Come on,' the cop said, and with surprising strength propelled him boldly through the aperture and outside the cell, which instantly relocked itself.

'Is it true about Cordon?' Nick asked the cop, the green pisser.

'Dunno.' The cop added, 'But if they did, it was a good idea. I don't know why they've kept him at Brightforth all this time; why couldn't they make up their minds? Well, that's what you get when you have an Unusual as Council Chairman.' He continued on up the hall, Nick following.

'You know Thors Provoni is back?' Nick asked. 'And with the help he promised?'

'We can handle them,' the cop said.

'Why do you think so?'

'Shut up and keep walking,' the cop said, his large head,

his New Man expanded cranium, bobbing venomously. He looked angry and aggressive, looking for an opportunity to use his metal stick on someone, and Nick thought, he'd snuff me right here and now if he could. But he has orders to fulfill.

Nonetheless, the cop frightened him: the concentration of hate on the man's face when Nick had mentioned Provoni. They may put up a hell of a fight, he realized. If this is representative of their collective feelings.

The cop stepped through a doorway; Nick followed ... and saw, in a single glimpse, the nerve-center of the police apparatus. TV screens, small, hundreds and hundreds of them, with a cop monitoring each cluster of four screens. A cacophony of noise hummed and clicked and buzzed through the big chamber; people, both men and women, hurried here and there ... performing little errands such as the one handed to this hate-ridden New Man cop escorting him. How damn busy it was. But the PSS was in the process of rounding up every Under Man they knew of; that alone would put a burden on their electronic-neurological equipment, and those operating it.

Just in that brief moment, he saw their fatigue. They did not look triumphant or happy. Well, he thought, doesn't the murder of Eric Cordon cheer you up? But they were looking ahead, as were the Under Men. The internal part, the bombing and raiding of the plants, the rounding up of Under Men – it had to be done in a matter of, probably, three days.

Why three days? he asked himself. The two messages hadn't permitted a fix on the ship – evidently – and yet it seemed to be everyone's assumption: they had a few days and that was all. But suppose he's a year out, Nick thought. Or five years.

'3XX24J,' his escort cop said, 'I am turning you over to a representative of the Council Chairman. He will be armed, so don't be heroic.'

'Okay, friend,' Nick said, feeling sheep-like at the rapid processes evolving all around him. A man in an ordinary business suit – purple sleeves, rings, turned-up-toes shoes – approached him. Nick scrutinized him. Tricky, devoted to his job – and a New Man. Above his body his great head wobbled; he was not using the customary neck support bracket in vogue among many New Men.

'You are 3XX24J?' the man asked; he examined a Xerox copy of some sort of document.

'I am Nick Appleton,' Nick said stonily.

'Yes, these number indent systems really don't work,' the rep of the Council Chairman said. 'You work – or worked – as a—' He frowned, then lifted his massive head. 'A what? A "tire regroover"? Is that correct?'

'Yes.'

'And today you joined the Under Men via your employer, Earl Zeta, whom the police have been watching, I believe, for several months. This is you I'm talking about, isn't it? I want to be sure I get the right man passed through. I have your fingerprints, here; we'll shoot them on to the print archives. By the time the Council Chairman sees you, the prints will be – or will not be – verified.' He folded up the document and carefully placed it in his purse. 'Come along.'

Once more, Nick gazed into the huge grotto-like chamber of the ten thousand TV screens. Like fish, he thought, the people gliding about; purple fish, both male and female, bumping together from time to time, like molecules of a liquid.

He had, then, a vision of hell. He saw them as ectoplasmic spirits, without real bodies. These police coming and going on their errands; they had given up life a long time ago, and now, instead of living, they absorbed vitality from the screens which they monitored – or, more precisely, from the people on the screens. The primitive natives in South America may be right, he thought, to believe that when someone takes a photograph of a person he steals the person's soul. What is this, if not a million, billion, endless, procession of such pictures? Eerie, he thought. I'm demoralized; I'm thinking in superstitious terms, out of fear.

'That room,' the rep of the Council Chairman said, 'is the data-source for the PSS all over the planet. Fascinating, isn't it? All those monitoring screens ... and you're seeing just a fraction of it; strictly speaking, you're seeing the Annex, established two years ago. The central nerve-complex is not

visible from here, but take my word for it, it's appallingly
large.'

' "Appallingly"?' Nick asked, wondering at the choice of
words. He sensed, weakly, a sort of sympathy for him on the
part of the Council Chairman rep.

'Almost one million police employees are maintained at
the peep-peep screens. A huge bureaucracy.'

'But did it help them?' Nick asked. 'Today? When they
made their initial roundup?'

'Oh yes; the system works. But it's ironically funny that it
ties up so many men and man-hours, when you consider that
the whole original idea was that—'

A uniformed police occifer appeared beside the two of
them. 'Get out of here and get this man to the Council Chairman.' His tone was nasty.

'Yes sir,' the rep said, and led Nick down a corridor to a
wide, transparent plastic front door. 'Barnes,' the rep said,
half to himself; he frowned with disarrayed dignity. 'Barnes
is the closest man to the Council Chairman,' he said. 'Willis
Gram has a council of ten men and women, and who does he
consult? Always Barnes. Does that indicate adequate cerebral processes to you?'

Another case of a New Man putting down an Unusual,
Nick realized; he made no comment as they got into a shiny
red squib, which had been decorated with the official government seal.

SIXTEEN

In a small, modern office, with one of the new spider
mobiles dangling above him, Nick Appleton listened listlessly
to piped in music. Right now the damn thing was playing
selections from Victor Herbert. Oh, Christ, Nick thought
wearily; he sat hunched over, his head in his hands. Charley,
he thought. Are you alive? Are you hurt, or are you okay?

He decided that she was okay. Charley wouldn't get
snuffed by anyone. She would live to a full life span: to well

over one hundred and twelve years, the population average.

I wonder if I can get out of here, he thought. He found himself faced by two doors, one through which they had come, the other leading to inner, more esoteric offices. Cautiously, he tried the knob of the first door. Locked. So, with utter stealth, he approached the door leading to the inner offices; he turned the knob, held his breath, and found it locked, too.

And it set off an alarm. He could hear it clanging. Damn, he said savagely to himself.

The inner door opened; there stood Police Director Barnes, impressive in his well-decorated green uniform, the lighter green variation worn by top police circles only.

They stood staring at each other.

'3XX24J?' Director Barnes asked.

'Nick Appleton. "3XX24J" is an apartment address, and not even my own. Or it was. Your men have probably looted it by now, looking for Cordonite material.' He thought, then, for the first time, about Kleo. 'Where is my wife?' he demanded. 'Was she hurt or killed? Can I see her?' And my son, he thought. Him especially.

Barnes twisted his head, called back over his shoulder, 'Check 7Y3ZRR and see if the woman's in good condition. The boy, too. Let me know at once.' He turned back to confront Nick. 'You don't mean that girl you had with you in that room at the 16th Avenue printing plant? You mean your legal wife.'

'I want to know about both of them,' Nick said.

'The girl with you at the plant is just fine.' He did not elaborate, but there it was, Charley had survived. He thanked God for that. 'Do you have any more questions you want to ask me before we meet with the Council Chairman?'

Nick said, 'I want an attorney.'

'You can't have one because of the enabling legislation passed last year forbidding legal representation to anyone already arrested. An attorney couldn't have helped you anyhow, even if you had seen him before your arrest, because your crime is political in nature.'

'What's my crime?' Nick said.

'Carrying Cordonite literature. That's ten years in a relocation camp. Being in the presence of other – known – Cordonites. Five years. Found in a building where illegal written material—'

'I've heard enough,' Nick said. 'About forty years in all.'

'As it stands in the books. But, if you're helpful to me and the Council Chairman, perhaps we could run your sentences simultaneously. Let's go in.' He pointed at the open door and Nick, wordlessly, passed on through, into a gloriously decorated office ... or was it an office? A huge bed filled half the room, and in the bed, propped up on pillows, lay Willis Gram, supreme ruler of the planet, his lunch on a tray resting on his middle. Scattered over the bed was every kind of written material possible; he made out the color-codes of a dozen government departments. It did not appear that they had been read – they were too perfect in condition: mint.

'Miss Knight,' Willis Gram said into the face microphone adhering to one flabby jowl, 'come take these chicken a la king type dishes away, I'm not hungry.'

A slender, almost bosomless woman entered and whisked the tray away. 'Would you like some—' she began, but Gram cut her off with a chopping motion of his hand. She became instantly silent and continued on out of the room with the tray.

'Do you know where my food comes from?' Willis Gram asked Nick. 'The building cafeteria, that's where. Why the hell—' He was speaking now to Barnes. 'Why the hell didn't I set up a special kitchen for myself alone? I must be insane. I think I'll resign. You New Men are right – we're just freaks, we Unusuals. We're not forged from the right material to rule.'

Nick said, 'I could take a cab over to a good restaurant like Flores' and pick you up—'

'No, no,' Barnes said sharply.

Gram turned to glance at him with curiosity.

'This man is here for an important reason,' Barnes said hotly. 'He is not a domestic servant. If you want a better

104

lunch, send out one of your staff. This is the man I told you about.'

'Oh, yes,' Gram said, nodding. 'Go ahead; interrogate him.'

Barnes seated himself in a stiffly-upright chair of the mid-eighteen twenties period, probably French. He brought forth a tape recorder, touched the on button.

'Your identity,' Barnes said.

Nick, seating himself on an overstuffed chair facing Barnes, said, 'I thought I was brought here to see the Council Chairman.'

'You were,' Barnes said. 'Chairman Gram will intervene from time to time to inquire further about the matter at hand . . . am I correct, Council Chairman?'

'Yeah,' Gram said, but his heart didn't seem to be in it. They're all exhausted, Nick thought. Even Gram. Especially Gram. It's been the waiting; it's undermined them. Now that the 'enemy' is here, they are too enervated to respond. Except, he thought, they did do a good job on the 16th Avenue press. Perhaps the ennui did not extend down to the lower levels in the police hierarchy, perhaps only those at the top, who knew the real situation . . . he stopped his thoughts abruptly.

'Interesting material circulating in your mind,' Gram, the telepath, said.

'That's right,' Nick said. 'I forgot.'

'You're absolutely right,' Gram said. 'I'm exhausted. But I can be exhausted most of the time; the work is carried on by department heads who I have complete trust in.'

'Your identity,' Barnes said.

'7Y3ZRR, but more recently 3XX24J,' Nick said, capitulating at last.

'Earlier today you were arrested at a Cordonite printing plant. Are you an Under Man?'

'Yes,' Nicholas Appleton said.

A moment of silence passed.

'When,' Barnes said, 'did you become an Under Man, a follower of the demagogue Cordon and his vicious publications that—'

105

'I became an Under Man,' Nick said, 'when we got back the results of our son's Civil Service test. When I saw how they had managed to test him on the basis of questions he could never possibly know or understand; when I realized that all my years of trust in the government had been wasted. When I recalled how many people had tried to wake me up, and had not so done. Until the test results came in, and, in reading over the Xerox copy of the test, realized Bobby had never had a chance. "What are the components, predicted by Black's formula, which will result in a network seizure on a single molecule-deep surface if the original entities at work are still operating, or if the original entities are operating, either alive or as if alive, in Eigenwelts that overlap only one—" '

Black's Formula. Comprehensible only to New Men. And they required a child to formulate a resultant *pari passu* based on the postulates of the unfathomable system.

'Your thoughts are still of interest,' Gram said. 'Can you tell me who administered your son's test?'

'Norbert Weiss,' Nick said. It would be a long time before he forgot that name. 'And another man's name was on the document. Jerome something. Pike. Pikeman.'

'So,' Barnes said, 'Earl Zeta's effect on you made its appearance only after this episode with your son. Up until then what Zeta pontificated had no—'

'Zeta never said anything,' Nick said. 'It was the news of Cordon's impending execution; I saw the effect on Zeta, and then I realized that—' He lapsed into silence. 'I had to protest,' he said, 'in some way. Earl Zeta opened the door to that way. We had a drink—' Breaking off, he shook his head, trying to clear it; the tranquilizer was still active in his system.

'Alcohol?' Barnes asked. He made a holographic note of that, using a small plastic notebook and a ballpoint pen which he held nearsightedly up to his face.

'Well,' Gram said, 'as the Romans said, "*In vino veritas.*" Do you know what that means, Mr. Appleton?'

' "There is truth in wine." '

Barnes said caustically, 'There is also the saying, "That's the bottle talking." '

'I believe in *"In vino veritas"*,' Gram said, and belched. 'I've got to eat,' he said plaintively. 'Miss Knight,' he said into his face microphone, 'send out to – where did you say, Appleton? That restaurant?'

'Flores',' Nick said. 'Their Alaskan baked salmon is a divine delight.'

'Where did you get the pops,' Barnes asked alertly to Nick, 'to eat in places like Flores'? On your income as a tire re-groover?'

Nick said, 'Kleo and I went there once. On our first anniversary. It took a week's pay, including the tips, but it was worth it.' He had never forgotten it; he never would.

With a curt gesture, Barnes continued with his interrogation. 'So smoldering resentments, which might never have risen to the level of acting out – these resentments became action when Earl Zeta presented you with a way of implementing your feelings by joining the movement. Had he *not* been an Under Man, your resentments might never have reached the surface.'

'What are you trying to prove?' Gram asked, annoyed.

'That once we destroy the axle of the Under Men, once we get men like Cordon—'

'We did,' Gram pointed out. To Nick, he said, 'Did you know that? That Cordon died of a long-term liver condition which was irreversible, and no transplant was available? You heard it on the radio? TV?'

'I heard it,' Nick said. 'That he had been shot to death by an assassin sent to his cell.'

'That's not true,' Gram said. 'He didn't die in his cell, he died on the operating table of the prison hospital during an attempt to put an artificial organ in him. We did everything we could to save him.'

No. Nick thought. No, you didn't.

'You don't believe me?' Gram said, reading his mind. He turned toward Barnes. 'There's your statistic: the embodiment of natural man, of Old Men, and he doesn't believe Cordon died naturally. Can we extrapolate from that that there will be a general planet-wide disbelief?'

'Sure can,' Barnes said.

'Well, damn it,' Gram said. 'I don't care what they be-lieve; it's all over for them. It's just rats here and there in the gutter, waiting for us to zarlp them one by one. Wouldn't you say that, Appleton? Joiners like you, you don't any-more have a place to go and leaders to listen to.' To Barnes he said, 'So when Provoni lands, there won't be anybody to greet him. No throngs of the faithful, they'll have melted away, as Appleton here would do. Only he got caught so it's southeast Utah for him or Luna, if he prefers. You prefer Luna, Mr. Appleton? Mr. 3XX24J?'

Nick said, choosing his words carefully, 'I've heard it said that whole families have gone intact to relocation camps. Is that true?'

'You want to be with your wife and son? But they're not charged.' Barnes bared a notched fang, pursuing the idea to its conclusion. 'We could charge them with—'

'You'll find a tract of Cordon's in our apartment,' Nick said. As soon as he said it he wished, God how he wished, he hadn't said it. Why did I do that? he asked himself. But we should be together. And then he thought of little tough Charley, with her large black eyes and her pushed-in nose. Her hard, slim, breastless body . . . and always her cheery smile, like a character out of Dickens, he thought. A chimney sweep. A Soho thug. Conning her way out of trouble, talking someone into something. Anyhow talking. Always talking. And always with her special lit-up smile, as if the world were a great furry dog which she longed to hug.

Could I go with her? he wondered. Instead of Kleo and Bobby. *Should* I go with her? If it's legally possible?

'It's not,' Gram said from his bed of enormous size.

'What's not?' Barnes demanded.

Gram said leisurely, 'He wants to go with that girl we found with him at the 16th Avenue printing plant. You re-member her?'

'The one you're interested in,' Barnes said.

Hot fear trickled its way down Nick's spine; his heart gave a deep shudder and a mighty heave, and, in his arms and legs, the blood circulation speeded rapidly up. Then it's true about Gram, he thought. What people say about his wenching around. His marriage—

'Is like yours,' Gram finished for him.

Presently, Nick said, 'You're right.'

'What's she like?'

'Feral and wild.' But he didn't have to say aloud, he realized. All he had to do was think of her, imagine her, relive in his mind the details of their short period together. And Gram would gather it up as fast as he thought it.

'She could be trouble,' Gram said. 'And this Denny, her boyfriend, he sounds psychopathic or something. The whole interaction between them, if you're remembering it right, it's sick. She's a sick girl.'

'In a sane environment,' Nick began, but Barnes cut him off.

'May I go on with my questions?'

'Sure,' Gram said, moodily withdrawing; Nick saw the heavyset old man turn his attention inward, to his own thoughts.

'If you were released,' Barnes asked, 'what would your reaction be, what would you do, if – and I say *if* – Thors Provoni returned? And with monstrous help? Help designed to enslave Earth for as long as—'

'Oh, God,' Gram groaned.

'Yes, Council Chairman?' Barnes asked.

'Nothing,' Gram groaned. He rolled over on his side, his gray hair spilling onto the whiteness of the pillows. Discoloring as if something that shunned the light had made its way among them, showing only its stringy pelt.

'Would you react in one of the following ways?' Barnes continued. 'One. Would you be hysterically joyful, without reservation? Two. Would you be wildly pleased? Three. Would you not care? Four. Would it make you uneasy? Five. Would it cause you to join a PSS or military organization prepared to fight the unnatural invaders? Which of these choices, if any, would you choose?'

Nick said, 'Isn't there something between "hysterically joyful without reservation" and "mildly pleased"?'

'No,' Barnes said.

'Why not?'

'We want to know who our enemies are. If you were "hysterically joyful" you would act. To help them. But if you were only "mildly pleased" you'd probably do nothing. That's what is being sorted out by the choices – would you act as an overt enemy of the establishment, and if so, in what direction and to what extent?'

Gram, his voice muffled by his covers, muttered, 'He doesn't know. My God, he just became an Under Man this morning! How the hell would he know how he'd act?'

'But,' Barnes pointed out, 'he's had years to think about Provoni's return. Don't forget that. His reaction, whatever it is, is deeply grounded.' To Nick he said, 'Choose an answer.'

After a pause, Nick said, 'It depends on what you do with Charley.'

'Try and extrapolate that,' Gram said to Barnes and chuckled. 'I can tell you what is going to be done to Charley. She'll be brought here, safe from the demented psychopath, that Denny or Benny or whatever his name is. So you shook off the Purple Sea Cow, very good. But she may have been lying when she said no one else ever had . . . you didn't think of that. She wound you around her little pseudopodium, didn't she? All of a sudden you were saying to your wife, "If she goes, I go." And your wife said, "Go." Which you did. And all that without any warning. You brought Charlotte to your apartment, made up a lie as to how you got involved with her, and then Kleo found the Cordonite tract, and blam, that was it. Because it gave her what a wife likes best: a situation in which her husband has to choose between two evils, between two choices neither of which is palatable to him. Wives love that. When you're in court, divorcing one, you get presented with a choice between going back to her or losing all your possessions, your property, stuff you've hung onto since high school. Yeah, wives really like that.' He buried himself deeper into the pillows. 'Interview's over,' he mumbled sleepily.

'My conclusions,' Barnes said.

'Okay,' Gram said muffledly.

'This man, 3XX24J,' Barnes said, indicating Nick, 'thinks in a manner parallel to your own. His primary concern is for his own personal life, not for a cause. If he is assured of possession of the woman he wants – if and when he finally decides – then he will stand by inert when Provoni arrives.'

'Which leads you to infer what?' Gram mumbled.

Barnes said briskly, 'That we announce today, *now*, that all relocation camps, both in Utah and on Luna, are to be abolished, and the detainees will be returned to their homes and families, or whomever else they wish.' Barnes' voice was jagged with harshness. 'We will, before Provoni arrives, give *them* what 3XX24J here wants – would settle for. Old Men live on a personal level; it is not the cause, the ideology, that motivates them. If they do enter a cause, it is to get back something in their personal lives, such as dignity or meaning. Like better housing, interracial marriage – you understand.'

Shaking himself like a wet dog, Gram sat up in bed and stared at him, his mouth turned down, his eyes bulging . . . as if, Nick thought, he's going to have a stroke.

'*Release* them?' Gram asked. '*All* of them? Like the ones we picked up today: hard core, even wearing uniforms of some kind of paramilitary type?'

'Yes,' Barnes said. 'It's a gamble but, on the basis of what citizen 3XX24J has said and thought, it's obvious to me that he is not thinking, "Will Thors Provoni save Earth?" He is thinking, "I'd certainly like to see that tough little bitch again." '

'Old Men,' Gram muttered. His face relaxed; now his flesh hung in wattles. 'If we gave Appleton his choice between having Charlotte or seeing Provoni be successful, he'd actually choose the former . . .' But then, all at once, his expression changed; it became furtive, cat-like. 'But he can't have Charlotte, I'm involved with her.' To Nick he said, 'You can't have her, so go back to Kleo and Bobby.' He grinned. 'There, I've made the decision for you.'

Clearly annoyed by the discussion, Barnes said to Nick, 'What would your reaction as an Under Man be if all the relocation camps – let's face it: the concentration camps –

were abolished and everyone was sent home, presumably to his friends and family. How would you feel if this were done for you, you too?'

Nick said, 'I think it's the most sensible, humane, rational decision a government could make. There would be a wave of relief and happiness that would cover the globe.' He felt, somehow, that he had expressed himself badly, in clichés, but it was the best he could do. 'Would you really do that?' he asked Barnes incredulously. 'I can't believe it. The number of people in those camps run into millions. It would be one of the most humane decisions by any government in history; it would never be forgotten.'

'You see?' Barnes said to Gram. 'Okay, 3XX24J; if this were done, how would you greet Provoni?'

He saw the logic. 'I—' He hesitated. 'Provoni went in search of help in destroying a tyranny. But if you release everyone, and presumably you would abolish the category of "Under Men"; there would be no more arrests—'

'No more arrests,' Barnes said. 'Cordonite literature will be allowed to circulate freely.'

Rousing himself, Gram rolled about in his bed, heaving and thrashing, managing at last a sitting position. *'They'd take it as a sign of weakness.'* He waggled his finger at first Nick, then more ominously at Barnes. *'They would assume we did it as a result of knowing ourselves to be defeated. Provoni would get the credit!'* He stared at Barnes in a mixture of emotions; his face flowed, mobile and agitated. 'You know what they'd do? They'd then force us to' – he glanced at Nick a little nervously – 'to make the Civil Service exams on the level. In other words, we'd give up our absolute control over who comes into the governmental apparatus and who goes out.'

'We need brain help,' Barnes said, chewing on the flat end of his ballpoint pen.

'You mean another double-dome superman like yourself?' Gram spat out the words. 'To overrule me? Why don't we have a plenipotentiary meeting of the Extraordinary Committee for Public Safety? At least that way we'll have your kind and my kind equally represented.'

Barnes said thoughtfully, 'I would like to have Amos Ild brought in. To get his opinion. It would take twenty-four hours to assemble the Committee; we could have Ild here in half an hour – he's in New Jersey working on the Big Ear, as you know.'

'That fucking enemy of the Unusuals! Up yours, Barnes. Up yours all the way! I'll never submit to the opinions of a head shaped like a pear with God knows what loose nuts and bolts floating around inside.'

Barnes said, 'Ild is the foremost intellectual on the planet today. We recognize him as that; obviously you do, too.'

Dithering, Gram said, 'He's trying to make me obsolete. He's trying to destroy the two-entity system that has made this world a paradise for—'

'Then I'll merely go ahead and have the camps opened,' Barnes said. 'With no concurring – or dissenting – opinions from anyone.' He rose to his feet, put his pad of paper and pen away, picked up his briefcase.

'Isn't it true?' Gram asked. 'Isn't he trying to undermine the Unusuals? Isn't that the real purpose of the Big Ear?'

'Amos Ild,' Barnes said, 'is one of the few New Men who has any concern for the Old. The Big Ear would give them parity powers, abilities equal to your own; it would draw them into the fabric of government. Citizen 3XX24J – his son could pass the ability test, the Special Achievement section, that got you into the government years ago. And look how high you've risen. Listen to me, Willis – the Old Men must be given back their franchise, but there's no use doing it if they simply lack, goddam simply lack, the skills, knowledge, aptitudes, that we have. We're not really falsifying the test results: all right, we do it now and then – we select, as Pikeman and Weiss did in Citizen 3XX24J's case. That's an evil, but not *the* evil. *The* evil lay in constructing a test which you and I could pass and he can't. We're not testing him by what he can do but by what *we* can do. So he gets questions involving Bernhad's Theory of Acausality, which no Old Man can understand. We can't give him a bigger cerebral cortex – we can't give him a New Man brain ... but we can provide him with extra talents that can compensate for it. As in your case. In all Unusual cases.'

'You're looking down at me,' Gram said.

Barnes, still on his feet, sighed. And sagged. 'Well, I've said all I can say right now. It's been a difficult day. I will not contact Amos Ild; I will simply go ahead and order the camps let open. Making it my own decision; mine alone.'

'Find Amos Ild; bring in Amos Ild,' Gram grated, and heaved about on the bed so that the floor under their feet vibrated.

Looking at his watch, Barnes said, 'Right. Within the next couple of days as a certainty. But it will take time to get him—'

'You said "half an hour",' Gram said.

Barnes reached for one of the fones on Gram's desk. 'May I?'

'Sure,' Gram said resignedly.

While Barnes made his call, Nick stood deep in thought, gazing out the immense window of the combination bed-room-office at the city around him, the city which stretched for miles – hundreds of miles.

'You are thinking,' Gram said, 'of ways of persuading me that you have a prior claim on that Charlotte girl.'

He nodded.

'You do,' Gram said. 'But it doesn't matter, because I'm who I am and you're who you are. A tire regroover. I'm passing a law against it, by the way. You'll be out of a job come next Monday.'

'Thanks,' Nick said.

'You always did feel guilty about it,' Gram pointed out. 'I pick up deep guilt from your mind. You worried about the people driving those squibs with the fake tread. Landing. Especially landing. That first bump.'

'True,' Nick said.

Gram said, 'Now you're thinking about Charlotte again, and devising ways of hustling her off. And at the same time you're asking yourself for the millionth time what you ethically should do . . . you can stop that and go back to Kleo and Bobby. And arrange for Bobby to take another—'

'I'll see her again,' Nick said.

114

SEVENTEEN

The fathers, Thors Provoni thought. Yes, that's what they are, our friends from Frolix 8. As if I managed to contact the Urvater, the primordial Father who built the eidos kosmos. They are upset and anxious because something is going wrong on our world; they care; they have empathy; they know how desperate our need is and how we feel; they know *what* we need.

He wondered if all three of his messages had reached the 16th Avenue printing complex, where the Under Man radio and TV transmission and receiving facilities were housed. And if the establishment had intercepted them.

And if they had intercepted them, what, he asked himself, would they do?

A purge. Most likely. But not a certainty. Old Willis Gram – if he was still in power – was an astute man, and he knew whom to milk – and how – of valuable information. Being a telepath did that; Gram could pick the minds of any-one brought close to him. But it remained to be seen who was brought close to him. Radical militants, such as the executives of the McMally Corporation? The members of the Extraordinary Committee for Public Safety? Police Director Lloyd Barnes? Probably Barnes, he was the smartest, and the most sane, of them all – at least among those at high level in the governmental apparatus. There were also independent research New Men scientists, such as the eerie Amos Ild. Ild! What if Gram consulted him? Ild would probably sketch out a shield that would protect Earth against *everything*. God help me, Provoni thought, if they've brought Ild – or Tom Rovere, for that matter, or Stanton Finch – into this. Fortunately the truly brilliant New Man gravitated toward abstract, academic studies: they became theoretical physicists, statisticians, and the like. Finch, for example, had, at the time Provoni left, been working on a system to duplicate the microsecond come third in the succession of creation of the universe; ultimately, under controlled conditions, he wished to work his way back to the first second and then, God forbid, push – in theory, in mathematical terms – the entropic flow back to the interval, called a valence-passage, before the first second.

But all on paper.

When he was finished, Finch would be able to show mathematically what situation was required for the big bang universe to come into existence. Finch could work with concepts such as negative time, as well as null-rate time ... probably by now it was all done, and Finch was involved with his hobby: the collecting of rare eighteenth century snuffboxes.

Now Tom Rovere. He had been working on the subject of entropy, basing his project on the arbitrary assumption that ultimately enough decay, and enough random distribution of ergs throughout the universe, would automatically start an anti-entropic flow backward, due to collisions between simple, indivisible bits of energy or matter with one another, out of which more complex entities would emerge. The frequency of the possibility of these gradually more complex entities would be in inverse proportion to their complexity. Once the process began, however, it could not be turned back until ultimately complex entities had been formed, with a unique – and uniquely complex – entity forming which would involve all the molecules in the universe. This would be God, but He would break down, and with His breaking down the force of entropy would assert itself ... as in the various laws of thermodynamics. Thus, Rovere demonstrated that the current epoch was slightly after that of the breaking-apart of the totally inclusive unique entity called God, and that a growing progression away from individuality and complexity was already under way. It would continue until the original equal distribution of waste heat occurred, whereupon, after much time, the anti-entropic force would, by randomness, by chance motion, manifest itself once more.

116

But Amos Ild. He differed from them: he was *building* something, rather than merely describing it in theoretical, mathematical terms. The government would make good use of him, if it did happen to occur to Gram. Yes, he would think of it, Provoni decided. Because by bringing Ild into top government levels, work on the Great Ear would slow down, perhaps even cease. It would take Gram time to figure this out, but eventually he would.

So I have to assume, Provoni thought, that we'll be up against Amos Ild. The brightest light the New Men possess – hence the most dangerous to us.

'Morgo,' he said.

'Yes, Mr. Provoni.'

'Can you construct a receiver out of yourself or out of parts of this ship by which you can monitor thirty meter band output by Earth transmitters? I mean ordinary transmitters, used for commercial purposes.'

'Why, may I ask?'

'They run regular news broadcasts at two spots on the thirty meter band. Hourly.'

'You wish to know what's happening on Earth politically?'

'No,' he said with sarcasm. 'I want to know the price of eggs in Maine.'

My temper's wearing thin, he realized.

'Sorry,' he said.

'No sweat,' the Frolixan answered.

Thors Provoni threw back his head and laughed. ' "No sweat" from a ninety ton gelatinous mass of protoplasmic slime that has engulfed this ship in its fluid body, that's on every side of me, like a barrel. And it says, "No sweat." '

This kind of usage would surprise the New Men, when they reached Terra. After all, it had learned his vocabulary *and* mannerisms – which were not the king's.

'I can pull the sixteen meter band,' Morgo said presently. 'Will that do? There seems to be considerable traffic on it.'

'Not the kind I want,' he said.

'The forty meter band, then?'

'Okay,' Provoni said irritably. He put on the headphone, turned the variable condenser of his receiving rig. Cross-talk came and went, and then, for an instant, he had a news broadcast.

'... the end of relocation camps on ... and Luna brought a ... who some of which for years ... coupled with this, the destruction of the subversive 16th Avenue printing ...' It faded out.

Did I hear that right? Provoni asked himself. The *end* of the relocation camps on Luna and southeastern Utah? Everyone freed? Only Barnes could have thought of that. But even Barnes ... it was hard to believe. Maybe as a whim of Gram's, he thought. A momentary panic reaction to our three radio messages to the 16th Avenue plant. But if it's been destroyed, perhaps they didn't receive the messages; perhaps they received only the first one or two.

He hoped both the government *and* the Cordonites had received the third message. It ran:

We will join you in six days and take over the task of operating the government.

To the Frolixan he said, 'Would you augment my transmission strength and beam the third message over and over again. Here, I can make you a rotary loop or tape.' He snapped on his tape recorder and read the words, grimly, and with ultra-clear articulation – and intense satisfaction.

'On a variety of frequencies?' Morgo asked.

'Every one you can manage. If you can get it up into the frequency modulation channels we might be able to print over a video image. Get it right into their TV sets.'

'Good. That will be enjoyable. It's a cryptic message; it does not, for example, mention that I am alone, that my brothers lag half a light year behind us.'

'Let Willis Gram figure that out when we get there,' Provoni grunted.

Morgo said, 'I have been meditating over the possible effect my presence will have on your Mr. Gram and his cronies. First of all, they will discover that I cannot die, and that will frighten them. They will see that I can grow, if fed properly, and in addition I am able to make nutritional use

118

of almost any substance. Third—'

'A thing,' Provoni said. 'You're a thing.'

'A thing?'

'That's what it's all about.'

'The psychological effect, you mean?'

'Right.' Provoni nodded somberly.

'I think,' Morgo said, 'that my ability to replace sections of living organisms with my own ontological substance will frighten them the most. When I manifest myself smally, as say a chair, consuming the actual object as a source of energy – this event, in miniature, so they can understand it, will panic them. As you have seen, I can replace any object with myself; there is no viable limit to my growth, Mr. Provoni, as long as I am fed. I can become the entire building in which Mr. Gram works; I can become an apartment building of five thousand people. And' – Morgo hesitated – 'there is more. But I will not at this time discuss it.'

Provoni meditated. The Frolixans had no specific shape; their historic method for survival was to mimic objects or other living creatures. Their strength lay in the fact that they could absorb creatures, become them, using them as fuel, and then abandoning their empty husks. This process, like that of cancer, would not easily be uncovered by Gram's detection-police apparatus; even when the transformation process reached vital organs, the imitated creature could function and survive. Death came when the Frolixan withdrew – ceased to provide counterfeit lungs, heart, kidneys. A Frolixan liver, for example, could function as well as the authentic liver it replaced . . . but it declined to remain once it had devoured everything of value.

Most frightening of all was the Frolixan invasion of the brain. The human – or other invaded organism – suffered from pseudo-psychotic thought-processes which he did not recognize as his own . . . and he would be correct; they would not be. And gradually, as the brain became absorbed and replaced, all of his thought-processes would be Frolixan. And at that point the Frolixan abandoned him, and he ceased to be, utterly empty of psychic content.

'Fortunately,' Provoni mused, 'you're selective in your

choice of hosts, since you have no interest in or intention of populating Earth and bringing to an end the life of human-oid organisms. All you're going after is the governmental structure.' And once that's done, he mused, you will retire. Won't you?

'Yes,' Morgo said, listening to his thoughts.

'You're not lying?' Provoni asked.

The Frolixan let forth a cry of pain.

'All right,' Provoni said hastily. 'I'm sorry. But suppose—' He did not finish, at least not aloud. But his thoughts jumped to the ultimate conclusion: I have sent a race of murderers to Earth, to destroy everyone equally.

'Mr. Provoni,' Morgo said, 'this is why I, and only I, am here with you: we want to try to settle matters without a physical conflict ... as would happen when my brothers arrive – happen then because we will not call on them unless needed for open warfare. I will negotiate a basic change in the establishment of your planet; that establishment will agree. In the news item you monitored, it mentioned that the concentration camps have been opened. They are doing it to placate us, are they not? Not from weakness on their part but from their desire to avoid an open fight, to present a united front. Your race is xenophobic. And I am the ulti-mate foreigner. I love you, Mr. Provoni; I love your people ... insofar as I know them through your mind. I will not do what I can do, but I will make them know what I can do. In your mind's memory-section there is a Zen story about the greatest swordsman in Japan. Two men challenge him. They agree to row out to a small island and fight there. The greatest swordsman in Japan, being a student of Zen, sees to it that he is last to leave the boat. The moment the others have leaped out onto the shore of the island he pushes off, rows away, leaving them and their swords there. Thus he proves his claim for what he is: indeed he is the finest swordsman in Japan. Do you see the application to my situa-tion? I can outfight your establishment, but I will do so by not-fighting ... if you follow my thought. It will be in fact be my refusal to fight – *yet showing my strength* – which will frighten them the most, because they cannot imagine such

120

power held but not used. Had they it, they would use it, your government. Your New Men, who to me are like the buzzing of flies. If I am obtaining an actual picture of them from your mind; if you do in fact know them.'

'I should know them,' Provoni said. 'I'm one of them. I'm a New Man.'

EIGHTEEN

Presently Morgo said, 'I knew. Hints of it, and your knowledge of it, have leaked into your conscious mind. Especially during sleep.'

'So I'm a double renegade,' Provoni said starkly.

'Why did you break with your fellows?'

Provoni said, 'There are six thousand New Men on Earth, ruling with the help, such as it is, from four thousand Unusuals. Ten thousand in a Civil Service hierarchy that cuts everyone else out ... *five billion* Old Men with no way—' He lapsed into silence and then he did a surprising thing: he raised his hand, and a plastic cup of water floated directly to him, depositing itself in the grip of his hand.

'You are an Unusual, too,' Morgo said. 'A t-k.' He added, 'That I did not guess.'

Provoni said, 'As far as I know, I'm the only fusion of New Man and Unusual. I'm a freak, splitting off from other freaks.'

'How far you could have gone in the Civil Service; consider, as you must have, what rating you could score.'

'Oh, hell; I was double-03. Not overtly, but when I had tests administered to me sub rosa. I could have challenged Gram. I could have challenged any of them.'

'Mr. Provoni,' the Frolixan said, 'I do not see why you failed to work from within.'

'I couldn't dislodge ten thousand civil servants, from G-1 to double-03, all the way up to the Extraordinary Committee for Public Safety and Council Chairman Gram.' But that

121

was not the reason, and he knew it. 'I was afraid,' he said, 'that if they found out they would kill me. My parents were afraid when I was a child. All of them, New Men, Unusuals ... and the Old Men and Under Men. I could harbinger a race of super supermen; if it became public the upheaval would be vicious and I would' – he gestured – 'disappear. And they would begin to watch for others like me.'

'It never occurred to anyone that a person might emerge who comprised both types,' the Frolixan said, 'That is, theoretically. Before they tested you.'

'Like I said, my tests were private. My father was at a G-4 rating, as a New Man, and he secretly arranged for the tests, after he saw my t-k ability and knew, in addition, that I had Nodes of Rogers sticking from my brain like pencil stubs. It was my father who made me wary, God rest his soul. You know, these great planet-wide and inter-planet-wide wars break out, and everyone is supposed to be thinking of the ideologies involved ... whereas in actuality most people simply want a good, safe night's sleep.' He added, 'A statement I read, literature on a pill. It said, in fact, that many persons who were suicidally inclined really wanted a good night's sleep and they thought they'd find it in death.' Where are my thoughts taking me? he wondered. I haven't thought of suicide in years. Not since I left Earth.

'You need sleep,' Morgo said.

'I need to know if my third message is getting through to Earth,' Provoni said gratingly. 'Can we really reach Earth in just six more days?' Ghosts had begun to haunt him: fields and pastures, the vast floating cities on Earth's blue oceans, the domes on Luna and Mars, New York, the kingdom of L.A. And especially San Francisco, with its quaint, fabulous, old-time BART 'rapid transit' system, built back in 1972 and for sentimental reasons still used.

Food, he thought. Steak with mushrooms, escargots, frogs legs ... which to be tender had to be frozen in advance, which most people did not know, including many otherwise good restaurants.

'Do you know what I want?' he asked the Frolixan. 'A glass of ice cold milk. Milk with ice in it. A half-gallon of it.

122

I want to just sit there and drink milk.'

'As you pointed out, Mr. Provoni,' Morgo said, 'a man's real interest is in the immediate and the small. We are on a voyage affecting the lives and hopes of six billion people, and yet when you imagine yourself there, at last, you imagine yourself sitting at a table on which rests a carton of milk.'

'But you see,' Provoni said, *they're the same way.* There is an invasion of Earth by nonterrestrials, and everyone – everyone! – wants merely to continue living. The myth of the seething, inarticulate mass that's searching for a spokesman, a leader – that would be Cordon. But how many people really care? Maybe even Cordon doesn't care ... not terribly. Do you know what the French gentry were afraid of during the Revolution? They were afraid someone would come in and smash their pianos. Their narrow vision . . .' He broke off. 'Which even I share,' he said aloud, 'to an extent.'

'You're homesick. It shows up in your dreams; nightly, you walk the paths of Earth's forests, and rise in majestic elevators to rooftop restaurants and drugbars.'

'Yes, drugbars,' Provoni said. He had run out of all medication long ago, fun and otherwise – including, of course, all the mind-affecting pills. I'll sit there at a drugbar, he said to himself, and have one capsule, pellet, tablet and spansule after another. I'll frost myself into invisibility. I'll fly like a raven, like a crow; I'll cackle and chirp my way across the fields of greenhouses, into the sunlight and out of it. In only six more days.

'There is one matter which we have not settled, Mr. Provoni,' the Frolixan said. 'Are we to make an initial public appearance, with great pomp and circumstance, or shall we land in some out-of-the-way area where we won't be seen? And begin operations slowly from there? You could move freely about, if the latter. You could see and enjoy your fields of wheat, your rows of Kansas corn; you could rest, take your pills, and, if you don't mind my saying it, shave, bathe, get clean clothes; freshen yourself up. Whereas if we drop down in the middle of Times Square—'

'It doesn't matter whether we land in the middle of Times Square or in a Kansas pasture,' Provoni said. 'They'll be maintaining constant radar alert, looking for us. They may even attack us, or try to attack us, with ships of the line, before we even reach Earth. We can't be inconspicuous, not with you weighing ninety or so tons. Our retrorockets will light up the sky like Roman candles.'

'They can't destroy your ship. I am wrapped around it entirely, now.'

'I understand, but they don't; they may try anyway.' How will I look when I emerge? he asked himself. Grimy, dirty, given to unclean habits ... but wouldn't they expect that? Wouldn't the crowd understand that? Maybe that is exactly the way I should appear.

'Times Square,' he said aloud.

'In the middle of the night.'

'No; even so it would be too crowded.'

'We'll fire warning bursts with the retrorockets. When they see that we're landing they'll retreat.'

'And then a hydrogen warhead shell from a T-40 cannon will blow us to bits.' He felt sardonic and savage.

'Mr. Provoni, remember that I am semi-matter, that I can absorb anything. I will be there, wrapped around your little ship and you, for as long as is necessary.'

'Maybe they'll go mad when they see me.'

'With enthusiasm?'

'I don't know. Whatever makes people go mad. Fear of the unknown; it may be that. They may retreat as far from me as is physically possible. They may retreat to Denver, Colorado, bunch up there like scared cats. You've never seen a scared cat, have you? I've always had cats, tomcats, unaltered, and always my cat is a loser. He's the one that comes back in shreds. You know how you can tell your cat's a loser? When he and another tom are about to fight, you go out to rescue yours, and if he's a winner, he at once jumps the other cat. And if he's a loser, he damn well lets you pick him up and take him indoors.'

'You will soon see cats again,' Morgo said.

'So will you,' Provoni said.

'Describe a cat for me,' Morgo said. 'Let it take shape in your mind. All your recollections and associations with cats.'

124

Thors Provoni thought about cats. It seemed a harmless thing to do as they waited out the six days until they reached Earth.

'Opinionated,' Morgo said at last.

'Me, you mean? On the subject?'

'No, I mean cats. And self-centred.'

Angrily, Provoni said, 'A cat is loyal to its master. But it shows it in a subtle way. That's the whole point, a cat gives himself to no one, and this has been his way for millions of years, and then you manage to knock a chink in his armor, and he rubs against you and sits on your lap and purrs. So, because of his love for you, he breaks the inherent genetic behavior-pattern of two million years. What a victory that is.'

'Assuming the cat is sincere,' Morgo said, 'rather than trying to cadge extra food.'

'You think a cat can be a hypocrite?' Provoni asked. 'I've never heard an insinuation of insincerity directed toward cats. Actually, much of the criticism comes from their brutal honesty; if they don't like a person then shit, they're off to someone else.'

'I think,' Morgo said, 'when we get to Terra I would like to have a dog.'

'A dog! After my meditation on the nature of cats – after all the wealth of material about dearly-loved cats from my past; I still think of one old tom named Asherbanopol, but we called him Ralf. "Asherbanopol" is Egyptian.'

'Yes,' the Frolixan said. 'You still moan deep in your heart for Asherbanopol. But when you die, as in the Mark Twain story—'

'Yeah,' he said morosely. 'They'll all be there, a row of them on each side of the road, waiting for me. An animal refuses to pass into Paradise without its master. They wait year after year.'

'And you fervently believe this.'

' "Believe it?" I know it's true; God is alive; that carcass they found in deep space back a few years ago, that wasn't God. You don't find God under such circumstances, that's Medieval thought. Do you know where you find the Holy

125

Spirit? It's not out in space – hell, it created space. It's here.'
He pointed to his chest. 'I – I mean, we – have a portion of
the Holy Spirit within us. Look at your decision to come and
give us help – you get nothing from it, perhaps injury, or
some kind of destruction that the military has but which we
haven't heard about.'

'I receive something from coming to your planet,' Morgo
said. 'I get to pick up and hold little life forms: cats, a dog,
a leaf, a snail, a chipmunk. Do you know – do you understand – that on Frolix 8 all life forms except ourselves were
sterilized, hence they long ago disappeared ... although I've
seen recordings of them, three dimensional recreations that
seem absolutely real. Wired directly to the ruling ganglia of
our central nervous systems.'

Fear overcame Thors Provoni.

'That bothers you,' Morgo said. 'That we would do that.
We ourselves; we were growing, dividing, growing. We
needed to urbanize every inch of our planet; the animals
would starve, and we preferred using a sterilizing gas, utterly
painless. They could not have lived in our world with us.'

'Your population has tapered off, now, has it?' Nick
asked. The fear still lay inside him, like a coiled snake.
Waiting to unwind, to show its poisonous fangs.

Morgo said, 'We always could use more room.'

Like Earth, Provoni thought.

'No, there's already a dominant sentient species, there.
We are forbidden by the civil wing of our ruling circles to—'
Morgo hesitated.

'Military,' Provoni said, in wonder.

'I am a commando. That's what caused them to pick me
to return to Sol 3 with you. I have a reputation for being
able to solve disputes by mixing reasoning and force. The
threat of the force makes them listen; the knowledge, my
knowledge, points out the way by which the best society
possible can succeed.'

'You've done this before?' Obviously it had.

'I am over a million years old,' Morgo said. 'I, backed by
the contingency of force, have solved wars so vast, with numbers so great, as to be impossible for you to imagine. I have

unscrambled politico–economic problems, sometimes by introducing new machinery or anyhow theoretical papers by which such devices could be achieved. And then I have passed by, and the rest is up to them.'

'Do you intervene only if called on?' Provoni said.

'Yes.'

'So, in essence, you help only civilizations which have been able to produce trans-stellar drives. To get their messenger there ... where at last you notice him. But some Medieval society, with longbows and pig-helmets—'

'Our theory,' Morgo said, 'as to this, is interesting. At the longbow level, in fact at the cannon level, and airships, water ships, bombs ... *it is none of our business.* We don't want it to be, because our theory tells us that they cannot destroy their race or their planet. But when hydrogen bombs are built, and technocracy has enabled them to build inter-stellar—'

'I don't believe it,' Provoni said flatly.

'Why?' The Frolixan explored his brain, deftly, but with his customary reverence. 'Oh, I see,' he said. 'You know that they create hydrogen bombs long before they develop an inter-stellar drive. You are right.' It paused. 'All right, then. We allow ourselves to get involved only when approached by a ship capable of inter-stellar flight. Because at that point the civilization is potentially dangerous to us. *They have found us.* A response of some sort on our part is indicated ... as, for instance, in your world's history, when Admiral Perry breached the wall surrounding Japan – and the entire country had to modernize within a matter of a few years. Bear this in mind: we could have chosen merely to kill every inter-stellar spaceman, instead of asking what we could add to help stabilize their culture. You would be incredulous if you knew how many cultures are in the grip of wars and power struggles and tyrannies ... some far advanced over yours. But you supplied us with our criterion: you reached us. So, Mr. Provoni, I'm here.'

Provoni said, 'I don't like that about the animals being exterminated.' He was thinking about the six billion Old Man population. Would they be treated like that? he won-

127

dered. Will they treat us all like that, New Man, Unusual, Old Man, Under Man – will they snuff us and inherit our planet with all its works?

Morgo said, 'Mr. Provoni, let me make two points which should serve to quiet your turmoil. First: we have known about your civilization for centuries. Our ships have entered and skimmed around in your atmosphere back to the time of whaling boats. We could have taken over any time, if we so desired; don't you think it would have been easier to defeat the "thin red line", the Redcoats, than to face cobalt and hydrogen tactical missiles as we would have to – are doing – now? I've been listening. You have several picket ships loitering in the area near the point at which Sol's gravitational field begins to affect us.'

'And second?'

'We will steal.'

' "Steal"!' Provoni was amazed. 'Steal what?'

'Countless diversions of yours: vacuum cleaners, type-writers, 3-D video systems, twenty-year batteries, computers – in exchange for ending the tyranny we will hang about a while, obtaining working models, if possible, or descriptions of every conceivable plant, tree, boat, power tool; you name it.'

'But you're technologically advanced over us.'

Morgo said in a pleased voice, 'It doesn't matter. Each civilization, on each planet, develops unique, idiosyncratic tools, manners, theories, toys, acid-resistant tanks, merry-go-rounds. Let me ask you this: suppose you could be transported back to England in the eighteenth century. And you could take back with you whatever pleased you. Wouldn't you cart away a good deal? Paintings alone – but I see that you understand.'

'We're quaint!' Provoni said furiously.

'Yes, that expresses it. And quaintness is one of the great use-constituents in the universe, Mr. Provoni. It is a sub-division of the principle of uniqueness, which your own Mr. Bernhad explained in his "Theory of Acausality Measured by Two Axes." Uniqueness is unique, but there are what Bernhad called "quasi-uniquenesses", of which many—'

'I ghosted Bernhad's theory for him,' Provoni said. 'I was a smart-assed young college kid, one of Bernhad's teaching assistants. We prepared all the data, the citations, everything – had them published in *Nature* – with only Bernhad's name on it. In 2103 I was eighteen. Now I'm one hundred and five.' He grimaced. 'An old man in a different sense. But I'm still alive and active; I can still piss and stink and eat and sleep and screw. Anyhow, you read about people living to be two hundred years old, born back around 1985, when the aging virus was isolated, and anti-geretelic compounds were mainlined by forty percent of the population.'

He thought, then, about the animals, and about Earth's six billion who were going nowhere, except, perhaps, the absolutely gigantic relocation camps on Luna with their opaque tank sides; the prisoners were not even allowed to see the landscape around them. Must be twelve to twenty million Old Men in those camps, he pondered. An army. Where'll they go on Earth? Twenty *million*? Ten million *apartments*? Twenty million jobs, and all non-G. Not Civil Service.

Gram may be handing us a hot potato, he said to himself. If we take over the functions of government even briefly, *we'll* have to process them. We might – incredibly – find ourselves putting them back in the camps on a 'temporary' basis. Jesus, he thought, how ironic can you get?

Morgo Rahn Wilc said suddenly, 'A man-of-war portside.'

'A what at what?'

'Check your radar screen. You'll see a blip – a ship, a large one, moving very fast, too fast for a commercial vehicle, coming directly at us.' A pause. 'On a collision course; they're going to sacrifice themselves to stop us.'

'Can they?'

Patiently, Morgo said, 'No, Mr. Provoni. Even when they have mounted .88 hydrogen warheads or four hydrogen warhead torpedoes.'

I'll wait, Provoni thought, as he bent over his radar screen, until I see it. Because this is obviously one of those fast new LR-82s – he rubbed his forehead wearily. 'No, that was ten years ago; I'm living in the past. Anyway,' he said, 'it's a fast ship.'

'Not as fast as ours, Mr. Provoni,' Morgo said. The *Gray Dinosaur* boomed and shuddered, as rocket engines were fired; then the characteristic whine that came from entering hyperspace.

The ship followed. There, on the screen once more, it hung, and it moved closer with each second, all its main engines firing in a brilliant nimbus of dancing, flaming, yellow light.

'I think it ends right here,' Provoni said.

NINETEEN

Notification reached Willis Gram with no delay. To the members of the Extraordinary Committee for Public Safety, gathered about his bed in his office-bedroom, he said, propping himself bolt upright among the pillows, 'Listen to this.'

Badger has *Gray Dinosaur* on its sighters. *Dinosaur* has begun evasive maneuvers. We are closing rapidly.

'I can't believe it,' Gram said happily. To the Committee members he said, 'I called you here because of this third transmission we got from Provoni. They'll be here in six days.' He stretched, yawned, grinned around at them. 'I was going to tell you how fast we have to act to open the relocation camps, as well as stopping our crackdown on Under Men still at large, and blowing up their transmitters and printing presses and like that. *But*: if *Badger* pulverizes *Dinosaur*, then that's it! We can go on as if nothing has happened, as if Provoni never made it back here at all.'

'But the first two notes were telecast,' Fred Rayner, the Interior Minister, said bitingly.

'Well, we'll not disclose it about the third message. About

them landing here in six days and "taking over the government", and all that.'

'Mr. Council Chairman,' Duke Bostrich, Minister of State, said, 'the third message is coming in – so help me God – on the forty meter band, so it's been picked up here and there all over the world. By this time tomorrow, everyone will know.'

'But if *Badger* gets *Dinosaur* it won't matter.' Gram inhaled deeply, reached to take an amphetamine capsule to soar even higher in this sudden, unexpected moment of greatness. 'You know,' he said to them all, especially Patty Platt, Minister of Defense, who had never liked or respected him, 'you know it was my idea to station ships like *Badger* out there five years ago . . . picket ships, not heavily armed. We know the *Gray Dinosaur* isn't armed. So even a picket ship can destroy it.'

'Sir,' General Hefele said, 'I am familiar with the T-144 class of picket ships, the class including *Badger*. Because of the long periods they must remain in space, and the distances they need to cover, they are built too clumsily to maneuver to where a bow shot, I use that as an example, could effectively be—'

'You mean,' Gram said, 'that my picket ships are obsolete? Why didn't you tell me?'

'Because,' General Rayburn with his thin, black moustache said, 'it never occurred to us that (one) Provoni might return, and (two) that a picket ship stationed in some vast area of empty space could sight Provoni if, or I suppose I should say when, Provoni returned.' He gestured. 'The number of parsecs it—'

'Generals Rayburn and Hefele,' Gram said, 'you will begin to compose resignation notes. Have them ready for me within an hour.' He lay back, then, abruptly started up; he pressed a button which turned on his general fone screen. It showed the Wyoming computer, or at least a section of it.

'Technician,' he instructed.

A white-smocked programmer appeared. 'Yes, Council Chairman.'

Gram said, 'I want a prognosis on this situation: a T-144

131

picket ship has encountered *Gray Dinosaur* at' – he reached for his desk, groping and straining and grunting – 'at these coordinates.' He read them to the technician, who was of course recording these instructions. 'I want to know,' he said, 'with all facts considered, what are the chances that a T-144 class ship could destroy the *Gray Dinosaur*?'

The technician rewound the tape, then plugged the deck into the computer's input and turned the switch to on. Behind plastic frames, wheels spun around; tapes wound themselves and rewound themselves.

Mary Scourby, Minister of Agriculture, said, 'Why don't we just wait and see the outcome of the battle?'

'Because,' Willis Gram said, 'that damn *Dinosaur* and that donkey Provoni driving it – plus their nonterrestrial friend – it may be all souped-up with weapons. And a fleet may be following.' To General Hefele, who was already painstakingly writing out his resignation, Gram said, 'Do our radar scopes sight anything else in that area? Ask *Badger*.'

From his coat pocket, General Hefele brought forth a transmitter-receiver. 'Any other blips seen by *Badger*?' A pause. 'No.' He returned to writing his resignation.

The technician in Wyoming said, 'Mr. Council Chairman, we have the 996-D computer's response to your query. It feels that the third message from Thors Provoni, the one we're picking up on all forty meter band frequencies, is the critical datum. The computer analyzes that the statement beginning, "We will join you in six days" implies that one of the aliens is with Provoni. Not knowing the alien's powers, it cannot compute, but it does go on to answer a correlative – the *Gray Dinosaur* cannot out-maneuver a T-144 picket ship for very long. So the unknown variable – the presence of the alien – is too great. It can't compute the situation.'

'I'm receiving a message from the crew monitoring *Badger*,' General Rayburn said suddenly. 'Be quiet.' He tilted his head on one side, toward the side of his ear-insert fone.

Silence.

'*Badger*'s gone,' General Rayburn said.

'*Gone?*' A half-dozen voices spoke up at once. 'Gone?'

132

Gram demanded. 'Gone where?'

'Into hyperspace. We'll know soon because, as has been abundantly shown, a ship can remain in hyperspace for ten, twelve, fifteen minutes at the most. We won't have to wait long.'

'*Dinosaur* took off right into hyperspace?' General Hefele asked, incredulously. 'That's only done as a last resort – the most extreme evasion measure possible. And they drew *Badger* into it after them. Maybe *Dinosaur* has been rebuilt; maybe its exterior surfaces are now of an alloy that does not decompose rapidly in hyperspace. Maybe they need only to wait until *Badger* blows up or returns to mutual or para-space. You know, the *Gray Dinosaur* that left this system ten years ago may not be the *Gray Dinosaur* that's coming back.'

'*Badger* recognized it,' General Hefele said. 'It's the same ship, and if modified, at least not so outwardly. Captain Greco of *Badger*, before he dropped down into hyperspace, said that it fitted the ident foto made fifteen years ago to the last jot and tittle, except—'

' "Except"?' Gram asked, grinding his molars. I've got to stop grinding my teeth, he realized; I broke right through that upper right cap, that time. That should have taught me. He leaned back, fooled with his pillows.

'Except,' General Hefele said, 'some of the exterior sensors were either missing or visibly changed, possibly damaged. And of course the hull was deeply pitted.'

'*Badger* could see all that?' Gram said wonderingly.

'The new Knewdsen radar scopes, the so-called eyepiece models, can—'

'Be quiet.' Gram was consulting his watch. 'I'll time them,' he said vigorously. 'It's been about three minutes already, hasn't it? I'll make it five, just to be on the safe side.' He sat in silence, studying his Omega watch; everyone else studied his own.

Five minutes passed.

Ten.

Fifteen.

Over in the corner, Camelia Grimes, the Minister of Job

133

Opportunities and Education, began to sniffle quietly into her lace handkerchief. 'He lured them to their death,' she half-spoke, half-whispered huskily. 'Oh, dear, it's so sad, just so sad. All those men lost.'

Gram said, 'Yeah, that's sad. It's also sad, too, that he got by a picket ship. One chance in – what? A billion? That a picket ship would pick it up in the first place. It almost looked like then and there we had him. Nailed down; snuffed, as a sight for his alien friends to witness.'

To General Hefele, General Rayburn said, 'Are there any other ships which might pick up the *Gray Dinosaur* when and if it emerges from hyperspace?'

General Hefele said, 'No.'

'So we won't know if it emerged,' Gram said. 'Maybe it was destroyed, too, along with *Badger*.'

'We'll know when and if it comes out of hyperspace,' General Hefele said, 'because as soon as it emerges, it'll begin transmitting that signal on the forty meter band, again.' To an aide he said, 'Have my com-net monitor for a renewed indication of their transmission.' To Gram he said, 'I'm assuming—'

'You may so assume,' General Rayburn said. 'No radio signal can pass out of hyperspace into paraspace.'

General Hefele said to his aide, 'Find out if Provoni's signal was cut off a few minutes ago.'

A moment later, through the intercom equipment which he wore from several neck straps, the tall, young aide had his message. 'Signal cut out twenty-two minutes ago and has not resumed.'

'They're still in hyperspace,' General Hefele said. 'And the signal may never resume; it may be all over.'

'I still want your resignation,' Gram said.

A red light lit up on the console of his desk. He picked up the appropriate fone and said, 'Yes? You have her with you?'

'Miss Charlotte Boyer,' his third-level clearance A receptionist said. 'Brought in here by two PSS men who had to drag her all the way. My goodness, their shins are going to be black and blue tomorrow, and she bit one on the hand; it tore a whole lot of flesh loose, and he's going to have to go to the infirmary right away.'

Gram said, 'Get four military MPs to spell the PSS men. When you have them, and they've got her completely under control, then let me know and I'll see her.'

'Yes sir.'

'If a certain individual named Denny Strong barges into the building looking for her,' Gram said, 'I want him arrested for trespassing and I want him in a jail cell immediately. If he tries to physically break into my office, here, I want the guards to snuff him. On the spot. The second his hand touches the handle to the door to this room.' *I could have done it once myself*, Gram thought. *But now I'm too old and my reflexes are too slow.* Nonetheless, he lifted the lid at the corner of his desk-top ... which brought the butt of a .38 magnum pistol within easy reach. *If Nicholas Appleton's mental image of him – and his knowledge of him – are correct, then I'd better be ready*, he thought. *And good God*, he thought, *I have to be ready vis-à-vis Nick Appleton – just because he left the building voluntarily and with no show of violence, there's no guarantee that he'll continue to go along with this.*

That's the trouble with being that age, he reflected. *You idealize the whole woman, her self, her personality ... but at my age it's simply how good a lay they'd make and that's that. I'll enjoy her, use her up, teach her a few things she probably doesn't know about sexual relations – even though she's 'been around' – that she hasn't dreamed up. She can be my little fish, for example. And once she learns them, does them, she'll remember them the rest of her life. They'll haunt her, the memory of them ... but on some level she'll be yearning for them again: they were so nice. Let's see what Nick Appleton, or Denny Strong, or whoever gets her after me, will do to gratify that. And she won't be able to force herself to tell him what it is that's the matter.*

He chuckled.

'Council Chairman,' General Hefele said, 'I have news from my aide.' His aide bent over him, covertly speaking into his ear. 'I regret to say – the forty meters' signal has resumed.'

'That's that,' Gram said stoically. 'I knew they'd come back out; they wouldn't have gone in if they hadn't known they could handle it . . . and *Badger* couldn't.' Laboriously, he heaved himself up to a sitting position, then rolled over, extended a massive leg, raised himself to a standing position. 'My bathrobe,' he said, looking around.

'I have it, sir,' Camelia Grimes said; she held it up for him to back into. 'Now your slippers.'

General Hefele said frigidly, 'They're right by your feet.' And thought, Do you need someone to put them on for you, Council Chairman? You gigantic mushroom that has to be waited on day and night, who lies in bed like a sick kid home from school, evading the realities of adulthood. And he's our ruler. He's the person primarily responsible for stopping the invaders.

'You always forget,' Gram said, facing him, 'that I'm a telepath. If you said the things you think, you'd be put up before a gas-grenade squad. And you know it.' He felt genuine anger, and it was rare for thoughts alone to ruffle him. But in this case it had gone too far. 'You want a vote?' he asked, waving his arm at them all, the collected assembly of the Extraordinary Committee for Public Safety, plus Earth's two top military planner-advisers.

' "A vote"?' Duke Bostrich asked, smoothing, reflexively, his distinguished silver hair. 'As to what?'

Fred Rayner, from Interior, said acidly, 'Mr. Gram's removal as Council Chairman, and someone else – of the group of us here in this room – taking his place.' He smiled starkly, thinking, Must it be spelled out, as with children? This is our chance to rid ourselves of the fat old fool; let him spend the rest of his life untangling his convoluted personal affairs . . . an example of which came up just now, this Boyer girl.

'I'd like a vote,' Gram said, after a pause. During the pause he had listened in on their various thoughts and knew that he would be given a support vote; hence he was scarcely worried. 'Go on,' he said, 'vote!'

136

Rayner said, 'He's read our thoughts; he knows how it'll come out.'

'Or he's bluffing,' Mary Scourby, Agriculture, said. 'He's read our thoughts and knows we can dislodge him, and will do so.'

'So,' Camelia Grimes said, 'we will have to vote after all.'

By a show of hands they derived a vote of six for retention of Gram and four against.

'Tiddly winks, old man,' Gram said scorchingly to Fred Rayner. 'Catch a woman if you can; if you can't catch a woman, catch a clean old man.'

'And the "clean old man",' Rayner said, 'is you. '

Throwing his head back, Willis Gram howled with delight. Then, stepping into his slippers, he stumped toward the main doors of the room.

'Council Chairman,' General Hefele said quickly, 'we may be able to contact *Dinosaur* and get some idea of the demands Provoni will be making, and to what extent his alien cohorts can and will—'

'I'll talk to you later,' Gram said, opening the door. He paused, then, and said, half to himself, 'Tear up your resignations, Generals. I was momentarily upset; it's nothing.' But you, Fred Rayner, he thought. I will get you, you double-domed monstrosity. I will see you snuffed for what you thought of me.

At third level, Willis Gram, in bathrobe, pajamas and slippers, sauntered up to the desk of his clearance A receptionist – a rating which permitted her to know about and deal with his most personal problems and activities. At one time Margaret Plow had been his mistress . . . she had then been eighteen. And look at her now, he said to himself. In her forties. The energy, the fire, was gone; all that remained was a brisk, efficient mask.

The walls of her cubicle had been made opaque. No one could observe their conversation. Only, he thought, a passing telepath might pick up something. But they had learned to live with that.

'Did you get the four MPs?' he asked Miss Plow.

'They have her in the next room. She bit one of them.'

'What did he do in return?'

'He slapped her halfway across the room, and that seemed to bring her out of it. She was – well, actually, not metaphorically a wild animal. As if she thought she was going to be snuffed.'

'I'll go talk with her,' he said, and passed on through the cubicle into the next room.

There she stood, her eyes screaming hatred and fear, like a trapped raptor – hawk eyes, he thought, which you better never look into. I learned that early, he reflected; don't look into the eyes of a hawk or an eagle. Because you won't be able to forget the hate that you saw ... and the passionate, insatiable need to be free, the need to fly. And oh, those great heights. Those dreadful drops on the prey; panic-stricken rabbit: that's the rest of us. Funny image: an eagle held prisoner by four rabbits.

The MPs, however, were not rabbits. He made out the kind of grip they had on her – where they held her and how tightly. She couldn't move. And they would outlast her.

'I could have you tranquilized again,' he said to her, in a conciliatory tone. 'But I know how you hate it.'

'You white bastard,' she said.

' "White"?' He did not understand. 'But there's no more white and yellow and black. Why do you say white?'

'Because you're the king of the tracks.'

One of the MPs said brusquely, ' "White" is still an insult in certain low-income strata.'

'Oh,' he said, nodding. He was picking up thoughts from her mind, now, and what he found amazed him. On the surface she was straining, taut, stationary only because four MPs held her. But inside—

A frightened, small girl, fighting in the manner of a child terrified of, say, going to the dentist. An irrational, abreactive return to prerational mentational processes. *She does not see us as human*, he realized. She distinguishes us as vague shapes, dragging her one way, then, almost at once, another, then doing this: forcing her – four big professional men forcing her – to stand in one spot, for God knows how long

138

and what for. Her mentational processes were, he estimated, on about the three-year-old level. But perhaps he could get somewhere talking with her. Perhaps he could drain off some of her fear, allowing her thoughts to resume a more mature quality.

'My name is Willis Gram,' he said to her. 'And do you know what I've just done?' He smiled at her, raised his hand, pointed at her, augmented his smile. 'I'll bet you can't guess.'

She shook her head. Briefly. Once.

'I've opened up all those relocation camps on the moon and in Utah, and all the people inside will come out.'

Her eyes huge and luminous, she continued to stare. But, in her thoughts, the data registered; it sent bewildering flows of psychic energy traveling throughout her cerebral cortex as she tried to understand.

'And we're not going to arrest anyone anymore,' he said. 'And so you're free.' At this, a wave of oceanic relief flooded through her mind; her eyes dimmed and then one tear spilled out, sliding down her cheek.

'Can—' She swallowed with difficulty and her voice shook. 'Can I see Mr. Appleton?'

'You can see anyone you want. Nick Appleton is free, too; we kicked him out of here two hours ago. He probably went home. He has a wife and child whom he's very fond of. He's undoubtedly gone back to them.'

'Yes,' she said distantly. 'I met them. The woman is a bitch.'

'But his thoughts about her – I spent quite a bit of time with him today. Fundamentally, he loves her; he just wants to have a bit of wild oat sowing . . . you realize I'm a telepath; I know things about other people that a non—'

'But you can lie,' Charlotte said, between clenched teeth.

'I'm not lying,' he said, although, as he well knew, he was.

Charlotte said, now suddenly calm, 'Am I really free to go?'

'There is one matter.' Gram felt his way carefully, his mind tuned to her thoughts, trying to pick them up before they turned into speech or action. 'You realize that we gave you a medical examination after PSS occifers brought you out of the ruins of the 16th Avenue printing plant . . . do you remember that?'

'A – medical exam?' She looked at him uncertainly. 'No, I don't remember. All I remember is being dragged by my arms through the building, with my head hitting the floor, outdoors, and then—'

'Hence the physical exam,' Gram said. 'We did this with everyone we captured at 16th Avenue. We also made cursory psychological exams. You registered rather badly; you were completely traumatized and in nearly a catatonic stupor.'

'So?' She eyed him mercilessly. The hawk-stare, it had never left her eyes.

'You need bed rest.'

'And I'm going to get it here?'

'This building,' Gram said, 'contains probably the finest psychiatric facilities in the world. After a few days of rest and therapy—'

The hawk eyes flamed up; thoughts shot through her mind, emanations from the thalamus which he could not follow, and then, all at once, in the twinkling of an eye, at the sound of the last trumpet, she contorted herself, limp, then, stiff, then spinning. Spinning! All four MPs had lost their holds on her; they reached out, and one of them brought forth a plastic club weighted with shot.

She backed lightning-fast, hunched over, squirming, opened the door behind her, ran down the hall. A PSS occifer, coming toward her, saw Willis Gram and the four MPs; sizing up the situation, he made a grab for her as she shot past him. He managed to get a grip on her right wrist . . . as he pulled her round she kicked him in the testicles. And he let go. She plunged on, toward the wide entrance doors of the building. No one else tried to stop her – not after they had seen the PSS occifer crumple to the floor in acute pain.

One of the four MPs brought out a 2.56 Richardson laser pistol, raised it, barrel ceiling-pointed. 'Shall I snuff her, sir?' he asked Willis Gram. 'I can get off one good shot if you tell me immediately.'

'I can't decide,' Gram said.

'Then I won't, sir.'

'Okay. Don't.' Willis Gram moved back into the office, slowly seated himself on the bed; he hunched forward, staring sightlessly at the patterns of the flooring.

'She's flurped, sir,' one of the MPs said to him. 'I mean, she's witless. Completely snurled.'

Gram said hoarsely, 'I'll tell you what she is – she's a gutter rat.' He had picked that phrase out of Nick Appleton's mind. 'A real one.' I can sure pick 'em, he thought. And so can he.

He told me, Gram thought, that he would see her again. And he will; she'll locate him somehow. He'll never go back to his wife.

Rising, he heavily made his way over to Margaret Plow's desk in the inner work cubicle. 'May I use your fone?' he asked.

'You can use my fone; in fact you can use my—'

'Just the fone,' he said. He dialed Director Barnes' private priority line; it would link up with Barnes wherever he was: in the bathroom taking a squat, on the freeway, even at his desk.

'Yes, Council Chairman.'

'I want one of your – special troops. Maybe two.'

'Who?' Barnes said stolidly. 'I mean, who do you want them to snuff?'

'Citizen 3XX24J.'

'You're serious? This isn't a whim, a mood? You really mean it? Remember, Council Chairman, you just now released him on the basis of him receiving complete amnesty along with everybody else.'

Gram said, 'He took Charlotte away from me.'

'Oh, I see,' Barnes said. 'She's gone.'

'Four MPs couldn't hold her; she becomes a maniac when she's trapped. I caught something in her mind about an elevator once, in her childhood, which wouldn't open; she was all alone. I think she was about eight. So she's got some variation of claustrophobia. Anyhow, she can't be restrained.'

'That's hardly 3XX24J's fault,' Barnes said.

'But,' Gram said, 'it's to him she's going.'

'Should it be done quietly? And made to look like an

141

accident? Or do you simply want the special troopers to merely walk in and do it and then walk out again, despite who sees them?'

'The latter,' Gram said. 'Like a ritualistic execution. And the freedom he's enjoying now' – and, he thought, his moment of joy when he finds Charlotte again – 'that's going to have to serve as the last meal they give condemned prisoners.'

'That isn't done any more, Council Chairman.'

'I think I will add one stipulation for your troopers,' Gram said. 'I want him snuffed while *she is there*. I want her to see it happen.'

'All right, all right,' Barnes said, nettled. 'Anything else? What's the latest about Provoni? One of the TV stations said that a picket ship detected the *Gray Dinosaur*. True?'

'We'll deal with it when we come to it,' Gram said.

'Council Chairman, that statement makes no sense.'

'Okay, we'll deal with that when we come to that.'

Barnes said, 'I'll let you know when my people have completed the exercise. With your permission, I'll send three men, one to have a tranquilizing gun ready for use on her, if, as you say, she becomes maniacal at times.'

'If she fights you,' Gram said, 'don't hurt her. His snuffdom will be enough. Goodbye.' He hung up.

Margaret Plow said, 'I thought you shot them afterward.'

'Girls, yes. Their men-friends, before.'

'How candid you are today, Council Chairman. There must be a terrible strain on you, the business with Provoni. That third message; he said six days. Just six days! And you're opening the camps and granting the general amnesty. It's too bad Cordon isn't alive to see this day; too bad his kidney ailment or liver ailment or whatever it was caused him to succumb just hours before—' She stopped abruptly.

' "Just hours before victory was in sight," ' he finished for her, reading the rest direct, like an iron oxide tape, from her basically empty mind. 'Well, he was a bit of a mystic. Maybe he knew.' Yes, maybe he did, Gram thought. He was an odd person. Maybe he'll rise from the dead. Oh, well, hell – we'll simply say he never died; it was a cover story. We wanted Provoni to think—

Good God, he thought. What am I thinking? Nobody's risen from the dead in 2100 years; they're not going to start to now.

After Appleton's death, he asked himself, do I want to make a one final try for Charlotte Boyer? If I could get my government psychiatrists working on her, they could iron out that feral streak, make her passive – as a woman should be. And yet – he liked her fire. Maybe that's the very thing about her that makes me find her attractive, he thought, that gutter rat streak, as Appleton put it. And maybe that's what hooked Appleton. Many men like violent women; I wonder why? Not merely strong women, or stubborn or opinionated, but simply *wild*.

I have to think about Provoni, he told himself. Instead of this.

Twenty-four hours later, a fourth message came from the *Gray Dinosaur*, monitored by the huge radio telescope on Mars.

We are aware that you have opened the camps and granted a general amnesty. That is not enough.

Certainly terse, Willis Gram thought, as he studied the message in written form. 'And we haven't been able to transmit back to them?' he asked General Hefele, who had brought him the news.

'I think we're reaching him, but he's not listening, either due to faulty circuitry in his receiving apparatus or due to his unwillingness to negotiate with us.'

'When he is approximately one hundred astronomical units out,' Gram asked, 'can't you get him with a cluster-missile? One of those that is tropic to—' He gestured.

'To life,' General Hefele said. 'We have sixty-four types of missiles we can try; I've already had their carrier-ships deploy them in the general area in which we expect to encounter the ship.'

'You don't know of any "general area in which we expect to encounter the ship". He could have come out of hyper-space anywhere.'

'Then let's say we have all our hardware available for use, once the *Dinosaur* is spotted. Maybe he's bluffing. Maybe he's come back alone. Exactly as he went, ten years ago.'

'No,' Gram said cannily. 'His ability to remain in hyperspace in that old 2198 tub. No, his ship has been rebuilt. And not by any technology we know.' A further idea struck him. 'God – he, he and the *Dinosaur*, may be *inside* the creature; it may have wrapped itself around the ship. So of course the hull didn't disintegrate. Provoni may be like some little internal parasite in the nonhumanoid entity, but one he's on good terms with. Symbiosis.' The idea struck him as plausible. Nobody, humanoid or otherwise, ever did anything for nothing; he knew that as one of life's verities, as sure as he knew his own name. 'They'll probably want our entire race, six billion Old Men and then us, to fuse with him in some kind of poly-encephalic jello. Think of that; how would you like that?'

'Everyone of us, Old Men included, would fight that,' General Hefele said quietly.

'It doesn't sound so bad to me,' Gram said. 'And I know, far better than you, what brain-fusion is like.' You know what we telepaths do every few months, he thought. We get together somewhere and weave our minds into a vast composite mind, a single mentational organism that thinks with the power of five hundred, six hundred men and women. And it is our joy-time, for all of us. Even for me.

Only this way, Provoni's way, *everyone* could be woven into the web.

But that might not be Provoni's idea at all. And yet – he had caught something in the four messages, the use of the word 'we'. A kind of concurrence between him and *it* seemed indicated. And in harmony, Gram thought. The messages, though terse, are frosty . . . as the kids say.

And the one he's bringing is the vanguard for thousands, he said morbidly to himself. *Badger*'s crew, the first casualties. There ought to be an alloy plaque set up somewhere, honoring them. They weren't afraid to take Provoni on; they dogged the *Dinosaur* and died in the attempt. Maybe with men with that courage we might fight and win after all.

144

And an inter-stellar war is hard to maintain – he had read that somewhere. Thinking this, he felt a trifle better.

Nicholas Appleton, after hours of fighting his way through crowds, managed to locate Denny Strong's apartment building. He entered the elevator, ascended to the fiftieth floor.

He rapped on the door. Silence. And then her voice, Charley's voice, came, 'Who the fuck is it?'

'It's me,' he said. 'I knew you would come here.' If Willis Gram wanted us not to see each other, he thought, he shouldn't have let both of us go.

The door opened. There stood Charley in a striped red-and-black shirt, hoop trousers, living sandals . . . and she had on a good layer of makeup, including enormous lashes. Even though he knew they were fake, the eyelashes got through to him. 'Yes?' she asked.

Part Three

TWENTY

Denny Strong appeared beside Charlotte Boyer. 'Hi, Appleton,' he said in a toneless voice.

'Hi,' Nick said warily; he remembered vividly how Denny – and Charlotte – had run amuck. And this time there existed no Earl Zeta to help him get out of there, when people began bouncing off the walls.

But Denny seemed calm. Wasn't that true of alcohol binges? A sine wave oscillation between murderous drunkenness and ordinary daytime civility ... and Denny was at the bottom of the sine wave, right now.

'How did you know I would come here?' Charley asked. 'How did you know I'd go back to Denny and we'd make up?'

'I had no other place to look,' he said, somberly. Of course she went back to Denny, he thought. All this, my trying to help her – wasted. And she probably knew it all along. I was a chess piece, used by Charley to punish Denny. Well, he thought, if the struggle is over, if she's back here – I see no use for myself, he thought. And said, 'I'm glad things are going so well for you, now.'

'Hey,' Denny said, 'you heard about the amnesty? And them opening the camps? Wheehee!' His slightly bloated face swelled with excitement; his bulging eyes danced as he smacked Charley on the rump. 'And Provoni's almost—'

'Don't you want to come inside?' Charley said to Nick, putting her arm round Denny's waist.

'No, I don't think so,' Nick said.

'Listen, man,' Denny said, squatting down on his haunches, doing, evidently, some sort of body-building exercises, 'I don't get like I was very often. It takes a lot to make me mad. And finding out this place wasn't clean ... that did it.' He retreated into the room, seated himself on the sofa. 'Sit down.' In a lower voice he said, 'I've got a can of Hamm's beer; we'll split it three ways.'

Alcohol, Nick thought. I'll drink with them, and then the insanity will come out in all three of us.

On the other hand, there existed but a single can. How drunk could they get on a third of a can of beer apiece?

'I'll come in for a minute,' he said, but what genuinely motivated him was not the presence of the beer but the presence of Charley. He yearned to gaze at her as long as possible. It was bitter-tasting, her going back to Denny; she had, in effect, rejected him, Nicholas Appleton, by doing so. The emotion affecting Nick was one he had rarely experienced: jealousy. Jealousy – and anger at her for betraying him as she had done; after all, he had given up his wife and child, repudiated them, by walking out of his apartment with Charley. They had been going to stay together . . . at the 16th Avenue plant, it had turned out. And now, because the plant had been bombed and raided, she had gone back, like a sick cat, to what she knew and understood, awful though it might be.

Studying her face, he saw a difference, now. Her face was stark, as if the makeup had been applied over a surface of metal or glass, anyhow something inorganic. That was it: Charlotte though apparently friendly and smiling, now seemed as brittle and hard as glass, and this was why she used so much makeup – to hide that quality, that lack of humanness.

Denny, slapping his crotch with glee, burbled, 'Hey, we can have six hundred tracts around the apartment now, and no trouble; I mean, no worry about a burst. And did you see the campers?'

He had seen them, all right, clogging the footlanes. Thin, cadaverous, looking horrifyingly identical in their government-issue olive drab denims . . . and he had seen the Red Cross soup kitchens set up to feed them. They were everywhere, wandering like ghosts, seemingly completely unable to relate to their new environment. Well, they had no money, no jobs, no places to live; anyhow they were out. And, as

148

Denny said, the general amnesty cleared everyone.

'But they never caught me,' Denny said, his face growing pale with aggressive pride. 'They caught you two, though. Shacking up at the 16th Avenue plant.' He clasped his hands before himself, rocked back and forth. To Charley he said, 'Even though you did your goddam best to get us bursted.' Reaching toward the coffee table he took the beer can, felt it, nodded. 'Cold enough still. Okay, here we go into dreamland.' He tore the metal strip from the top of the beer can. 'You first, Appleton, as our guest.'

'I'll have a little,' Nick said; he took only a small sip.

'Guess what happened to Charley,' Denny said as he took a deep swallow. 'You probably think she's been here a day or so, from the time she got out of the 16th Avenue plant. But that's not true. She just got here an hour ago; she's been hiding and running.'

'Willis Gram,' Nick said hoarsely. Once more the sick fear ruled him, made him tense up and feel terribly cold.

'Because,' Denny said lazily, teasingly, 'he has these beds in rows in what he calls the "building infirmary". But in fact—'

'Stop it,' Charley said gratingly, between clenched jaws.

'Gram offered her a little "bed rest". Did you know Gram is that type of man, Appleton?'

'Yes,' Nick said tightly.

'But I got away,' Charley said; she giggled, mischievously. 'They had four army MPs and I got away.' To Denny, she said, 'You know how I am when I'm mad, really mad. You saw me, Nick, when we first met; you saw Denny and I fighting; right? Aren't I awful?'

'So Gram didn't get you,' Nick said. And I am seeing you again, he reflected. But – not really. I am seeing you made up for Denny, back to your disguises and falsifying forms. Legality has come to your work, but habits remain. You want to be elegant – at least, elegant as you conceive it – and you want to go riding in the Purple Sea Cow again, at high speeds, speeds great enough that were you to hit anything, the body-shell of the squib would disintegrate. But before that happens it's still plenty of fun. And you two can walk into prastical parlor or a scenera smokery or a drugbar and everyone's reaction will be, 'What a beautiful girl.' And, beside you, Denny can leer a leer which says, 'Hey, guys, look what I get to lay.' And their envy will be enormous. So to speak.

Rising to his feet, he said, 'I guess I'll go.' To Charley he said, 'I'm glad you got away from Gram. I knew he wanted you and I assumed he'd get you. That makes me feel a lot better.'

'He still may,' Denny said, grinning and sipping beer.

'Then get out of this apartment,' Nick said. 'If I can find her, they can find her.'

'But they don't know her address,' Denny said, propping his feet up on the table; he wore genuine leather shoes ... which had probably cost him plenty. But which gained him entry to the most notorious scenera smokeries on the planet, including those in Vienna.

That was it. They both looked dressed and groomed for a tour of drugbars and smokeries. Alc was not their only thing – it was merely one more of their illegal things. Smokery-hopping was legal, and so, by assuming certain trappings, certain makeup, they could circulate with the elite of a world in which even New Men and Unusuals participated. *Everyone*, government workers included, liked the new derivation of opium, called scenera after its discoverer, Wade Scenera, a New Man. It had, like miniature plastic statuettes of God, become a planet-wide craze.

'You see, Appleton,' Denny said, handing the virtually empty can of beer to Charley, 'she carries completely false ID cards, all the official ones' – he gestured – 'you know, the ones you have to have, not like, say, a Union Oil credit card. And they're faked so good that they'll fit into those little slots in those little electronic boxes the pissers carry. Right, you little bitch?' He affectionately reached to put his arm around her.

'I'm a bitch all right,' Charley said. 'And that's what got me away from the Federal Building.'

'They'll find her here,' Nick said patiently.

Arrogantly, and at the same time exasperated, Denny

said, 'Look, I explained it to you. When they picked up you and her at the printing plant they—'

'Who is this apartment in the name of?' Nick asked him.

Frowning, Denny said, 'Me.' He brightened. 'They don't know – as far as they're concerned, I don't exist. Listen, Appleton, you have to have more guts; you're a crybaby, a crasher. Boy, if I was in the sky, I'd sure hate to have you around.' He laughed, but this time it was an insulting laugh, one of denigration.

'You're sure her name has never come up officially in connection with this apartment?' Nick asked.

'Well, she's paid the rent a couple of times by check. But I fail to see how that—'

'If she signed a check,' Nick said, 'for this apartment, her name would be fed automatically into the New Jersey computer. And not just her name – it would receive and store the information as to where her name had come from. And she has a file with the PSS, like the rest of us. They'll ask the New Jersey computer to spill out everything it has on you – they'll match it up to the police file . . . for instance, were you two ever in the Purple Cow when you got cited?'

'Yeah,' Denny grunted. 'Speeding.'

'They took her name, too, as a witness.'

Denny, his arms folded, slowly slumping back against the sofa and down into it, said, 'Yes.'

Nick said, 'That's all they need. They've got the connection with you, then with this apartment, then God knows what the PSS folder on her may show.'

A look of consternation flew across Denny's face, a shadow, moving from right to left. His eyes shone with suspicion and agitation; he looked, now, as he had looked the time before. The mixture of fear and hate toward the authorities, the father symbols. Denny was thinking rapidly; the expression on his face changed, now, second by second. 'But what could they get *me* on?' he said hoarsely. 'God.' He rubbed his head. 'I'm grassed by this alc; I can't think. Could I talk my way out of it? Goddam it – I have to take something.' He disappeared into the bathroom, rummaged in the medicine cabinet. 'Methamphetamine hydrochloride,' he said, getting a bottle down. 'That'll clear my brain. My brain has got to be clear if I'm going to get out of this.'

'So you've lost the grassy from the alc,' Charley said tauntingly, 'by gulleting the mess.'

'Don't lecture me!' Denny said, coming back into the living room. 'I can't stand it; I'll go crazy.' To Nick, he said, 'Take her away from here. Charlotte, you stay with Nick; don't try to come back here to the apartment. Nick, you got any pops on you? Enough to rent a motel room for a couple of days?'

'I guess so,' Nick said, and felt delight swim through him – he had twisted Denny up enough to ace himself out.

'Then find a motel. And don't fone me – the line's probably tapped. They're probably ready to close in right now.'

'Paranoid,' Charley said coldly. She then glanced at Nick and—

And two blackers, black uniformed police, 'black pissers' as they were called, entered the apartment without touching the knob or using a key – the door simply swung open for them.

The black pisser on the left held something out to Nick. 'Is this a photograph of you, sir?'

'Yes,' Nick said, staring at the photograph. How had they gotten it? The picture – one print – lay in a bottom drawer of his dressing cabinet at home.

'You're not getting me,' Charley said. 'You're not getting me.' She strode toward them, and, raising her voice, she yelled, 'Get out of here.'

The black pisser reached for his regulation issue heavy-duty laser gun. So did the other.

Denny sprang onto the pisser doing the backup; together they rolled, like cats in a fight, on the floor: a buzzsaw of motion.

Charley kicked the first pisser in the groin, then, raising her arm up and back, caught his windpipe with the sharp bone of her elbow, moving at high speed so that to Nick it was only a blur of motion . . . and then the pisser lay on the floor, struggling to breathe, whooping loudly and vainly in a struggle for air.

'There'll be one more,' Denny said, rising successfully from his catfight. 'Downstairs, probably, or up on the roof field. Let's take a chance on the field; if we can get in the Sea Cow we can outrun one of their ships. Did you know that, Appleton? I can outrun a police cruiser; I can get her up to 120 m.p.h.' He started toward the door. Nick followed, numbly.

'They weren't after you,' Denny said to Charley as they rose via the elevator. 'They were after Mr. Clean, here.'

'Oh,' she said, with an oops expression. 'Well, Jesus – so we saved him instead of me. Isn't he important.'

Denny said to Nick, 'I wouldn't have fought them if I knew it was you they wanted. I don't even know you. But I saw that one going for his gun and I recognized him as a special forces commando. So I knew they were here for a snuff.' He smiled, a liquid, luminous smile from his big sensual blue eyes. 'You know what I've got?' He reached into his back pocket and brought out a tiny pistol. 'A self-defense weapon. Made by Colt. Shoots a .22 short, but with damn high muzzle velocity. I didn't have time to use it; I wasn't prepared. But I am now.' He held the gun at his side until they reached the roof field.

'Don't go out,' Nick said to Charley.

'I'll go out alone first,' Denny said. 'Because I have the gun.' He pointed. 'There she is, the Cow. Christ, if they've pulled out the ignition wires . . . that car had goddam well better start or I'll go back downstairs and kill both those pissers.'

He stepped from the elevator.

A black pisser leaned from behind the parked vehicle, pointed his laser tube at Denny, and said, 'Stop right there.'

'Hey, occifer,' Denny said congenially, showing bare hands. The gun was in his sleeve, now. 'What's up? I'm going for a spin, that's all. You still trying to nail Cordonites? Don't you know—'

The black pisser shot him with his laser tube.

Charley touched the *one* button on the elevator control panel; the doors lumbered shut. She then pressed *emergency express*. The elevator dropped deadfall.

153

TWENTY-ONE

Exactly forty-four hours later, Kleo Appleton turned on her TV set. *Marge At Large*, her favorite mid-afternoon program. Something cranked out by clever New Men to lull Old Men into thinking their plight was not so bad ... but, when the screen lit, there was nothing on it. Only a smear of herringbone patterns, and, from the four speakers, only the rush of static.

She tried another channel. The same.

She tried *all* sixty-two channels. All off the air.

Provoni must be almost here, she realized.

The apartment door opened and Nick strode in, going directly to the closet.

'Your lovely clothes,' Kleo said. 'Yes, don't forget to take them. And there's still your personal things in the bathroom; I can box them for you, if you want to wait a minute.' She did not feel anger, only a vague anxiety. Caused by the disruption of their marriage, his fling with the Boyer child.

'That's very nice of you,' Nick said solemnly.

'You can always come back,' Kleo said. 'You have a key – use it any time, day or night. As long as I live I'll have a bed for you to sleep in – not my own, but a bed of your own. So you can feel more distant from me. Distance from me is what you want, really, isn't it? That Charlotte Boyer – or is it Boyd? – girl is only an excuse. Your main relationship is still with me, even though momentarily it's negative. But you'll find she can't give you anything. All she is is a wall of makeup. Like a robot or something, painted to look like a human.'

'Android,' he said. 'No, she's not that. She's the tail of a fox and a field of wheat. And the light of the sun.'

'Leave some of your shoes here,' she said, trying not to make her sound a pleading one, but ... she was pleading.

154

'You won't need ten pairs of shoes. Take two or three at the most. Okay?'

'I'm sorry,' Nick said, 'to be doing this to you. I never sowed my wild oats; I guess, as you say, I'm doing it now.'

'You realize that Bobby will be given a new test, a fair one. Do you realize that? Answer me. Do you?'

Nick stood staring at the TV screen. All at once he dropped his load of clothes and hurried to the set.

'On all channels it's the same,' Kleo said. 'Maybe the cable is out.' She added, 'Or it's Provoni.'

'Then he can't be more than fifty million miles out.'

Kleo said, 'How did you find an apartment for you and – this girl? All those people from the relocation camps ... haven't they rented every apartment in the U.S.A.?'

'We're staying with friends of hers,' he said.

'Could you give me the address?' she asked. 'Or the fone number? In case I have to reach you about something important. For instance, if Bobby is injured in some way, you'd want to—'

'Be quiet,' Nick said. He crouched down before the TV set, scrutinizing the screen. The white-noise roar of static had all at once ceased. 'That means a transmitter's on,' Nick said. 'They were off, all off; Provoni negated their signals. Now he'll try to transmit.' He turned toward his wife, his face enflamed, his eyes wide and staring like a child. Or as if he's gone flump, she thought with vague alarm.

'You don't know what this means, do you?' Nick asked.

'Well, I guess that—'

'That's why I'm leaving you. Because you don't understand anything. What does Provoni's return mean to you? The most important event in history! Because with him—'

'The Thirty Years War was the most important event in history,' Kleo said, practically. She had majored in that era of Western culture and she knew what she was talking about.

On the screen appeared a face, jutting chin, massive ridges over the eyes, and the eyes small and fierce, like holes punched through the fabric of reality, of the envelope surrounding them, holding back utter darkness. 'I am Thors

Provoni,' he said, and the reception was good; his voice came in even more accurately than the video image. 'I am living inside a sentient organism that—'

Kleo burst into laughter.

'Shut up!' Nick snarled.

' "Hello world," ' Kleo mimicked. ' "I am alive and living inside a giant worm." Oh, God, it strikes me up; it really—'

He slapped her, throwing her backward with the force of his blow. And then returned to the TV screen.

'—in approximately thirty-two hours,' Provoni was saying, in a hoarse, measured voice . . . he looked exhausted in a way that Nick had never seen in a human before. He spoke with massive efforts, as if each word spoken cost him a little more of his remaining vital energy. '—our missile screen has repelled over seventy types of missiles. But the body of my friend surrounds the ship, and he—' Provoni took a deep, shuddering breath. 'He handles them.'

To Kleo, who had sat up, rubbing her cheek dazedly, Nick said. 'Thirty-two hours. Is that the time he lands? Is he that close? Did you hear?' His voice rose almost to hysteria.

Tears filled her eyes; she turned away without answering and disappeared into the bathroom. To lock herself in until she was finished crying.

Cursing he ran after her; he pounded on the locked bathroom door. 'God damn it, our lives depend on what Provoni does. And you won't listen!'

'You hit me.'

'Christ,' he said, futilely. And hurried back to the TV set. But the visual image was gone and the white-noise roar of static had resumed, too. And now, by degrees, the regular transmission of the network was fading back in.

The screen showed Sir Herbert London, the major news analyst for NBC. 'We have been off the air,' London said, in his calming, half-ironic, half-boyish way, 'about two hours. So have all other video transmitters in the world; that is to say, we have been without any form of visual transmissions, even on closed, private circuits, such as the police use. Just now you heard Thors Provoni – or someone claiming to be him – inform the world that in thirty-two hours his ship, the

156

Gray Dinosaur, will land in the middle of Times Square.' Turning to his news partner, Dave Christian, he said, 'Didn't Thors Provoni, if that's who he is, look terribly, terribly tired. As I listened to him speak and watched his face – the video signal was not as strong as the audio, but that would be natural – I got the distinct impression that here's a man who has worn himself out, who has been defeated and knows it. I can't see how he's going to be able to do much of anything politicalwise for a while, not for a long, long period of rest.'

'You're right, Herb,' Dave Christian said, 'but it may be the alien with him who will conduct business . . . if that's the right term. Anyhow, do what they're here to do.'

'Thors Provoni,' Sir Herbert said, 'in case you don't know or have just forgotten, set out ten years ago in a commercial craft modified with a supra-C engine . . . he modified it himself, so we really don't know what velocities he's capable of. Anyhow, here he is, back, and apparently with the alien or aliens he vowed to bring, his "help" for the billions of Old Men, whom, he thinks, are being treated unfairly.'

'Yes, Herb,' Dave said, 'his feeling was quite intense; he maintained the idea that the Civil Service tests were rigged . . . although a blue ribbon inquiry failed to run anything up concrete. So I think we can say they, of course, are not. But what we do not know – and this is perhaps the most vital question – is whether Provoni will try to negotiate with the Extraordinary Committee for Public Safety and Council Chairman Gram – in other words, will they sit down, assuming (chuckle) this alien can sit, and *talk* about it. Or are we simply going to be attacked thirty-two hours from now. Provoni has let us in on the fact that our government has sent a fairly large number of missiles into space, in his direction, but—'

'Herb,' Dave interrupted, 'if I may. Provoni's claim that he and his alien ally destroyed a large and varied number of interplan missiles may be untrue. The government may deny it. Provoni's "success" at destroying the alleged missile-strikes may be merely propaganda, trying to implant in our minds the idea that they have technological powers greater than our own.'

157

'His ability to block video transmission throughout Earth,' Herb said, 'shows a certain amount of power; it must have been a terrific drain, and this might be part of the reason for Provoni's obvious, blatant fatigue.' The newscaster shuffled with papers. 'Meanwhile, all over the Earth, gatherings are planned for the moment Provoni – and friends – land. There had been plans for gatherings in each city, but now that Provoni has said he will land in Times Square, it will be there that we can expect to find the greatest mob ... some there out of Under Man convictions and faith in Provoni, or mere curiosity. Probably, in most cases, the latter.'

Nick said, 'Notice the little twists they give the news. "Mere curiosity." Doesn't the government realize that, just by returning, he has already created a revolution? The camps are empty; the tests are no longer rigged—' He broke off as a thought came to him. 'Maybe Gram will capitulate,' he said slowly. That was one thing he had not – nor had anyone else he knew – thought of. Immediate, total capitulation. The reins of government turned over to Provoni and the aliens.

But that wasn't Willis Gram's way. He was a fighter who had made his way to the top, literally, over a pile of bodies. Willis Gram is planning what to do right now, he realized. The total military capability will be compressed to take aim on this one ship, a ten-year-old junk heap ... or maybe it wasn't anymore. Maybe it shone like a god at day. A god visible in the shimmering sun.

'I'm going to stay locked in the bathroom until you're gone,' Kleo said sniffily from behind the locked door.

'Okay,' he said. Lugging his armload of clothes, he headed for the elevator.

'I am Amos Ild,' the tall man with his huge white hairless head, his hydrocephalic-like head, supported by thin tubes of very strong plastic, said.

They shook hands. Ild's paw was damp and cold, like his eyes, Gram thought. And then he thought, He never blinks. My God, he's had his eyelids removed. He probably takes pills and works around the clock, twenty-four hours a day.

158

No wonder Great Ear was progressing so well.

'Sit down, Mr. Ild,' Council Chairman Gram said. 'It is very nice of you to come here, considering the immense value of your work.'

'The officials who brought me here,' Amos Ild said in a high-pitched squeaky voice, 'tell me that Thors Provoni has returned and will land within less than forty-eight hours. Surely this is a far more important matter than Great Ear. Tell me – or give me the documents – that contain all that's known about the aliens Provoni has reached.'

Gram said, 'Then you believe it is Provoni? And he really has an alien or a bunch of aliens with him?'

'Statistically,' Amos Ild said, 'by the third order of neutrologics, the analysis would have to deduce itself to that summation. It *probably* is Provoni; he *probably* has one or more aliens with him. They say he blacked out all video transmissions and then transmitted both video and audio bits from his ship. What else?'

'Missiles,' Gram said, 'which reach his ship, do not detonate.'

'Even if they're not set on contact-detonation but proximity-detonation?'

'Right.'

'And he remained in hyperspace more than fifteen minutes?'

'Yes,' Gram said.

'Then you should infer that he has an alien with him.'

'On the TV program he said it was "wrapped around his ship", you know – sort of sheltering it.'

'Like a mother hen sheltering her eggs,' Amos Ild said. 'We may all be that, soon. Unhatched eggs sat on by a cosmic chicken.'

Gram said, 'Everyone said I should get your opinion as to what to do.'

'To destroy it; concentrate all your—'

'We can't destroy it. What I want from you is the answer as to how we should react when Provoni lands and emerges from it. Should we make one last try, with him *outside* the ship? Where the alien can't help him? Or if we got him upstairs here, to my office, got him alone . . . it couldn't follow.'

'Why not?'

'If it wrapped up his ship, it must weigh tons. The elevator couldn't take it.'

'Couldn't it be a thin sort of shroud? Like a veil?' Ild leaned toward him. 'Have you calculated the weight, the mass, of his ship?'

'Sure. Here.' Gram riffled through a bunch of reports, found one, handed it to Ild.

'One-eight-three million tons,' Ild read. 'No, it's not a "thin sort of shroud." It has enormous mass. I understand it's landing in Times Square. You'll have to have riot squads clear the area in advance; that's obvious and mandatory.'

'So what if he doesn't have room to land on, except on the heads of his supporters?' Gram asked irritably. 'They know he's coming; they know he's going to plop down, retro-rocketwise. If they're too damn dumb to—'

Amos Ild said, 'If you are going to consult with me, you must do precisely what I tell you. You will consult no other advisors, form no other opinions. In effect, I will become and act as the government until the crisis is over, but, of course, every decree will carry your signature. I particularly do not want you consulting Police Director Barnes. And secondly, you should not consult the Extraordinary Committee for Public Safety. I will stay with you twenty-four hours a day until this is over; I see you notice my missing eyelids. Yes, I take zaramide sulphate. I never sleep – I can't afford to. There's too much to be done. You will also stop consulting with whatever odd individual happens along, as you customarily do. I am the only one who will advise you, and if this is not satisfactory, I will return to Great Ear.'

'Jesus,' Gram said, aloud. He tuned himself into the brain of Amos Ild, searching for additional data. The interior thoughts were identical to the expression in words; clearly, Ild's mind did not work like other people's, who said one thing and thought another.

And then an idea came to him from his *own* mind, something Ild had missed. Ild would be his *advisor*. But Ild had not stipulated *that he had to take the advice*; he was under no obligation to do more than merely hear it.

'I have taped what you just now said,' he told Ild. 'What we both said. Oral swearing is legal swearing, as ruled in Cobb versus Blaine. I swear to do as you say. And you swear to give me your undivided attention; during this crisis you have no employer but me. Agreed?'

'Agreed,' Ild said. 'Now give me all the information you have dealing with Provoni. Biographical material, papers he did in graduate school, news reports; I want all news dispatched to me here in this building the moment it's picked up by the media. They will pipe it to me and I will decide whether it should be publicly broadcast or otherwise released.'

'But you can't stop it from being released,' Gram said. 'Because he takes over the channels; he—'

'I know that. I mean all news additional to the direct speeches made by Provoni over TV.' Ild pondered. 'Please have your technicians rerun Provoni's telecast. I want to see it myself, immediately.'

Presently, on the far screen of the room, light appeared, the roar of static . . . and then the static cut out, and, after a moment, Provoni's massive, weary face appeared on the screen.

'I am Thors Provoni,' he declared. 'I am living inside a sentient organism that has not absorbed me but is protecting me, as it will you, soon. In approximately thirty-two hours his protection will manifest itself throughout Earth and there will be no more physical warfare. So far, our missile screen has repelled over seventy types of missiles. But the body of my friend surrounds the ship, and he' – a weary pause – 'he handles them.'

'That's sure true,' Gram said aloud.

'Do not fear physical confrontation,' Provoni said. 'We will hurt no one, and no one can hurt us. I will talk to you' – he panted with fatigue; his eyes stared fixedly, rigidly – 'at a later time.' The video image shut off.

Amos Ild scratched his rather long nose and said, 'The prolonged space voyage has nearly killed him. Probably the alien is keeping him alive; without it he would die. Perhaps

161

he expects Cordon to make speeches. Do you know if he is aware that Cordon is dead?'

'He may have monitored a newscast,' Gram admitted.

'The killing of Cordon was good,' Ild said. 'Also the opening of the camps and the general amnesty – that was good too; it made the Old Men misjudge the *quid pro quo*: they thought they gained, but Cordon's death far outweighs the factor of the opening of the camps.'

'Do you think,' Gram said, 'that the alien is one of those things that lands like a spider on the back of your neck, bores a hole to the upper ganglia of your nervous system, and then controls you like you're a puppet? There was some very famous old book, back around 1950, where these creatures caused people to—'

'Was it done on an individual basis?'

' "Individual"? Oh, I see, one parasite for each host. Yes, it was one for each person.'

'Evidently what they do will be done on a bulk basis.' Ild pondered. 'Like erasing tape. The whole reel at once, without passing the tape across the erase head.' He seated himself, stabilizing his gigantic head with his hands as he did so. 'I am,' he said slowly, 'going to assume it's a bluff.'

'By that you mean there's no alien? He didn't find them, he didn't bring one back?'

'He brought something back,' Ild said. 'But so far everything we've seen could have been done on a technological basis. Repelling the missiles, blanking out the TV – gadgets that he picked up on some world in another star system. They rebuilt his hull so that he could travel in hyperspace ... maybe forever, if he wants. But I'm going to choose the choice neutrologics dictates. We have seen no alien; ergo until we see it, we must assume that probably it does not exist. Probably, I say. But I have to choose now, in order to arrange our defenses.'

Gram said, 'But Provoni said there'd be no warfare.'

'None by him. Only by us. Which there will be. Let's see – the largest laser system on the East Coast is in Baltimore. Can you have it moved to New York, set up in Times Square, before the thirty-two hours elapse?'

'I guess so,' Gram said. 'But we've used laser beams on his ship out there in space and they've done nothing.'

'Mobile laser systems, such as are found on warships,' Ild said, 'put out an insignificant beam compared with a large stationary system such as Baltimore has. Will you please use your fone and make arrangements immediately? Thirty-two hours is not long.'

It sounded like a good idea; Willis Gram picked up his line-4 fone and got a trunk call through to Baltimore, to the technicians in charge of the laser system.

Across from him, as he made the arrangements, sat Amos Ild, massaging his great head, his attention focused on everything that Gram said.

'Fine,' Ild said, when Gram hung up the fone. 'I have been calculating the probabilities of Provoni finding a scientific race superior enough to our own that they could impose their political will on us. So far, inter-stellar flights have located only *two* civilizations more advanced than our own . . . and they were not very greatly advanced: perhaps a hundred years or so. Now, notice that Provoni has returned in the *Gray Dinosaur*; that is important, because had he actually encountered such a superior race they most certainly would have come here *in one or more of their ships*. Look at him; look at his fatigue. He is virtually blind and dead. No, neutrologics says to decide that he is bluffing; he could so easily have proved he was not, merely by returning in an alien vessel. And' – Amos Ild grinned – 'there would have been a flotilla of them, to impress us. No, the same ship he left in, the way he looked on TV—' His head wobbled with intensity; on the bald scalp veins stood out, throbbing.

'Are you all right?' Gram inquired.

'Yes. I am solving problems; please be quiet for a moment.' The lidless eyes stared, and Willis Gram felt uneasy. He momentarily dipped into Ild's mind but, as was so often the case with New Men, he found thought-processes he could not follow. But this – it wasn't even a language; it took the form of what appeared to be arbitrary symbols, transmuting, shifting . . . hell, he thought, and gave up.

All at once Amos Ild spoke. 'I have reduced the proba-

163

bility to zero, through neutrologics. He does not have any alien with him, and the only threat he poses is the technological hardware which some highly evolved race has provided him.'

'You're sure?'

'According to neutrologics it is an absolute, not a relative certainty.'

'You can do that with your neutrologics?' Gram asked, impressed. 'I mean, instead of it being like 30-70 or 20-80 you express it in the terms a precog can't; all he can give is probabilities because they're a bunch of alternate futures. But you say "absolute zero". Then all we need to get is' – he saw the reason, now, for having the Baltimore laser system set up – '*just Provoni.* The man himself.'

'He'll be armed,' Amos Ild said. 'With very powerful weapons, both mounted on his ship and hand weapons besides. And he'll be within a shield of some kind, a protective area that moves with him. We will keep the Baltimore laser gun pointed on him until it penetrates his shield; he will die; the mobs of Old Men will see him die; Cordon is already dead; we are not far from the finish. In thirty-two hours it may all be over.'

'And then my appetite will come back,' Gram said.

Amos Ild said, smiling slightly, 'It looks to me as if it never went away.'

You know, Gram thought to himself, I don't trust this 'absolute zero' business; I don't trust their neutrologics – maybe because I don't understand it. But how can they maintain that an event in the future *must* happen? Every precog I've ever talked to has said that hundreds of possibilities lie at every point in time ... but they don't understand neutrologics either, not being New Men.

He picked up one of his fones. 'Miss Knight,' he said, 'I want a convocation of as many precogs as I can get within, say, the next twenty-four hours. I want them patched into a network by telepaths and, myself being a telepath, I'll contact all the precogs and see, if working in unison, they can come up with a good probability. Get on this right away

164

– it has to be done today.' He rang off.

'You've violated our arrangement,' Amos Ild said.

'I just wanted to integrate the precogs via the telepaths,' Gram said. 'And get their' – he paused – 'opinion.'

'Call your secretary back and cancel your request.'

'Do I have to?'

'No,' Amos Ild said. 'But if you go ahead, I'm going back to Great Ear and continue my work there. It's up to you.'

Gram picked up the fone again and said, 'Miss Knight, cancel that about the precogs, what I just said.' He hung up, feeling gloomy and morose. Extracting information from the minds of others was his chief *modus operandi* in life; it was hard to give up.

'If you go to them,' Ild said, 'you're back with probabilities; you'll be back with 20th century logic, a tremendous step back; well over two hundred years.'

'But if I got ten thousand precogs patched in by 'paths—'

'You would not know,' Amos Ild said, 'as much as I have already told you.'

'I'll let it go,' Gram agreed. He had elected Amos Ild as his source of information and opinion, and it was probably the right thing to do. But ten thousand precogs . . . aw hell, he thought. There really isn't enough time anyhow. Twenty-four hours – that's nothing. They'd all have to assemble in one spot, and twenty-four hours wouldn't do it, modern sub-surface transportation notwithstanding.

'You're really not going to sit here in my office,' he said to Amos Ild, 'continually, without a break, all the way through this?'

Ild said, 'I want the bio material on Provoni; I want everything I enumerated.' He sounded impatient.

With a sigh, Willis Gram pressed a switch on his desk; it opened the circuits to all the major computers throughout the world. He rarely – if ever – used this mechanism. 'Provoni comma Thors,' he said. 'All material, and then an abstract in terms of relevance. At ultimate high-speed run, if possible.' He remembered to add, 'And this takes priority over everything else.' He released the switch, turned away from the mike. 'Five minutes,' he said.

Four and one half minutes later, a stack of paper oozed from a slot in his desk. That was a rundown of all information. Then, coded in red, the summation: one or two pages.

He handed it all over to Ild without looking at it. Reading anything more about Provoni did not appeal to him; he had read, seen, heard endlessly about the man, it seemed, during the last few days.

Ild read the summation first, at great speed.

'Well?' Willis Gram asked. 'You made your zero prognosis without the material; now does having seen the material alter your neutrologics in any way?'

'The man's a showman,' Ild said. 'Like many Old Men who are intelligent, but not intelligent enough to enter the Civil Service. He's a con man.' He tossed the summary down and began to look over the great volume of material; as before, he read at fantastic speed. Then, all at once, he scowled. Once more the great egg-like head bobbed unsteadily; Amos Ild reached up reflectively to stop its near gyrations.

'What is it?' Gram asked.

'One small datum. Small?' Ild laughed. 'Provoni refused public testing. There's no record of him ever having taken a Civil Service examination.'

'So what?' Gram asked.

'I don't know,' Ild said. 'Perhaps he knew he'd fail. Or perhaps' – he fiddled with the papers, moodily – 'or perhaps he knew he would pass. Perhaps' – he fixed his unwinkable eyes on Gram – 'perhaps he's a New Man. But we can't tell.' He held up the mass of material angrily. 'It's not here either way. The datum is simply missing; no records of *any* aptitude testing of Provoni are here – and never were here.'

'But mandatory testing,' Gram said.

'What?' Ild stared at him.

'In school. They give mandatory tests, IQ and aptitude tests to see which channel of education the students should receive. He would have taken one every four years or so, from three years of age on.'

'They're not here,' Ild said.

Gram said, 'If they're not here, Provoni or somebody working in the school-system for him, *got them out.*'

'I see,' Amos said presently.

'You care to withdraw your "absolute zero" prediction?' Gram asked acidly.

After a pause, in a low, controlled voice, Amos Ild said, 'Yes.'

TWENTY-TWO

Charlotte Boyer said, 'Scrup the authorities. I'm going to be at Times Square when he lands.' She inspected her wristwatch. 'Two hours from now.'

Nick said, 'You can't. The military and the PSS—'

'I heard the newscaster,' Charley said. 'Same as you. "A dense, enormous mass of Old Men, numbering perhaps in the millions, has converged on Times Square, and—" Let's see; how did he put it? "And for their own protection they're being removed by balloon 'copters to safer places." Such as Idaho. Did you know you can't get a Chinese dinner in Boise, Idaho?' She rose, paced the room. 'Sorry,' she said to Ed Woodman, the owner of the apartment in which she and Nick were staying, 'What do you say?'

Ed Woodman said, 'Look at the TV screen. They're hustling everyone anywhere near Times Square into those goddam huge 4-D transports and flying them out of the city.'

'But more people are arriving,' his wife Elka said. 'They're falling behind; more people are coming in than are being gotten out.'

'I want to go,' Charley said.

'Watch on TV,' Ed said. He was an older man, in his early forties, heavyset, good-natured, but keenly alert. Nick had found his advice worth listening to.

On TV, the announcer was saying, 'Rumors that the largest laser gun in the eastern United States has been moved from Baltimore and set up near Times Square seem to have a basis in fact. At about ten this morning, New York time, a large object, which observers said looked like a complete

167

laser system, was landed by air on the roof of the Shafter Building, which overlooks Times Square. If – and I repeat *if* – the authorities intend to use a very powerful laser beam on Provoni or Provoni's ship, this would be the spot where the laser gun would most likely be placed.'

'They can't keep me from going there,' Charley said.

Ed Woodman, swiveling his chair to turn toward her, said, 'Yes, they certainly can. They're using tranquilizing gas; they're knocking everyone out and then shoveling them aboard those big 4-D transports like so many sides of beef.'

'Clearly,' the TV newscaster said, 'the moment of confrontation will come when, having landed his ship, and assuming he does so, Thors Provoni exits from the ship and displays himself for what he undoubtedly expects to be an adoring public. His distress will be, shall we say, acute? To find no one there, just police and army barricades.' The newscaster smiled amiably. 'Over to you, Bob?'

'Yes,' Bob Grizwald, another of the endless gnat-army of TV newscasters said, 'Provoni is in for a disappointment. No one, repeat: no one, will be allowed near his ship.'

'That laser cannon mounted on the roof of the Shafter Building may give him a welcome,' the first newscaster said; Nick had not picked up his name, but it didn't matter – they were interchangeable men, all smooth, all buttoned down, unable to lose their poise no matter what calamity occurred. The only emotion which they allowed themselves to express was an occasional wry smile. They were doing this now.

Charley said, 'I hope Provoni wipes out New York.'

'And seventy million Old Men?' Nick asked.

Ed Woodman said, 'You're too savage, Charlotte. If the aliens have come to destroy the cities, they'll destroy the Old Men rather than the New Men out there in the country on those floating sky-rafts. That would hardly coincide with Provoni's wishes. No, it's not cities they want – *it's the apparatus.* The thing that governs.'

Nick said to him, 'If you were a New Man, Ed, would you be nervous right now?'

'I'd be nervous,' Ed said, 'if that laser cannon doesn't hurt him. In fact I'd be nervous anyhow. But not nervous

168

like a New Man, no, indeed not. If I were a New Man or an Unusual, and I saw that laser beam bounce off Provoni, I'd find a ditch to hide in; I wouldn't be able to get away fast enough. They probably don't feel that way: they've ruled for so long, held power for so long, that heading for a ditch, literally and physically, wouldn't enter their minds.'

'If they gave all the news,' Elka said severely, 'they'd mention how many New Men and Unusuals have been leaving New York during the last eight or nine hours. You can see, look.' She pointed out the window. The skyscraper was blackened by a sea of dots. Airborne squibs radiating out from the downtown section of the city: their old and familiar stamping grounds.

'Turning now to other news,' the newscaster said, 'it has been officially reported that the noted New Man theoretician and builder of the Great Ear, the first electronic telepathic entity, Amos Ild, has been appointed by Council Chairman Gram to a special post. "Advisor to the Council Chairman", it is designated. Word from the enormous Federal Building in Washington—'

Ed Woodman shut the set off.

'Why did you do that?' Elka asked, slender and tall in her inflated balloon trousers and fishnet drawstring blouse, her tawny red hair tumbling down the back of her neck. In some ways, Nick had noted, she resembled Charley. They had been friends, he was informed, back into school years; back to something like the As level, which was virtually infancy.

'Amos Ild,' Woodman said. 'There is a really strange one. I've been interested in him for years; Christ, he's considered one of the three or four brightest men in the whole Sol System. *Nobody* understands his thinking, except perhaps the one or two in the same class – near the same class, I mean – with him. He's' – he gestured – 'a screwball.'

'But we can't tell,' Elka said. 'We can't follow their neutrologics.'

'But if other New Men can't understand him—'

'Einstein was the same way with his Unified Field Theory,' Nick said.

'Einstein's Unified Field Theory was understood theoretically, but it took twenty years to *prove* it.'

'Well, when Great Ear comes on, we'll know about Ild,' Elka said.

'We'll know about him before that,' Ed said. 'We'll know as we watch the government make decisions in this Provoni crisis.'

'You never were an Under Man,' Nick said to Ed.

'Afraid not. Too gutless.'

'Does it make you want to fight?' Charley asked, coming over to infuse herself into their conversation.

'Fight? Against the government? Against the PSS and the military?'

'With help on our side,' Nick said. 'The help of the nonterrestrials. Such as Provoni is bringing – or so he claims.'

'He probably is,' Ed Woodman said. 'There's no point in returning to Earth empty-handed.'

'Get your coat,' Charley said to Nick. 'We're flying to Times Square. Either that or we're through with each other.' She got her own coat, her rawhide leather jacket, marched to the apartment door, opened it, stood.

Ed Woodman said, 'Well, you can fly into the area, and a PSS or army 'copter will grapple you and drag you down. And they'll run Nick's name through their computers and come up with the fact that the black pissers have him on their snuff-list. So they'll shoot him, and you can come on back here.'

Rotating, as if on an axis, Charley reentered the apartment, hung up her coat. Her full lips protruded in a grim pout, but she yielded to the logic. After all, this was why they were hiding out here, staying with friends of hers she hadn't seen in two years.

'I don't understand,' Charley said. 'Why did they want to kill Nick? If it had been me – and we thought it was, all of us – I could understand that, because that old goat was trying to get me into one of those "infirmary" beds for convalescing girls ... but Nick – he let you go when he had you earlier. He didn't feel the need of killing you then; you just walked out of the building, as free as the air we breathe.'

'I think I know,' Elka Woodman said. 'He could stand her leaving him per se, but he knew where she was going: back to you. And he was right; you were.'

'I saw her and Denny,' Nick said. 'If Denny—' He decided not to finish the sentence. If Denny were alive, she'd be with him, not me, he thought. And that did not please him, in a sense. But anyhow the opportunity for him was there, and many a man before, in such situations, had moved to take advantage of it. It was part of the expertly waged battle of sexual possessiveness, the 'look who I get to lay' syndrome, carried to its logical conclusion: the opposition is snuffed. Poor Denny, he thought. Denny was so sure that if they once got into the Purple Sea Cow he could get away, get all three of them away. Maybe he could have. They would never know because they had decided not to be lured back by the Cow; as far as he and Charley knew, it remained on the roof field of the apartment building, where Denny had left it.

It was too dangerous to go back. They had fled on foot, lost themselves in the crowds of Old Men and releasees from the camps; New York, in the last couple of days, had become a mass of humanity which rolled, tide-like, toward Times Square, broke on the rocks which were the PSS and army barricades, and then fell back.

Or were flown off, God knew where. After all, Willis Gram had only promised to open the old camps – he hadn't promised not to build new ones.

Charley asked aggressively, 'We *are* going to watch on TV, aren't we?'

'Sure,' Ed Woodman said, leaning forward and clasping his hands together between his knees. 'Missing it is out of the question; they've got TV cameras on every roof in that region. Let's upon this occasion hope Provoni doesn't decide to grab the airways again.'

'I hope he does,' Elka said. 'I want to hear him talk.'

'He'll be on the air,' Nick said. He was positive of it. 'We'll see everything, hear everything. But not as arranged by the networks.'

'Isn't there a law against cutting into TV transmissions?' Elka said. 'I mean, didn't he break the law when he cut off all the other TV stations and telecast from his ship?'

'Oh, God,' Charley said, giggling, her hand over her eyes. 'Don't mind me, but it's too funny. Provoni returns after ten years with a monster from another star system to save us, and he's arrested for tampering with people's TV reception. That's how they can get rid of him; that makes him a wanted felon!'

It is now, Nick thought, less than an hour and a half.

And all this time, he realized, as the *Gray Dinosaur* approaches Earth, they're lobbing missiles at it. They've stopped mentioning it to the public: they know the missiles aren't doing any good. But there's a *mathematical* chance that a missile will somehow penetrate the ship's shield, no matter what kind it is, that the creature 'in which the ship is wrapped' will become tired or in some way inoperative – perhaps only for an instant, but in that instant even a small missile could probably completely knock out *Dinosaur*.

At least the government is trying, he said to himself grimly. As well they damn sure ought to be.

'Turn the TV back on,' Charley said.

Ed Woodman did so.

On the screen an old inter-stellar ship, its retrojets sputtering, was lowering itself in the dead center of Times Square. An antiquated ship, pitted, corroded, with jagged metal pieces brustling: the remains of once-functioning sensory apparatus.

'He fooled them!' Ed Woodman said. 'He's an hour and a half early! Do they have their laser cannon ready to fire? God, he's got their timing off! They bought the thirty-two hour story absolutely.'

Police 'copters and squibs hurried away like dancing gnats, avoiding the blast of the retrojets. On the ground, PSS occifers and soldiers scurried away, scrambling for cover.

'The laser beam,' Ed Woodman said in a monotone, his eyes fixed on the screen. 'Where is it?'

'You want it to show up?' Elka demanded.

'They'll get it going sooner or later,' Ed said. 'Let the test come now. Jesus, the poor bastards; they must be scurrying around the roof of the Shafter Building like ants.'

From the roof of the Shafter Building, a red beam of force bored straight at the now parked ship. Over the TV they could hear its furious whine as it wound up, higher and higher in intensity. It must be almost on full now, Nick thought. And – the ship remained intact.

Something huge and ugly materialized about the ship and he knew what it was. They were seeing the alien being. Like a snail, he thought. It rippled slightly, extended two pseudopodia, oozed more directly into the path of the laser beam . . . as the beam bored at it, it became larger and more palpable. *It's feeding on the beam,* he realized. *The longer they keep the beam on it the stronger it will become.*

The TV newscaster, for one time in his life disconcerted, blurted out, 'It seems to thrive on the laser beam.'

His companion put in, 'A creature from another star system, impossible to believe, but there it is. It must weigh thousands of tons; it's engulfed the ship—'

The hatch of the ship slid aside.

Thors Provoni, wearing a gray underwear-like garment, emerged, helmetless, weaponless.

The laser beam, redirected by the technicians operating it, moved until it focused on Provoni.

Nothing happened. Provoni remained unaffected.

Nick, peering, saw a web-like tent structure imposed over Provoni. From the alien. The laser people were out of luck.

'It wasn't a bluff,' Elka said quietly. 'He did bring back a creature with him.'

'And it has great power,' Ed said huskily. 'Do you realize the strength of that laser beam? Calculated in ergs—'

To Nick, Charley said, 'What are they going to do now? Now that the laser beam didn't work?'

In mid-sentence the newscaster was abruptly cut off. There, standing beside his ship, Thors Provoni lifted a microphone to his lips. 'Hello,' he said, and his voice issued from the TV set; Provoni did not trust the networks, obviously: once again he had taken over the many channels, but this time their audio portion only. The video image still emanated from network cameras.

Nick said, 'Hello, Provoni. It's been a long trip.'

TWENTY-THREE

'His name,' Provoni said into his microphone, 'is Morgo Rahn Wilc. I want to talk to you about him in detail. First this. He is ancient. He is telepathic. He is my friend.'

Nick walked away from the TV set, went into the bathroom and got some pills down from the cabinet; he chose a pair of phenmetrazine hydrochloride tablets, swallowed them, then added one twenty-five milligram tablet of chlordiazepoxide hydrochloride. His hands, he discovered, were shaking; he had trouble holding the glass of water and then he had trouble getting the pills down.

At the door of the bathroom Charley appeared. 'I need something. What do you recommend?'

'Phenmetrazine and chlordiazepoxide,' he said. 'Fifty milligrams of the former; twenty-five of the latter.'

'That's swellers and shrinkers together,' she said.

'But a good combination; the chlordiazepoxide intensifies the capacity of the cerebral cortex, while the phenmetrazine stimulates the thalamus, giving a general overall brain-metabolism boost.'

Nodding, she took the pills which he recommended.

Shaking his head, Ed Woodman entered the bathroom, took several pills from the rows of bottles. 'Wow,' he said. 'They just can't kill him; he just won't die. And that thing eats energy; they're just pumping it full of juice every passing second, the stupid bastards. He'll be the size of Brooklyn in another half hour; it's like pumping up an infinitely large balloon with no popping point.'

On the TV, Thors Provoni was saying, '—I never saw his world. He met me in deep space; he was on patrol and picked

174

up automatic radio signals my ship was emanating. There, in deep space, he rebuilt my ship, consulting telepathically with his brothers on Frolix 8, and was given permission to accompany me back here. He is only one of many. I think he can do what we must do. If he can't, there are a hundred more like him waiting one light year away. In ships capable of passing through by hyperspace. So, if necessary, they could be here in a very short time.'

'Now there he's bluffing,' Ed Woodman said. 'If they can travel through hyperspace, Provoni and this thing would have done so; as it is, they came through regular space, but using a supra-C drive, of course.'

'But,' Nick said, 'he used *his* ship, the *Gray Dinosaur*. Their ships might be built for hyperspace; *Dinosaur* isn't.'

'Then you believe him?' Elka asked.

'Yes,' Nick said.

'I believe him,' Ed Woodman said, 'but he is a showman. This business of appearing eight hours before expected – it threw everybody off, and was undoubtedly deliberate. And he has been standing there letting them laser him with billions of volts of power. And his "friend", Morgo something; he's got him out and visible, to impress us.' He added acidly, 'And I am impressed.'

Charley went to the living room window, opened it, leaned out and yelled, 'Hey, you all gonna eat up Nu Yohk? Don' you all do that, y'hear?' She closed the window, her face expressionless.

'That ought to throw them off,' Nick said.

'New York is my home town,' Charley said. Abruptly, she pressed her fingers against her forehead. 'I felt something. Like a – a sweep, a probe. Passing through me and leaving.'

Acutely, in an instant of instinctive insight, Nick said, 'He's looking for New Men.'

'Oh, God,' Elka moaned. 'I just felt it, just for an instant. He *is* looking for New Men. What's he going to do with them? Snuff them? Do they deserve that? They never snuffed us.'

'Denny,' Charley said. 'And me, very nearly; they almost took a shot at me in the Federal Building. And they sent assassins to snuff Nick. If you – what's the word? – extrapolate from that—'

'It's a high average,' Nick said. And Cordon, he said to himself. Shot, probably. We'll never really know – just that he's dead. Does Provoni know yet? he wondered. God help us, he may go berserk.

Over the TV audio circuit, Provoni said, 'Monitoring Earth's transmissions, we learned of Eric Cordon's death.' His massive face retracted, as if retreating into itself with pain. 'Within an hour, we will know the circumstances – the actual ones, not those transmitted over the media – and we will—' He paused. Nick thought, He's conferring with the alien. 'We will—' Again he paused. 'Time will tell,' he said at last, cryptically, his great head bent downward, his eyes shut; a convulsive shudder passed across his features, as if he were trying with difficulty, great difficulty, to regain control of himself.

'Willis Gram,' Nick said. 'That's who did it. That's where the order came from. Provoni knows that; he knows where to look. That snuffing is going to color everything that happens from now on, everything Provoni does, says; what his friend does. It dooms the ruling circles; I think Provoni is the kind of man who—'

'You don't know what effect the alien may have had on him,' Ed pointed out. 'It may moderate Provoni's bitterness and hatred.' To Elka, he said, 'When it probed your mind, did it seem – cruel? Hostile? Destructive?'

She pondered, then glanced at Charley. Charley shook her head no. 'I don't think so,' Elka said. 'It was just – so strange. And it was looking for something it didn't find in me. So it went on. It only took a fraction of a second.'

'Can you imagine that thing,' Nick said, 'probing minds by the hundreds? Maybe thousands. All at once.'

Ed said quietly, 'Maybe millions.'

'In that short time?' Nick asked.

Charley, irritably, said, 'I feel lousy. I feel like my period is coming on. I'm going to lie down.' She disappeared into the bedroom; the door shut after her.

'I'm sorry, Mr. Lincoln,' Ed Woodman said, 'I just don't

have time right now to listen to the notes you've made for your Gettysburg address.' His face was harsh and sardonic, and he had flushed a dark, furious red.

Nick said, 'She's afraid; that's why she's gone in there. It's too much for her. Isn't it too much for you, really? Aren't you taking it in intellectually, but emotionally it really isn't registering? I see the screen; I know what I'm seeing, but' – he gestured – 'only the frontal lobe of my brain comprehends what I see. And hear.' He walked to the bedroom door, opened it slightly. She lay on the bed, at an odd angle, her face turned to one side, eyes wide open. Nick shut the door after him, came over slowly, seated himself on the edge of the bed.

'I know what it's going to do,' she said.

'Do you?'

'Yes.' She nodded expressionlessly. 'It's going to replace portions of their minds and then withdraw, leaving nothing. A vacuum. They'll be living hollow shells. Like a lobotomy. Do you remember that from school, reading about the insane psychiatric practices of the 20th century? Debrained, that's what they, the doctors, made people. That thing will remove the Nodes of Roger and more – it won't stop with just making them like us. It hasn't affected Provoni; he's convinced it.'

'How do you know that?' Nick asked.

'Well, it's not a long story. Two years ago I forged a set of G-2 completed tests – showing satisfactory results. So for a time I had access to government records, and one time just for the hell of it I asked for info on Provoni, the so-called "Provoni file", and I sneaked it home, under my coat – it was mostly microfilm. And I sat up all night reading it.' She explained, 'I read very slowly.'

'And he's like that? Vengeful?'

'He's obsessed. He's what Cordon wasn't; Cordon was a rational man, a rational political figure, who happened to be living in a society where no dissent is allowed. In another society he would have been a major statesman. But Provoni—'

'Ten years may have changed him,' Nick pointed out.

'Alone most of that time ... there must have been a good deal of introspection and self-analysis during those years.'

'Couldn't you hear it today? Just now?'

'No,' he said, truthfully.

'I got fired from the job and fined p350, and that gave me a criminal record which I've added to.' She was silent for a moment. 'Denny, too. He fell a few times.' She lifted her head. 'Go back and watch the TV. Please. If you don't, I'll go in there and I really can't, so you go, okay?'

'Okay,' he said. He left the bedroom, turned his attention to the TV set.

Is she right? he asked himself. About Provoni, what sort of man he is? That's not what we've heard ... heard from the Under Man presses. If she felt that way, how could she be a Cordonite, distributing and selling his pamphlets? But they were Cordon's pamphlets, he reflected. Maybe she liked him enough to overcome her distrust of Provoni.

In the name of God, he thought, I hope she's wrong about what they intend to do to the New Men – lobotomize them, all of them, ten million! Including the Unusuals. Like Willis Gram.

Something swept into his mind, a wind like that of hell. He clapped his hands to his forehead, bent over in – pain? Not pain; more a sort of strange sense, that of peering down into a great, dark pit and then, very slowly, beginning to tumble slow-motion into it.

The feeling abruptly departed.

'I just got scanned,' he said shakily.

'How'd it feel?' Elka asked.

Nick said, 'He showed me the universe empty of stars. I never want to see it again as long as I live.'

Ed Woodman said, 'Listen. On the tenth floor of this building a low-order New Man lives ... apartment BB293-KC. I'm going down there.' He headed for the door. 'Anyone want to come? Maybe just you, Nick.'

'I'll come,' Nick said. He followed after Ed Woodman, caught up with him in the silent, carpeted hall.

'He's probing,' Ed said as they reached the elevator and pressed the button. He indicated all the apartment doors,

178

the rows and rows of them that filled this one building. *'Behind every one of those doors he's probing.* God knows what it's like for some of them; that's why I want to see this New Man ... Marshall, I think his name is. G-5, he told me once. So you can see he's small fry; that's why he's in a building filled mostly with Old Men.'

The elevator came; they entered and descended.

'Listen, Appleton,' Ed said. 'I'm afraid. I got probed, too, but I didn't say anything. He's looking for something and he didn't find it in the four of us, but elsewhere he may find it. And I want to know what he does when he finds it.' The elevator stopped; they stepped into the hall. 'This way,' Woodman said, striding rapidly along; Nick hurried to keep up with him. 'BB293KC. I'm going down there.' He headed for the door, came to it, halted; Nick caught up with him.

Ed Woodman knocked.

No answer.

He turned the knob. The door opened. Carefully, Ed Woodman pushed the door aside, stood, then moved out of Nick's way.

On the floor, crosslegged, sat a slender man with a small black board, dressed in expensive hashair robes.

'Mr. Marshall?' Ed Woodman said softly.

The slender, dark man lifted his inflated, balloon-like head; he regarded them, smiling. But he did not speak.

'What are you playing with, Mr. Marshall?' Ed Woodman asked, bending down. He turned to Nick. 'An electric mixer. He's making the blades turn.' He straightened up. 'G-5. Approximately eight times our mental abilities. Anyway, he's not suffering.'

Going over, Nick said, 'Can you talk, Mr. Marshall? Can you say anything to us? How do you feel?'

Marshall began to cry.

'You see,' Ed said, 'he has emotions, feelings, even thoughts. But he can't express them. I've seen people in hospitals after a stroke, when they can't talk, can't communicate in any way, and they cry like that. If we leave him alone he'll be all right.'

Together, Nick and Ed left the apartment; the door shut

179

after them. 'I need some more pills,' Nick said. 'Can you suggest anything helpful, really helpful, at this point?'

'Desipramine hcl,' Ed said. 'I'll give you some of mine, I noticed you don't have any.'

They made their way to the elevator and pressed the up button.

'We better not tell them,' Ed said, as they ascended.

'They'll know soon anyhow,' Nick said. 'Everyone will know it. If it's happening everywhere.'

'We're close to Times Square,' Ed said. 'He may be probing in concentric rings; Marshall got it now, but New Men in Jersey may not get it until tomorrow.' The elevator halted. 'Or the next week. It may take months, and by that time Amos Ild – it would have to be Ild – can think of something to do.'

'You want him to?' Nick asked, as they stepped from the elevator.

The light in Ed Woodman's eyes flickered. 'That's—'

'That's hard for you to decide,' Nick said, finishing Ed's halting statement.

'What about you?'

Nick said, 'I couldn't be more pleased.'

Together, they walked back to their apartment. Neither man spoke: a wall had settled into place between them. There simply was nothing to talk about. And both men knew it.

TWENTY-FOUR

'They'll have to be cared for,' Elka Woodman said. She had wormed the account of Mr. Marshall's condition out of the two of them. 'But there are billions of us; we can do it. Centers, like playareas, could be set up for them. And dorms. And meals.'

Charley sat on the couch, silently pulling the stitches out of a skirt. She wore a petulant, disapproving look; Nick did not know why, and at the moment he did not care.

'If it's got to be done,' Ed Woodman said, 'couldn't he do it slowly? So we can arrange care? They may starve to death or walk into passing squibs, they're like infants.'

'The ultimate vengeance,' Nick murmured.

'Yes,' Elka said. 'But we can't let them die helpless and' – she gestured – 'retarded.'

' "Retarded," ' Nick said. Yes, that's what they were, not like children but like *brain-damaged* children. Hence, Marshall's frustration when they tried to question him.

And it was brain damage. The cerebellum of their brains had been injured, from within, from the probing thing.

The TV set, still on, now carried the voice of the regular network newscaster. '—was just twelve hours ago that the famous physicist Amos Ild, retained by Council Chairman Willis Gram as his special advisor in the crisis, predicted over all television networks that there was no chance – repeat: no chance – that Thors Provoni had brought back an alien life form with him.' For the first time, Nick heard authentic anger in the announcer's voice. 'It would appear that the Council Chairman has relied on the – what's the expression? Staff of bending oats or something; I don't know. God in heaven.' On the screen the announcer bowed his head. 'It looked – to us, anyhow – like a good idea, the Baltimore laser system, trained on *Dinosaur*'s hatch. I guess, looking back now, it was too simple. Provoni wasn't going to get himself snuffed like that after ten years in space. Morgo Rahn Wilc, we have that down as the name or title of the alien.' Turning his face away from the microphone, the announcer said to someone invisible, 'For the first time in my life I'm glad I'm not a New.' He did not seem to realize that his words were being picked up by the world, nor did he care: he sat rubbing his eyes, shaking his head, saying nothing. Then his image disappeared and another announcer, evidently preempting him, appeared. He looked grave.

'Neurological tissue-damage seems to be deliberately—' he began, but at that point Charley took hold of Nick's hand and led him from the set.

'I want to listen,' he said.

'We're going to take a drive,' Charley said.

'Why?'

'Instead of sitting around here feeling unhooked. We'll go fast. We'll go in the Purple Sea Cow.'

'You mean go back to where they killed Denny?' He stared at her in absolute disbelief. 'The black pissers probably have a stake-out, an alarm system—'

'They don't care now,' Charley said quietly. 'First of all, they were all called in for crowd control, and secondly, if I can't go riding in the Cow for a few minutes, up real high and real fast, I'll probably try to kill myself. I mean that, Nick.'

'Okay,' he said. In a way she was right: there was no real point in staying here, glued to the TV set. 'But how'll we get over there?'

'Ed's squib,' Charley said. 'Ed, can we borrow your squib? For a little drive?'

'Sure.' Ed handed her the keys. 'You may need gas, though.'

Together, Nick and Charley ascended the stairs to the roof: only two floors were involved, so the elevator was not needed. For a time, neither of them spoke; they devoted themselves to locating Ed's squib.

Seated inside the squib, behind the tiller, Nick said, 'You should have told him where we're going. About the Cow.'

'Why worry him?' That was her sole, complete answer; she gave no more.

He sent the squib up into the sky; it was, now, virtually free of traffic. Presently, they hovered about Charley's former apartment building. There, on the roof field, stood the Purple Sea Cow.

'Shall I go down there?' Nick asked her.

'Yes.' She peered. 'I don't see anybody around. Really, they don't care anymore. It's the end of everything, Nick. The end of the PSS, the end of Gram, or Amos Ild – can you imagine what that thing will do when it gets to him?'

He shut off the squib's motor, glided silently down to come to rest beside the Cow. So far so good.

Charley got swiftly out, key in hand; she strode to the door of the Cow, inserted the key. The door opened; she at once squeezed in behind the tiller, motioned him to open the other door. 'Hurry,' she said. 'I can hear an alarm somewhere, probably on the ground floor. But what the hell now?' She smashed savagely down on the gas pedal, and the Cow raced upward, skimming like a barn swallow, like a flat disc.

'Look back,' Charley said, 'and see if anybody's following us.'

He did so. 'Nothing in sight.'

'I'll take evasive maneuvers,' she said, 'as Denny called it. We do a lot of spirals and Immelmanns. It's really frosty.' The squib dived, roared up a canyon between high rise buildings. 'Listen to those pipes,' Charley said, and pressed down even harder on the gas pedal.

'If you drive like this,' he said, 'you will pick up an occifer.'

She turned her head. 'Don't you understand? *They don't care now*. The whole establishment, everything they were supposed to protect – it's all gone. Their superiors are like the man you and Ed found downstairs.'

'You know,' he said, 'you've changed since I met you.' Since a couple of days, he realized. The bubbling vitality was gone from her; she had become hard in an almost cheap sort of way: she still wore her makeup but it had become a complete mask, now, inanimate. He had noticed it before, but it was coming up from deeper levels now. Everything about her, even when she was talking or moving, seemed inanimate. As if she no longer feels, he thought. But consider what's happened: first, the attacking of the 16th Avenue printing plant, then her horrible encounter with rutting Willis Gram, then Denny's death. And now this. She had nothing left by which to feel.

As if reading his thoughts, Charley said, 'I can't drive this thing the way Denny did. He was a master pilot; he could get it up to 120—'

'In town?' Nick asked. 'In traffic?'

'On the big freeway tacks,' Charley said.

'You both would have been killed by now.' Her driving

183

made him acutely uneasy; she had, by degrees, increased their velocity. The dial read 130. That was fast enough for him.

'You know,' Charley said, gripping the tiller with both hands, and staring fixedly ahead, 'Denny was an intellectual, a real one. He read all Cordon's pamphlets and tracts, all his writing. He was very proud of that; it made him feel superior to everybody else. You know what he used to say? He said he – Denny – could never be wrong, and that once he had a premise he could deduce from it with exact certainty.'

She slowed down, turned the squib down a side street between smaller buildings. Now she seemed to have a destination in mind – formerly she had driven just for the joy of flight, but now she slowed, lowered the squib ... he peered down, saw a square without buildings.

'Central Park,' she said, glancing at him. 'You ever been here before?'

'No,' he said. 'I didn't think it still existed.'

'Most of it doesn't. It's been cut down to a single acre. But it's still grass; it's still a park.' Somberly, she said, 'Denny and I found it one day, cruising around late at night, about 4:00 A.M. It frosted us out of our shoes; it really did. We'll land there.' The squib dipped down, slowed until it barely moved forward, and then she let the rubber tires touch the ground. The squib, its wings withdrawn, became, all at once, a surface vehicle.

Opening the door on her side, Charley got out; he did so, too, and was astounded at the texture of the grass under his feet. He had never walked on grass before in his life.

'How are your tires?' he asked.

'What?'

'I'm a regroover, remember? If you'll give me a flashlight, I'll look them over and see if any are regrooved. It could cost you your life, you realize. To have a regrooved tire and not know it.'

Charley lay down, stretched herself out on the grass, arms folded to prop up her head. 'My tires are okay,' she said. 'We only use the Cow at night, when there's room to fly. We don't take it as a surface vehicle during the day except in an emergency. Like the one that killed Denny.' She was silent, then, for a protracted length of time, simply lying on her back in the damp, cold grass, staring up at the stars.

'Nobody comes here,' Nick said.

'Never. They'd obliterate it completely, but Gram has a soft spot about it. Seems he played here as a child.' She raised her head and said wonderingly, 'Can you imagine Willis Gram as a baby? Or Provoni, for that matter. You know why I brought you here? So we could make love.'

'Oh,' he said.

'You're not surprised?'

'It's been hanging in the back of both our minds since we met,' he said. Anyhow it was true for him; he suspected it in her, too, but of course she could deny it.

'Can I take your clothes off for you?' she asked, rummaging in the pockets of his coat to see if he had anything of value which might fall out and get lost in the grass. 'Car keys?' she asked. 'Ident tabs? Oh, what the hell. Sit up.' He did so, and she removed his coat, which she carefully laid out on the ground near his head. 'Next your shirt,' she said, and so it went. Until, at last, she began on her own clothing.

'What small breasts you have,' he said, perceiving her in the dim starlight.

'Listen,' she said brusquely, 'it's not like it's costing you anything.'

That melted his heart. 'No, of course not,' he said. 'I don't want you to do this—' He put his hand on her shoulder. 'It's just that you did it here, with Denny.' For you, he thought, it may be like old times, but for me there's a specter hanging over me: the Dionysian face of the young boy ... all that life, and snuffed out just like that. 'It reminds me of a part of a poem,' he said, 'by Yeats.' He helped her take off her alliforgict sweater: they were easy to get on, hard to get off, once they had molded themselves to the curves of the body.

'I should just spray myself with paint,' she said, as the sweater came off.

'You don't get the texture of fabric that way,' he said. He paused a moment and said, hopefully, 'Do you like Yeats?'

'Was he before Bob Dylan?'

'Yes.'

'Then I don't want to hear about him. As far as I'm concerned, poetry started with Dylan and has declined since.'

Together, they removed the rest of their clothing; for a time they lay naked in the cold, wet grass, and then, simultaneously, they rolled toward each other; he rolled himself onto her, held her, gazed down at her face.

'I'm ugly,' she said. 'Aren't I?'

'You think *that*?' He was appalled. 'Why, you're one of the most attractive women I've ever met.'

'I'm not a woman,' she said matter-of-factly. 'I can't give back. I can only accept, not give. So don't expect anything of me, just that I'm here now.'

'It's statutory rape,' he told her, presently.

Charley said, 'Look, the end of the world has come; we're being taken over and neurologically destroyed by an unkillable thing. So at a time like this, what pisser is going to cite you? Anyway, there'd have to be a complaint made, and who would do it? Who would witness it?'

' "Witness it," ' he echoed, holding her close to him for a moment. PSS monitoring systems ... they probably had one set up on Central Park, forgotten as it was. He withdrew from her, then, leaped to his feet. 'Get your clothes on fast,' he said, reaching for his own.

'If you're thinking of a pisser monitor of this park—'

'I am.'

'Believe me, they're all watching Times Square. Except those who're New Men, like Director Barnes. They'll be tending to the damaged ones.' A thought struck her. 'That means Willis Gram.' She sat up, buried her hands in her ruffled, grass-wet hair. 'I'm sorry,' she said, 'but I sort of liked him.' She began to get her own clothes, and then she dropped them to the ground and beseechingly said, 'Look, Nick, the PSS isn't coming to get us. I'll tell you what I'll do, you take me a little longer, maybe just five minutes or so. And you can read that – what is it? – poem to me.'

'I don't have the book with me and you know it.'

'Do you remember it?'

'I guess so.' Fear, like a tide rising in his heart, made him

186

tremble as he put his own clothes back down and approached the supine girl. As he put his arms around her he said, 'It's a sad poem; I was thinking about Denny and this spot, here, where you used to come in the Cow. It's as if his spirit's buried here.'

'You're hurting me,' Charley complained. 'Do it more slowly.'

Once again he got to his feet. He began methodically to dress. 'I can't take the chance of being picked up,' he said, 'with those assassins, those black pissers, out for me.'

She lay unmoving. And then she said, 'Tell me the poem.'

'Will you get dressed? While I'm saying it?'

'No,' she said, arms behind her head, staring upward at the stars. 'Provoni came from up there,' she said. 'God, I'm just so goddam glad I'm not a New Man right now—' She clenched her fists and ground out the words, harshly. 'He's doing right, but – you have to feel sorry for them, the New Men. Lobotomized. Their Nodes of Rogers gone and God knows what else. Surgery out of space.' She laughed. 'Let's write it all up and call it *THE COSMIC SURGEON FROM A DISTANT STAR*. Okay?'

He crouched down, gathering up her items. Purse, sweater, underwear. 'I'll tell you the poem and then you'll understand why I can't go with you to places you and Denny went; I can't replace him, like a new Denny. Next you'll be giving me his wallet, which is probably ostrich hide, his watch, a Criterion, his agitite cuff links—' He broke off. ' "I must be gone: there is a grave where daffodil and lily wave, and—" ' He paused.

'Go on,' she said. 'I'm listening.'

' "And I would please the hapless faun, buried under the sleep ground, with mirthful songs before the dawn." '

'What does "mirthful" mean?' she asked.

He ignored her and spoke on. ' "His shouting days with mirth were crowned; and still I dream he treads the lawn, walking ghostly in the dew." ' Pierced, he thought, by my glad singing through. But he could not say it aloud; it affected him too much.

'You like that?' Charley asked. 'That kind of old stuff?'

Nick said, 'It's my favorite poem.'

'Do you like Dylan?'

'No,' he said.

'Tell me another poem.' Dressed, now, she sat beside him, knees bent, head bowed.

'I don't know any others from memory. I don't even remember how the rest of it goes, and I've read it a thousand times.'

'Was Beethoven a poet?' she asked.

'A composer. Of music.'

'So was Bob Dylan.'

Nick said, 'The world began before Dylan.'

'Let's go,' Charley said. 'I feel like I'm catching cold. Did you enjoy it?'

'No,' he said truthfully.

'Why not?'

'You're too tense.'

'If you had gone through the things I've gone through—'

'Maybe that's what's the matter. You know too much. Too much and too soon. But I love you.' He put his arm around her, hugged her, kissed her on the temple.

'Really?' Some of her old vitality returned; she leaped up, spread her arms wide, spun in a circle, arms extended.

A police cruiser, its siren and red light off, came gliding up behind them, silently landing.

'The Cow,' Charley said; she and he sprinted for the Cow, scrambled in, with Charley behind the tiller. She started it up; the Cow rolled forward as its wings extended themselves.

The red light of the PSS skunk car came on; so did its siren. And, on a bullhorn, the cruiser blared at them, words they could not decipher; the words echoed and echoed until Charley screeched with suffering.

'I'll lose him,' she said. 'Denny did it a thousand times; I learned from him.' She crushed the gas pedal, flattened it. The roar of full-throated pipes thundered behind Nick, and at the same time his head was snapped back, as the Cow suddenly gained speed. 'I'll show you the engine in this sometime,' she said, her eyes moving back and forth. And the Cow continued to gain speed; he had never been in a

188

squib hopped-up like this, although he had seen many hopped-up ones brought onto the lot for resale. They were not like this, however.

'Denny put every pop of money he owned into the Cow,' she said. 'He *built* it for like this, for getting away from the pissers. Watch.' She touched a switch, sat back, her hands no longer on the controls. The squib dropped abruptly, almost to the ground; Nick tensed himself – it looked like sure impact – and then, on some sort of automatic pilot system, unfamiliar to him, the ship glided at enormous speed up narrow streets, between old wooden stores – gliding at about three feet from the ground.

'You can't navigate this low,' he said to her. 'We're lower than if the wheels were down and we were landcrawling.'

'Now watch this.' She turned her head, studied the PSS cruiser behind her – it had followed, allowed himself to fly at their level – and then she yanked the rise-gear network into the ninety degrees' position.

They shot upward, into the darkness, the cruiser right behind them.

And now, from the south, a second cruiser appeared.

'We ought to give up,' Nick said, as the two cruisers joined together. 'They could open fire any time, now, and get us. In another minute, if we don't comply with that flashing red light, they'll do so.'

'But if we're caught, they'll snuff you,' Charley said. She increased their flight angle, and still, behind them, the two police cruisers howled their sirens and flashed their lights.

The Cow dropped once more, deadfall, until the automatic system halted it several feet above the pavement. The police cruisers followed. They dropped, too.

'Oh, God,' Charley said. 'They've got the Reeves-Fairfax margin control system, too. Let's see.' Her face worked frantically. 'Denny,' she said. 'Denny, what'll I do? What'll I do now?' She turned a corner – scraping a street lamp, he noticed. And then a bursting cloud of fire manifested itself directly ahead of them.

'Grenade launchers or thermotropic missiles,' Nick said. 'A warning shot. Turn on your radio to the police band.' He

189

reached toward the control board, but she savagely grabbed his hand and pushed it back.

'I'm not going to talk to them,' she said. 'And I'm not going to listen to them.'

Nick said, 'They'll destroy us with the next shot. They have the authority to do it; they will.'

'No,' Charley said. 'They're not going to shoot down the Cow. Denny, I promise you.'

The Cow ascended, did an Immelmann, did one again, then a barrel roll . . . and the cruisers remained on their tail.

'I'm going – do you know where I'm going?' Charley said. 'To Times Square.'

He had been waiting for this. 'No,' he said. 'They're not letting any ships into that area; they have it sealed off. You'd run into a solid phalanx of black-and-whites.'

But she continued on. He saw searchlights ahead, and several military vehicles circling. They were almost there.

'I'm going to go to Provoni,' she said, 'and ask him for sanctuary. For both of us.'

'For me, you mean,' he said.

Charley said, 'I'll ask him straight-out to let us into his protective web. He will; I know he will.'

'Maybe,' Nick said, 'he will.'

Abruptly, a shape loomed ahead. A slow army vehicle, carrying ammunition for hydrogen warhead-firing cannon; it had its warning lights lit from end to end.

Charley said, 'Oh, God I can't—' And then they hit.

TWENTY-FIVE

Light flashed in his eyes. He heard – felt – movement about him. The light hurt and he reached to put his hand up, to shut away the light, but his arm would not move. But I feel nothing, he said to himself. He felt completely rational. We're on the ground, he said to himself. It's a PSS occifer

190

shining his flashlight into my eyes, trying to see if I'm unconscious or dead.

'How is she?' he asked.

'The girl in the ship with you?' A leisurely, calm voice. Too calm. Uncaring.

He opened his eyes. A green-clad PSS occifer stood over him with a flashlight and gun. Wreckage, mostly from the ammunition carrier, lay spread out everywhere; he saw an ambulance, white-clad men working.

'The girl is dead,' the PSS occifer said.

'Can I see her? I have to see her.' He struggled, trying to get to his feet; the occifer helped him, then brought out a notebook and pen.

'Your name?' he asked.

'Let me see her.'

'She looks bad.'

Nick said, 'Let me see her.'

'Okay, buddy.' The PSS occifer led him, by the use of his flashlight, through the mounds of debris. 'There she is.'

It was the Purple Cow. Charlotte was still inside. There had never been a doubt from the first as to whether she was alive: her skull had been neatly halved by the tiller, into which she had fallen with enormous force when the Cow hit the big tub of an ammunition ship.

Someone had, however, dragged the tiller away from her, leaving the opening the tiller had made. The cerebral cortex could be seen, wet with blood, convoluted, pierced in half. Pierced, he thought, as in the Yeats poem; pierced by my glad singing through.

'It had to happen,' he said to the cop. 'If not this way, then some other way. Some fast way. Maybe someone on alcohol.'

'Her ID cards,' the cop said, 'say she's only sixteen.'

'That's right,' Nick said.

A tremendous boom sounded, shaking the ground under them. 'H-head cannon,' the cop said, busy with his pad and pen. 'More firing at that Frolixan thing.' He braced himself. 'It won't do any good. It's into people's mind all over the planet. Your name?'

'Denny Strong,' Nick said.

'Let me see your mandatory ID.'

Nick turned and ran, as best as he could.

The cop called after him, 'Slow down. I won't take a shot at you. What do I care any more? I'm just sorry about the girl.'

Slowing to a halt, Nick looked back. 'Why?' he asked. 'Why do you care about her? You didn't know her. Why don't you care about me? I'm on a black pisser snuff list; does that matter to you?'

'Not really. Not since I got a look at my boss over the v-fone; not since I saw him. A New Man, you know. Like a baby. He was playing with things on his desk, stacking them up in piles, according to color, I guess.'

'Could you give me a ride?' Nick asked.

'Where do you want to go?'

'The Federal Building,' Nick said.

'But that's a nuthouse, now. All those New Men in their cubicles, stay out of there.'

'I want to see Council Chairman Gram.'

'He's probably like the others, the other Unusuals and New Men.' Thoughtfully, the occifer said, 'However, I don't know if it has done anything to the Unusuals, actually. It's the New Men.'

'Take me there,' Nick said.

'Okay, buddy, but you're hurt – you've a broken arm and possibly, very possibly, internal injuries. Wouldn't you rather go to City Hospital?'

'I want to see Council Chairman Gram.'

The occifer said, 'Okay, I'll fly you there. And just leave you off on the roof field. I don't want to get mixed up with what's going on – I don't want it to start affecting me.'

'You're an Old Man?' Nick asked.

'Yeah, sure. Like you. Like most people. Like this whole city, except in places like the Federal Building where New Men—'

'It won't start affecting you,' Nick said. He walked shakily, but unassisted, toward the nearby parked PSS skunk car. Walking – and trying not to pass out. Not now, he said to

192

himself. Gram comes first; then it doesn't matter anyhow. Maybe he was spared; as the cop said, it seems mostly directed at New Men, not Unusuals.

The cop leisurely got into the car, waited for him, then started up into the sky.

'That really is a shame about the girl,' the cop said. 'But I noticed what sort of mill it had, souped up like crazy. Was it hers?'

Nick said nothing, he held his right arm, his mind empty of thoughts. Merely feeling the buildings pass below as the squib-cruiser headed for the Federal Building, fifty miles outside of the city of New York, in the satrapy of Washington, D.C.

'Why was she going so fast?' the cop asked.

'For my sake,' he said. 'That's why she went so fast. That's what killed her.'

The squib wheezed on, making its familiar vacuum cleaner sound.

TWENTY-SIX

The roof field of the Federal Building was alive with light as vehicles came and went. Only official squibs could be seen, however; the field was obviously closed to the public . . . God knew for how long.

The PSS occifer said, 'I have clearance to land.' He pointed to a pulsing green light on the intricate instrument panel of his squib.

They settled to a landing; Nick, with the occifer's help, managed to get out, to stand up unsteadily.

'Good luck, buddy,' the occifer said, and in an instant he had gone; his squib became invisible in the sky above, its red blinking lights blending with the stars.

At the entrance ramp, at the far end of the field, a line of black pissers barred his way. All carried carbines with feather-point bows. And all of them looked at him as if he were offal.

'Council Chairman Gram—' he began.

'Lose yourself,' one of the black pissers said.

Nick said, '—asked me to come here and see him.'

'Don't you know there's a forty thousand ton alien that's—'

'I'm here because of the emergency,' Nick said.

One of the black pissers spoke into a wrist mike, waited in silence, listening to his ear speaker, then nodded. 'He can go on in.'

'I'll escort you there,' another of the black pissers said. 'The whole fucking place is in a shambles.' He led the way, and Nick followed, moving as best he could.

'What's the matter with you?' the occifer said. 'You look like you've been in a squib accident.'

'I'm all right,' Nick said.

They passed, then, a New Man who stood with a written directive in his hands, obviously trying to read it. Some residual sense told him that he should read it, but there was no comprehension in his eyes, only frightened confusion.

'This way.' The black-clad PSS occifer led him through a series of cubicles; Nick caught glimpses of New Men here and there, some seated on the floor, some trying to do things, to handle objects, others merely sitting or lying, staring emptily forward. And some, he saw, were having violent rages; evidently, flown in for the emergency, Old Men employees were trying to keep them under control.

The final door opened; the occifer stepped aside, said, 'Here,' and strode off, back the way they had come.

Willis Gram was not in his big, rumpled bed. He sat, instead, on a chair at the far end of the room, evidently at peace; his face seemed composed and tranquil.

'Charlotte Boyer,' Nick said, 'is dead.'

'Who?' Gram blinked, turned to focus his attention on Nick. 'Oh. Yeah.' He lifted his hands, palms up. 'They took away my telepathic ability. I'm just an Old Man now.'

An intercom on his desk said suddenly, 'Council Chairman, we have installed the second laser system, this one on the roof of the Carriager Building, and twenty seconds from now it will have focused its beam on the same spot as the Baltimore laser system.'

Gram said loudly, 'Provoni's still standing there?'

'Yes. The Baltimore beam is directly on him. When we add the Kansas City beam, we will virtually double the power at function-level.'

'Keep me informed,' Gram said. 'Thanks.' He turned to Nick. Today, Gram was fully dressed: business pantaloons, silk blouse with frilly sleeves, pie-plate shoes. He was groomed, nattily dressed, and calm. 'I'm sorry about the girl,' he said. 'I'm sorry, but not really sorry – not if you really get down to the bottom of it – as I might have been if I'd known her better.' He rubbed his face wearily, it had been freshly powdered, and a white layer came off on his hands; he slapped them together irritably. 'I'm not wasting any tears for the New Men,' he said, his lips twisting. 'It's their fault. You know about a man, a New Man, called Amos Ild?'

'Of course,' Nick said.

' "Absolutely no possibility," ' Gram said, ' ' "That he's brought an alien back with him." ' Neutrologics, which the rest of us, Old Men and Under Men and Unusuals, can't understand. Well, there's nothing to understand, it doesn't work. Amos Ild was just an eccentric, fiddling with millions of components for his Great Ear project. He was insane.'

'Where is he now?' Nick said.

'Off somewhere playing with paperweights,' Gram said. 'Setting up intricate balance-systems for them, using rulers as the support bars.' He grinned. 'And he'll be doing it the rest of his life.'

'How far has the destruction of neurological tissue spread, geographically speaking?' Nick asked. 'Over the whole planet? To Luna and Mars?'

'I don't know. Most communications circuits aren't being manned; there's nobody, just plain nobody, on the other end. Which is eerie.'

'You've called Peking? Moscow? Sumatra One?'

195

'I'll tell you who I've called,' Gram said. 'The Extraordinary Committee for Public Safety.'

Nick said, 'And they no longer exist.'

Nodding, Gram said, 'He – it – killed them. Scooped out their skulls, left them empty. Except for the diencephalon, for some reason. They left that.'

'The vegetative functions,' Nick said.

'Yeah, we could have kept them alive like vegetables. But it wasn't worth it; I told the different doctors to let them die, once I knew the extent of brain damage. That applies only to the New Men, however. There are two Unusuals on the Public Safety Committee, a precog and a telepath. Their talents are gone, same as mine. But we're alive. For a while.'

'It won't do anything more to you,' Nick said. 'Now that you're an Old Man, you're in no more danger than I.'

'What did you want to see me about?' Gram asked, turning to face him. 'To tell me about Charlotte? To make me feel guilty? Christ, there're a million little bitches like her slinking around in the world; you can get yourself another in half an hour.'

Nick said, 'You sent three black pissers to kill me. They killed Denny Strong instead, and because of his death we couldn't handle the Sea Cow; hence the crash. Hence her death. You set up the train of circumstances; it all emanated from you.'

'I'll call off the black troopers,' Gram said.

'That's not enough,' Nick said.

The intercom burbled into life. 'Council Chairman, both laser beams are now directed at the target spot, Thors Provoni.'

'What results?' Gram asked, standing rigidly, supporting his great bulk by holding onto the desk.

'They're being passed to me now,' the intercom said.

Gram, silently, waited.

'No visible change. No, sir, no change.'

'Three laser systems,' Gram said huskily. 'If we brought in the one from Detroit—'

'Sir, we can't really operate *what we have* properly. The

mental illness that's attacking the New Men means we lack—'

'Thanks,' Gram said, and shut the intercom off. ' "Mental illness," ' he said, in ferocious mockery. 'If only that's what it was. Something you could cure in a sanitarium. What do they call that? Psychogenic?'

Nick said, 'I'd like to see Amos Ild. Balancing paperweights on rulers.' The greatest intellect produced so far by the race of man, he thought. Neanderthal, homo sapiens, then New Men – evolution. And using the New Man neutrologics, he had struck out; he had batted 000. But maybe Gram is right, he thought. Maybe Amos Ild was always insane ... but we had no way of measuring a unique brain like his, no standard by which to judge.

It's a good thing we're rid of Ild, he thought. It's a good thing we're rid of all of them, he thought. Maybe all the New Men, in one sense or another, were insane. It's just a question of degree. And their neutrologics – the logic of the insane.

'You look lousy,' Gram said. 'You better get medical help; I can see that your arm's broken.'

'To your infirmary?' Nick said. 'As you call it?'

'They're competent medically,' Gram said. 'It's strange,' he said, half to himself, 'I keep listening for your thoughts and they never come. I have only your words to go on.' He cocked his shaggy head, studied Nick. 'Did you come here to—'

'I wanted you to know about Charlotte,' Nick said.

'But you're unarmed; you're not going to try to snuff me. You were searched; you didn't know it but you passed five checkpoints. Are you?' With unusual swiftness for a man of his bulk, he spun deftly, touched a stud on his desk. Instantly, five black troopers were in the room; they did not seem to have come there; they just were. 'See if he's armed,' Gram said to the black troopers. 'Look for something small, like a knife made of plastic, or a microtab of germs.'

Two of them searched Nick. 'No sir,' they informed the Council Chairman.

'Stay where you are,' Gram instructed them. 'Keep your tubes pointed at him and kill him if he moves. This man is dangerous.'

'Am I?' Nick asked. 'Is 3XX24J dangerous? Then six billion Old Men are dangerous, too, and your black pissers aren't going to be able to hold them back .They're all Under Men, now; they've seen Provoni; they know he's back, as he promised; they know your weapons can't hurt him; they know what his friend, the Frolixan, can do – has done – to the New Men. My broken arm is paralyzed; I couldn't pull a trigger anyhow. Why couldn't you have let us alone? Why couldn't you let her come to me, and be together? Why did you have to send those black pissers after us? *Why?*'

'Jealousy,' Gram said quietly.

'Are you going to resign as Council Chairman?' Nick asked. 'You have no special qualifications. Will you let Provoni rule? Provoni and his friend from Frolix 8?'

After a pause, Gram said, 'No.'

'Then they'll kill you. The Under Men will. They'll be coming here as soon as they understand what's happened. And those tanks and weapons-squibs and black squads aren't going to stop more than the first few thousand of them. Six billion, Gram. Can the military and the black pissers kill six billion men? Plus Provoni and the Frolixan? Do you have any real chance of any sort? Isn't it time to pass control of the government, the whole establishment apparatus, to someone else? You're old and you're tired. And you haven't done a good job. Snuffing Cordon – that alone should, by a constituted court of law, hang you.' And very well may, he thought. For that and other decisions Gram had made during his tenure.

Gram said, 'I'm going to go and talk with Provoni.' He nodded to the black-clad troopers. 'Get me a police squib; get it all ready.' He pressed a button on his desk. 'Miss Knight, ask communications to try to establish voice contact between me and Thors Provoni. Tell them to start on it right now. Top priority.'

He rang off, stood, then said to Nick, 'I want—' He hesitated. 'Have you ever tasted Scotch whiskey?'

'No,' Nick said.

'I have some twenty-four-year-old Scotch, a bottle I've never opened, a bottle for a special occasion. Wouldn't you say this is a special occasion?'

'I guess it is, Council Chairman.'

Going to the bookshelf on the right-hand wall, Gram lifted several volumes out, reached behind those that remained, came out holding a tall bottle of amber fluid. 'Okay?' he said to Nick.

'Okay,' Nick said.

Gram seated himself at his desk, tore the metal seal from the top of the bottle, removed the stopper, then looked around and among the clutter until he found two paper cups. He dumped their contents into a nearby wastebasket, then poured Scotch into each of the cups. 'What'll we drink to?' he asked Nick.

'Is that part of the ritual of taking alcohol?' Nick asked.

Gram smiled. 'We'll drink to a girl that wrestled herself loose from four six-foot-tall MPs.' He was silent a moment, not drinking. Nick, too, held his cup without lifting it. 'To a better planet,' Gram said, and drank the cupful down. 'To a planet where we won't need our friends from Frolix 8.'

'I won't drink to that,' Nick said; he set his cup down.

'Well, then just drink! Find out what Scotch tastes like! The finest of the whiskies!' Gram stared at him in bewilderment and resentment ... the latter grew until his face was dark red. 'Don't you realize what you're being offered? You've lost your perspective on things.' He pounded angrily on the walnut surface of his mighty wooden desk. 'This whole thing has made you lose your values! We have to—'

'The special squib is ready, Council Chairman,' the intercom said. 'On the roof field at port 5.'

'Thanks,' he said. 'What about voice contact? I can't go until I get voice contact and establish that I'm not going to do them any harm. Switch off the laser beams. Both of them.'

'Sir?'

He repeated his order. Hurriedly.

'Yes sir,' the intercom said. 'And we'll continue to try for voice contact. Meanwhile, we'll hold your ship ready.'

Picking up the bottle, Gram poured himself more Scotch. 'I can't understand you, Appleton,' he said to Nick. 'You come here – what for, in God's name? You're injured but you refuse—'

'Maybe that's why I came here,' Nick said. ' "In God's name." As you put it.' To stare you down, he thought, until you are ready to die. Because you and those like you must pass away; you must make room for what is coming. For what *we* are going to do. *Our* projects, instead of such semipsychotic constructs as the Great Ear.

The Great Ear – what a superb device for a government to own, to help keep everyone in line. Too bad it'll never be completed, he thought. We will see to that, although Provoni and his friend already have. But we will make it final.

'We have video and audio contact, Council Chairman,' the intercom said. 'Line 5.'

Gram picked up the red v-fone, said, 'Hello, Mr. Provoni.'

On the screen appeared Provoni's rugged, bony face with its shadows, its furrows, its crags and pits . . . his eyes held in them the absolute emptiness which Nick had felt during the moment the probe passed through him . . . but the eyes held more: they gleamed animal-like, eyes of a breathing, willful, intense creature that strove and sought for what it wanted. An animal which had burst out of its cage. Strong eyes, set in a strong face, tired as it obviously was.

'I think it would be a good thing for you to come up here,' Gram said. 'You've done vast harm; rather the irresponsible organism with you has done vast harm. Thousands of men and women, important in the government and industry and in the sciences—'

'We should meet,' Provoni interrupted hoarsely, 'but it would be difficult for my friend to move himself so far.'

'We shut off the laser beams as an act of good faith,' Gram said, with tension, his eyes unblinking.

'Yes, thank you for the laser beams.' Provoni's rock-like face split open to disclose a stubbled smile. 'Without that energy source, he would have been unable to do his task. At least unable to right away. Over a few months – well, it

200

would eventually have been accomplished; our work would have been done.'

'Are you serious?' Gram asked, ashen. 'About the laser beams?'

'Yes. He converted the energy of the laser system; it re-vitalized him.'

Gram turned away from the fone screen for a moment, evidently to get control of himself.

'Are you all right, Council Chairman?' Provoni asked.

Gram said, 'Here you could shave, bathe, get a rubdown, a physical examination, rest for a time ... and then we could confer.'

'You will come here,' Provoni said calmly.

After a pause Gram said, 'All right. I'll be there in forty minutes. Do you guarantee my safety and my freedom to leave?'

'Your "safety",' Provoni echoed. He shook his head. 'You still don't comprehend the magnitude of what's happened. Yes, I'll be glad to guarantee your safety. You'll leave in the state you arrived, at least as far as our actions are concerned. If you have a coronary seizure—'

'All right,' Gram said.

And so, in a matter of one minute, Willis Gram had capitulated his position entirely; it was he who went to Provoni, not the other way around ... nor even to a neutral, middle point, divided equally between them. And it was a necessary, rational decision; he had no other choice.

'But there will be no coronary seizure,' Gram said. 'I am ready to face anything necessary. Any condition that has to be met. Off.' He hung up the fone. 'Do you know what haunts me, Appleton? The fear that other Frolixans might come, that this might be only the first.'

'No more are needed,' Nick said.

'But if they want to take over Earth—'

'They don't want to.'

'They have. In a way. Already.'

'But this is it. There won't be any more damage done. Provoni has what he wants.'

201

'Suppose they don't care about Provoni and "what he wants". Suppose—'

One of the black troopers said, 'Sir, to reach Times Square in forty minutes – we should start now.' He had braid on him: a pisser of high rank.

Grunting, Gram picked up a heavy woolex greatcoat and tugged it on over his shoulders. One of the troopers assisted him. 'This man,' Gram said, indicating Nick, 'is to be taken to the infirmary and given medical treatment.' He inclined his head, and two of the troopers approached Nick, menacingly, their eyes weak and yet intense.

'Council Chairman,' Nick said, 'I have a favor to ask. Can I see Amos Ild for a time, before I go to the infirmary?'

'Why?' Gram asked, as he started toward the door with the two other black troopers.

'I just want to talk to him. See him. Try to understand all this, all that's happened to the New Men, by seeing him. Seeing him on the level he now—'

'Cretin level,' Gram said harshly. 'You don't want to come with me when I meet Provoni? You could express the wishes of—' He gestured. 'Barnes said you were representative.'

'Provoni knows what I want – what everyone wants. What happens between you and him will be simple: you will resign your office and he will take on the office in your place. The Civil Service system will be radically revised; many positions will be elective, rather than appointive. Camps will be set up for the New Men where they will be happy; we have to think of them, their helplessness. That's why I want to see Amos Ild.'

'Then go do that.' Gram nodded to the two troopers, one on each side of Nick. 'You know where Ild is – take him there, and when he's finished, then the infirmary.'

'Thanks,' Nick said.

Lingering, Gram asked, 'Is she really dead?'

'Yes,' Nick said.

'I'm sorry.' Gram held out his hand, to shake. Nick declined it. 'You were the one I wanted to see dead,' Gram said. 'Now – hell, now it doesn't matter. Well, I've finally

202

untangled my personal life from my public life; my personal life is over.'

'As you said,' Nick said icily, ' "there's a million little bitches like her crawling this world." '

'That's right,' Gram said stonily. 'I did say that.'

He set off, then, with his two guards. The door slid shut after him.

'Come along,' one of the two remaining black pissers said.

'I will come at the rate I feel like,' he said; his arm hurt violently and he was beginning to feel sick at his stomach. Gram was right – he would have to go downstairs to the infirmary very soon.

But not until he saw, with his own eyes, Amos Ild. The highest intellect born of man.

'In here.' One of the guards indicated a door which was guarded by a PSS occifer wearing regulation green. 'Step aside,' the black pisser said.

'I'm not authorized to—'

The black trooper lifted his gun. As if to hit him with it.

'Whatever you say,' the occifer in green said, and stepped aside.

Nicholas Appleton entered the room.

TWENTY-SEVEN

In the center of the room sat Amos Ild, his great head held in place by the collar of metal spokes. He had surrounded himself with a variety of objects: paperclips, pens, paperweights, rulers, erasers, sheets of paper, cartons, magazines, abstracts ... he had torn pages out of the magazines, crumpled them up and tossed them away. Now, at this moment, he was drawing on a piece of paper.

Nick came over. Stick men, a huge circle in the sky which represented the sun.

'Do the people like the sun?' he asked Amos Ild.

Ild said, 'It makes them warm.'

203

'So they go out into it?'

'Yes.' Amos Ild drew on another sheet, now, tired of that one. He drew what appeared to be an animal.

'A horse?' Nick asked. 'A dog? It's got four legs; is it a bear? A cat?'

Amos Ild said, 'It's me.'

Pain constricted Nick Appleton's heart.

'I have a burrow,' Ild said, drawing a flattened, irregular circle, low down, with a brown crayon. 'It's there.' He placed his large finger over the flattened brown circle. 'I go inside it when it rains. I keep warm.'

Nick said, 'We'll make you a burrow. Exactly like that.'

Smiling, Amos Ild crumpled up the drawing.

'What are you going to be,' Nick asked, 'when you grow up?'

'I am grown-up,' Ild said.

'What are you, then?'

Ild hesitated. Then he said, 'I build things. Look.' He got up from the floor, his head swaying ominously . . . God, Nick thought, it'll snap his spine. Proudly, he showed Nick the network of paperweights and rulers which he had built.

'Very nice,' Nick said.

'If you take one weight away,' Ild said, 'it collapses.' A mischievous expression appeared on his face. 'I'm going to take a piece away.'

'But you don't want it to fall down.'

Amos Ild, towering above Nick, dominating with his huge head and its elaborate support, said, 'What are you?'

'I'm a tire regroover,' Nick said.

'Is a tire what a squib has on it that goes around and around?'

'Right,' Nick said. 'The squib lands on it. On them.'

'Could I do that, sometime? Be a—' Ild hesitated.

'A tire regroover,' Nick said with patience. He felt calm. 'It's a very bad job. I don't think you'd enjoy it.'

'Why not?'

'Because, you see, there are treads on the tires . . . and you dig them deeper so it looks like there's more rubber than there is, but the person who buys it might have a flat tire because of that. And then they might have an accident, and be hurt, too.'

'You're hurt,' Ild said.

'My arm's broken.'

'Then you must hurt.'

'Not exactly. It's paralyzed. I'm still in shock, somewhat.'

The door opened and one of the black troopers looked in, his narrow eyes taking in the scene.

'Could you bring me a morphine tablet from the dispensary?' Nick asked him. 'My arm—' He indicated it.

'Okay, fella,' the trooper said, and departed.

'It must really hurt bad,' Amos Ild said.

'Not so bad. Don't worry about it, Mr. Ild.'

'What's your name?'

'Mr. Appleton. Nick Appleton. Call me Nick and I'll call you Amos.'

'No.' Amos Ild said. 'We don't know each other that well. I'll call you Mr. Appleton and you call me Mr. Ild. I'm thirty-four, you know. Next month I'll be thirty-five.'

'And you'll get lots of presents,' Nick said.

Ild said, 'I just want one thing. I want—' He became silent. 'There's an empty place in my mind; I wish it would go away. It didn't used to be there.'

'The Great Ear,' Nick said. 'Do you remember that? Building that?'

'Oh, yes,' Ild said. 'I did that. It's going to hear everyone's thoughts and then' – a pause – 'we can put people into camps. Relocation camps.'

'Is that nice to do?' Nick asked.

'I – don't know.' Ild put his hands to his temples and shut his eyes. 'What are other people? Maybe there aren't any others; maybe they're make-believe. Like you – maybe I made you up. Maybe I can make you do anything I want.'

'What would you want me to do?' Nick asked.

'Pick me up,' Amos Ild said. 'I like to be picked up and then there's a game – you spin around, holding me by my hands. And cen – trifugal force —' He stumbled over the word, gave up. 'You make me fly out horizon—' Again he stumbled. 'Could you pick me up?' he asked plaintively, looking down at Nick.

'I can't, Mr. Ild,' Nick said. 'Because of my broken arm.'

'Thank you, anyway,' Amos Ild said. He shuffled meditatively over to the window of the room, gazed out at the night sky. 'Stars,' he said. 'People go there. Mr. Provoni went there.'

'Yes,' Nick said. 'He certainly did.'

'Is Mr. Provoni a nice man?'

Nick said, 'He is a man who did what had to be done. No, he isn't a nice man – he's a mean man. But he wanted to help.'

'Is that good, to help?'

'Most people think so,' Nick said.

'Mr. Appleton,' Amos Ild asked, 'do you have a mother?'

'No, not living.'

'I don't either. Do you have a wife?'

'Not really. Not anymore.'

'Mr. Appleton, do you have a girl friend?'

'No,' he said, harshly.

'Did she die?'

'Yes.'

'Just a little while ago?'

'Yes,' he grated.

'You must get a new one,' Amos Ild said.

'Really?' he asked. 'I don't think so – I don't think I ever want a girl friend again.'

'You need one that'll worry about you.'

'This one worried about me. It killed her.'

'How wonderful,' Amos Ild said.

'Why?' Nick stared at him.

'Think how much she loved you. Imagine anybody loving you that much. I wish someone loved me that much.'

'Is that important?' Nick asked. 'Is that what it's all about, instead of invasions by aliens, the destruction of ten million superlative brains, the transfer of political power – all power – by an elite group—'

'I don't understand those things,' Amos Ild said. 'I just know how it's wonderful, someone loving you that much.

And if someone loved you that much, you must be worth loving, so pretty soon someone else will love you that way, too, and you'll love them the same way. Do you see?'

'I think so,' Nick said.

'Nothing exceeds that, where if a man gives his life for a friend,' Amos Ild said. 'I wish I could do that.' He pondered, seated, now, on a swivel chair. 'Mr. Appleton,' he asked, 'are there other grown-ups like me?'

'Like you in what way?' he asked, stalling.

'That can't think. That have an empty place there.' He placed his hand on his forehead.

'Yes,' Nick said.

'Will one of them love me?'

'Yes,' Nick said.

The door opened; there stood the black trooper with a paper cup of water and a morphine tablet. 'Five more minutes, fella,' the trooper said, 'and then you're going to the infirmary.'

'Thanks,' he said, taking the pill at once.

'Brother, you really are in pain,' the trooper said. 'And you look like you're about to topple over. It wouldn't be good for that kid' – he paused, corrected himself – 'for Mr. Ild to see that: it'd worry him, and Gram doesn't want him worried.'

'There'll be camps for them,' Nick said. 'Where they can relate on their own level. Instead of trying to be like us.'

The trooper grunted, shut the door after him.

'Isn't black the color of death?' Ild asked.

'It is, yes,' Nick said.

'Then are they death?'

'Yes,' Nick said. 'But they won't hurt you.'

'I wasn't afraid they'd hurt me; I was thinking that you already have a broken arm and maybe they did that.'

'A girl did that,' Nick said. 'A short, snub-nosed little gutter rat. A girl I'd sell my life – make all this unhappen – for. But it's too late.'

'She's your girl friend who died?'

He nodded.

Amos Ild took a black crayon and drew. Nick watched as

stick figures emerged. A man, a woman. And a black, four-legged, sheep-headed animal. And a black sun, a black land-scape with black houses and squibs.

'All black?' Nick asked. 'Why?'

'I don't know,' Amos Ild said.

'Is it good that they're all black?'

After a pause, Amos Ild said, 'Wait.' He scribbled over the picture, then tore the paper into strips, wadded them up and threw them away. 'I can't think anymore,' he complained peevishly.

'But we're not all black, are we?' Nick asked. 'Tell me that, and then you can stop thinking.'

'I guess the girl is all black. And you're partly black, like your arm and parts inside you, but I guess the rest isn't.'

'Thank you,' Nick said, standing dizzily up. 'I think I'd better be going to go see the doctor now,' he said. 'I'll see you later.'

'No you won't,' Amos Ild said.

'I won't? Why not?'

'Because you found out what you wanted. You wanted me to draw the Earth and show you what color it is, if it's black especially.' Taking a piece of paper he drew a large circle – in green. 'It's alive,' he said. And smiled at Nick.

Nick said, ' "I must be gone: there is a grave where daffodil and lily wave, and I would please the hapless faun, buried under the sleepy ground, with mirthful songs before the dawn. His shouting days with mirth were crowned; and still I dream he treads the lawn, walking ghostly in the dew, pierced by my glad singing through." '

'Thank you,' Amos Ild said.

'Why?' Nick said.

'For explaining.' He began another picture. With his black crayon he drew the woman, underground and horizontal. 'There's the grave,' he said, pointing. 'That you have to go to. That's where she is.'

'Will she hear me?' Nick asked. 'Will she know I'm there?'

'Yes,' Amos Ild said. 'If you sing. But you have to sing.'

The door opened and the black trooper said, 'Come along, mister. To the infirmary.'

He lingered. 'And should I put daffodils and lilies there?' he asked Amos Ild.

'Yes, and you have to remember to call her name.'

'Charlotte,' he said.

Amos Ild nodded. 'Yes.'

'Come on,' the trooper said, taking him by the shoulder and leading him out of the room. 'There's no point in talking to the kiddies.'

' "Kiddies"?' Nick asked. 'Is that what you're going to call them?'

'Well, we've sort of started to. They're like children.'

'No,' Nick said, 'they are not like children.' They are like saints and prophets, he thought. Soothsayers, old wisemen. But we will have to take care of them, they won't be able to manage by themselves. They won't even be able to wash themselves.

'Did he say anything worth hearing?' the trooper asked him.

Nick said, 'He said she can hear me.'

They had reached the infirmary. 'Go on in there,' the trooper said, pointing. 'Through that door.'

'Thanks,' Nick said. And joined the line of men and women already waiting.

'What he said,' the black trooper said, 'wasn't very much.'

'It was enough,' Nick said.

'They're pathetic, aren't they?' the trooper asked. 'I always wished I was a New Man, but now—' He grimaced.

'Go away,' Nick said. 'I want to be able to think.'

The black-clad trooper strode off.

'And your name, sir?' the nurse said to him. She held her pen poised.

'Nick Appleton,' he said. 'I'm the tire regroover.' He added, 'And I want to think. Maybe if I could just lie down—'

'There are no beds left, sir,' the nurse said. 'But your arm' – she touched it gingerly – 'we can set that.'

'Okay,' he said. And, leaning against the nearby wall for support, waited. And, as he waited, thought.

Attorney Horace Denfeld briskly entered the outer office of Council Chairman Willis Gram. He had his briefcase with him, and the expression he wore, even unto the way he walked, showed a further development of his sense of negotiating from strength.

'Tell Mr. Gram that I have further material pertaining to his alimony and property—'

At her desk, Miss Knight glanced up and said, 'You're too late, counselor.'

'I beg your pardon? You mean he's busy now? I'll have to wait?' Denfeld examined his diamond-surrounded wristwatch. 'I can wait fifteen minutes at the longest. Please convey that news to him.'

'He's gone,' Miss Knight said, folding her fingers beneath her sharp chin, a lazy, confident gesture not lost on Denfeld. 'All his personal problems, you and Irma in particular – they're all over with.'

'You mean because of the invasion.' Denfeld rubbed the side of his nose irritably. 'Well, we'll follow him with a writ issued by the court,' he said, scowling and looking his most terrible look. 'Wherever he's gone.'

'Willis Gram,' Miss Knight said, 'has gone where no writs can follow him.'

'You mean he's dead?'

'He is outside our lives, now. Beyond the Earth we live on. He's with an enemy, an old enemy, and with what may be a new friend. At least we can hope so.'

'We'll find him,' Denfeld said.

'Do you want to bet? Fifty pops?'

Denfeld hesitated. 'I—'

Returning to her typing, Miss Knight said, between peck-pecks, 'Good day, Mr. Denfeld.'

By her desk, Denfeld stood – something had caught his eye, and he now reached to pick it up: a small plastic statuette of a man in robes. He held it for a time – Miss Knight tried to ignore him but there he was – fingering the statuette, studying it closely, solemnly. On his face an expression of wonder had appeared, as if, with each passing moment, he saw something more in the plastic figure.

'Who is this?' he asked Miss Knight.

'A statue of God,' Miss Knight said, and paused in her busy typing to study him. 'Everybody has one, it's a fad. Haven't you seen one of those before?'

'Is that how God looks?' Denfeld asked.

'No, of course not; it's only—'

'But it is God,' he said.

'Well, yes.' She watched him; she saw the wonder in his eyes, his consciousness narrowed down to this one artifact . . . and then she realized: Of course, *Denfeld is a New Man*. And I'm seeing the process; he is becoming a kiddy. Rising from her chair, she said, 'Sit down, Mr. Denfeld.' She led him over to a couch and got him seated . . . his briefcase forgotten, she realized. Forgotten now; forgotten forever. 'Can I get anything for you?' she asked; she was at a loss as to what to say. 'Some Coke? Zing?'

Denfeld gazed up at her wide-eyed and hopeful. 'Could I have this? To keep?'

'Certainly,' she said, and felt compassion for him. One of the least and last of the New Men to go, she thought. And where is his arrogance now? Where is everybody's?

'Can God fly?' Denfeld asked. 'Can He hold out His arms and fly?'

'Yes,' she said.

'Someday—' He broke off. 'I think every living thing will fly or anyhow trudge or run; some will go fast, like they do in this life, but most will fly or trudge. Up and up. Forever. Even slugs and snails; they'll go very slow but they'll make it sometime. All of them will make it eventually, no matter how slow they go. Leaving a lot behind; that has to be done. You think so?'

'Yes,' she said. 'A very great lot behind.'

'Thank you,' Denfeld said.

'For what?'

'For giving me God.'

'Okay,' she said. And stoically resumed her typing. While Horace Denfeld played endlessly with the plastic statuette. With the vastness of God.

Panther Science Fiction – A Selection from the World's Best S.F. List

More Great Science Fiction Books from Panther

Isaac Asimov, Grand Master of Science Fiction, in Panther Books

All-action Fiction from Panther